I0647234

A Text Book Of

ENERGY MANAGEMENT

For

Third Year Diploma in Chemical Engineering and Technology Group and also for Electrical Engineering Students

Semester V

As Per MSBTE's 'G' Scheme Syllabus

D. B. DHONE

B. Sc., B. Tech., M.S.,
LMISTE, MIE
Chartered Engineer
Head of Training and Placement,
Bharati Vidyapeeth's J.N.I.O.T.,
PUNE

SAMIR NIMKAR

M. E. (Chemical)
Energy Auditor
Lecturer, Bharati Vidyapeeth's I.O.T.,
MUMBAI

NIRALI PRAKASHAN
ADVANCEMENT OF KNOWLEDGE

N3152

ENERGY MANAGEMENT (CHEMICAL ENGINEERING)

ISBN 978-93-83971-96-1

First Edition : June 2014

© : **Authors**

The text of this publication, or any part thereof, should not be reproduced or transmitted in any form or stored in any computer storage system or device for distribution including photocopy, recording, taping or information retrieval system or reproduced on any disc, tape, perforated media or other information storage device etc., without the written permission of Authors with whom the rights are reserved. Breach of this condition is liable for legal action.

Every effort has been made to avoid errors or omissions in this publication. In spite of this, errors may have crept in. Any mistake, error or discrepancy so noted and shall be brought to our notice shall be taken care of in the next edition. It is notified that neither the publisher nor the authors or seller shall be responsible for any damage or loss of action to any one, of any kind, in any manner, therefrom.

Published By :
NIRALI PRAKASHAN
Abhyudaya Pragati, 1312, Shivaji Nagar,
Off J.M. Road, PUNE – 411005
Tel - (020) 25512336/37/39, Fax - (020) 25511379
Email : niralipune@pragationline.com

DISTRIBUTION CENTRES

PUNE

Nirali Prakashan
119, Budhwar Peth, Jogeshwari Mandir Lane
Pune 411002, Maharashtra
Tel : (020) 2445 2044, 66022708, Fax : (020) 2445 1538
Email : bookorder@pragationline.com

Nirali Prakashan
S. No. 28/25, Dhyari,
Near Pari Company, Pune 411041
Tel : (020) 24690204 Fax : (020) 24690316
Email : dhyari@pragationline.com
        bookorder@pragationline.com

MUMBAI

Nirali Prakashan
385, S.V.P. Road, Rasdhara Co-op. Hsg. Society Ltd.,
Girgaum, Mumbai 400004, Maharashtra
Tel : (022) 2385 6339 / 2386 9976, Fax : (022) 2386 9976
Email : niralimumbai@pragationline.com

DISTRIBUTION BRANCHES

NAGPUR
Pratibha Book Distributors
Above Maratha Mandir, Shop No. 3, First Floor,
Rani Jhanshi Square, Sitabuldi, Nagpur 440012,
Maharashtra, Tel : (0712) 254 7129

BENGALURU
Pragati Book House
House No. 1, Sanjeevappa Lane, Avenue Road Cross,
Opp. Rice Church, Bengaluru – 560002.
Tel : (080) 64513344, 64513355,
Mob : 9880582331, 9845021552
Email:bharatsavla@yahoo.com

JALGAON
Nirali Prakashan
34, V. V. Golani Market, Navi Peth, Jalgaon 425001,
Maharashtra, Tel : (0257) 222 0395
Mob : 94234 91860

KOLHAPUR
Nirali Prakashan
New Mahadvar Road,
Kedar Plaza, 1st Floor Opp. IDBI Bank
Kolhapur 416 012, Maharashtra. Mob : 9855046155

CHENNAI
Pragati Books
9/1, Montieth Road, Behind Taas Mahal, Egmore,
Chennai 600008 Tamil Nadu, Tel : (044) 6518 3535,
Mob : 94440 01782 / 98450 21552 / 98805 82331, Email : bharatsavla@yahoo.com

RETAIL OUTLETS

PUNE

Pragati Book Centre
157, Budhwar Peth, Opp. Ratan Talkies,
Pune 411002, Maharashtra
Tel : (020) 2445 8887 / 6602 2707, Fax : (020) 2445 8887

Pragati Book Centre
Amber Chamber, 28/A, Budhwar Peth,
Appa Balwant Chowk, Pune : 411002, Maharashtra,
Tel : (020) 20240335 / 66281669
Email : pbcpune@pragationline.com

Pragati Book Centre
676/B, Budhwar Peth, Opp. Jogeshwari Mandir,
Pune 411002, Maharashtra
Tel : (020) 6601 7784 / 6602 0855

PBC Book Sellers & Stationers
152, Budhwar Peth, Pune 411002, Maharashtra
Tel : (020) 2445 2254 / 6609 2463

MUMBAI
Pragati Book Corner
Indira Niwas, 111 - A, Bhavani Shankar Road, Dadar (W), Mumbai 400028, Maharashtra
Tel : (022) 2422 3526 / 6662 5254, Email : pbcmumbai@pragationline.com

www.pragationline.com   info@pragationline.com

PREFACE

We take an opportunity to present this book entitled as **'Energy Management'** to the students of Fifth Semester of Chemical Engineering and Technology Group as well as useful to Fifth Semester of Electrical Engineering as elective subject. This book has been written as per Revised 'G' Scheme Syllabus prepared by MSBTE for Chemical Engineering.

The aim of this book is to provide knowledge to the students related to Energy Management as well as several Fundamental Strategies in improving occupational safety and implementation & evaluation of safety programs.

We take this opportunity to express thanks to Principal Dr. R. B. Reshmlal; Principal W. G. Kharche, Prof. Navale; Shriram Polytechnic, Airoli, Prof. Bobade and Prof. Mandalik; Datta Meghe Polytechnic, Nagpur.

We would like to thanks our family members for their support.

We are also thankful to publisher Mr. Dineshbhai Furia, Mr. Jignesh Furia, Mr. M. P. Munde and its supporting staff Mr. Santosh, Mrs. Prachi Sawant, Mrs. Roshan Khan, Miss. Chaitali Takle, Mr. Ravi and Mr. Damodar for their constant followup and encouragement in bringing out the book in short period of time.

Authors

SYLLABUS

1. ENERGY SCENARIO (Hrs. 06, Marks 12)

- Primary and secondary energy sources
- Commercial and noncommercial energy sources
- Global primary energy reserves
- Indian energy scenario
- Energy security
- Energy conservation and its importance
- Features of perform achieve and trade-PAT scheme
- Salient features of EC act 2001

2. BASICS OF ENERGY (Hrs. 08, Marks 16)

- Concept of Calorific value, Specific heat, Modes of heat transfer,
- Combustion (concept and calculations)- Basics of combustion, 3 T's of combustion, Stoichiometry of combustion, Excess air in combustion
- Fuels- Types and examples of fuel, Properties of fuel, Storage of fuel
- Electrical Energy (Concept and calculations)- DC and AC, Power factor, Energy demand
- Electricity generation from thermal power plant (Concept and block diagram)

3. ENERGY AUDIT (Hrs. 10, Marks 20)

- Concept of energy audit
- Need for energy audit
- Types of energy audit - Preliminary & Detailed
- Energy audit instruments
- Structure of audit report
- Energy benchmarking
- ENCON recommendation
- Simple payback period (Definition and Calculation)

4. ENERGY EFFICIENCY IN THERMAL AND ELECTRICAL UTILITIES (Hrs. 14, Marks 32)

Boilers

- Types of boiler – salient features of fire tube, water tube, package, FCB
- Boiler evaporation ratio
- Efficiency calculation by direct method
- Advantages and disadvantages of direct method
- Steps to check performance assessment of boiler
- Energy conservation measures in boiler

Heat Exchangers

- Concept of heat exchanger
- Types of heat exchangers - by construction and flow
- LMTD
- Overall heat transfer coefficient
- Steps to check performance assessment of heat exchanger

Pumps
- Working of centrifugal Pump
- Pump performance
- Hydraulic, shaft and electrical input power
- Pump operating point
- Effect of oversizing pump
- Energy loss in throttling
- NPSH
- Effect of speed variation, Impeller trimming
- Performance assessment of pump (only method)
- Energy conservation opportunities in pump

Cooling tower
- Types of cooling tower
- Components of cooling tower
- Cooling tower performance
- Efficient system operation
- Energy saving opportunities

5. **NON-CONVENTIONAL ENERGY SOURCES**   (Hrs. 10, Marks 20)

Solar Energy
- Solar constant
- Solar insolation
- Solar water heater – construction and working flat plate collector
- Solar thermal energy
- Solar photovoltaic energy
- Construction and working of box type and parabolic solar cooker

Wind Energy
- Wind generation
- Power available in wind
- Components of wind mill
- Capacity factor

Biomass Energy
- Types of biomass
- Direct combustion of biomass
- Gasification of biomass
- Construction and working of Biogas plant
- Biofuels- types, raw material and use
  Concept of fuel cell
  Concept of wave and tidal energy
  Concept of geothermal energy
  Comparison of conventional and non-conventional energy

•••

CONTENTS

•••

Chapter 1

ENERGY SCENARIO

Objectives

Students will study and understand the following:

- Classify sources of energy
- Describe energy security measures
- State salient features of EC Act 2001

1.1 INTRODUCTION

- World moves on energy. A fluctuation in supply and price of energy imparts bad effects. Like air, water and food, man needs energy in different forms. Energy has always played an important role in human and economic development and in society's well-being.

- Without heat and electricity from fuel combustion, economic activity would be limited and restrained. Modern society uses more and more energy for industry, services, homes and transport.

- This is particularly true for oil, which has become the most traded commodity, and part of economic growth is linked to its price.

- Fuel is a substance burned as a source of heat or power. The heat is derived from the combustion process in which carbon and hydrogen in the fuel substance combine with oxygen and release heat.

- The provision of energy as heat or power in either mechanical or electrical form is the major reason for burning fuels.

1.1.1 Classification of Energy (W-13)

Energy can be classified into several types based on the following criteria:

- Primary and Secondary energy
- Commercial and Non-commercial energy
- Renewable and Non-renewable energy

- Primary energy such as crude oil, hard coal, natural gas, secondary energy which is produced from primary energy. Secondary energy comes from the transformation of primary or secondary energy.

(1.1)

- The generation of electricity by burning fuel oil is an example. Other examples include petroleum products (secondary) from crude oil (primary), coke-oven coke (secondary) from coking coal (primary), charcoal (secondary) from fuelwood (primary), etc.

- Both electricity and heat may be produced in a primary or secondary form.

- Primary heat is the capture of heat from natural sources (solar panels, geothermal reservoirs) and represents the arrival of "new" energy into the national supplies of energy commodities.

- Secondary heat is derived from the use of energy already captured or produced.

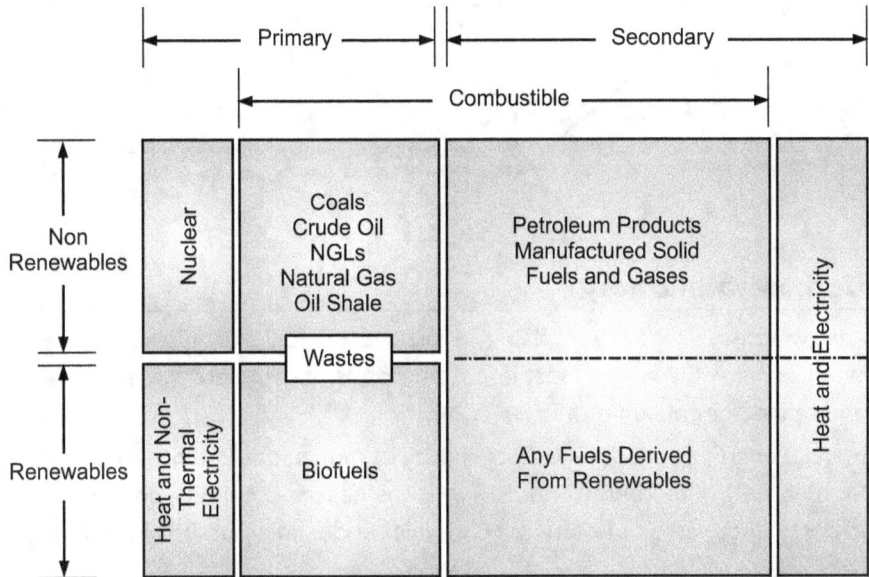

Fig. 1.1

- Primary energy may also be divided into fuels of fossil origin and renewable energy. Fossil fuels are taken from natural resources which were formed from biomass in the geological past.

- By extension, the term fossil is also applied to any secondary fuel manufactured from a fossil fuel.

- Renewable energy, apart from geothermal energy, is drawn directly or indirectly from current or recent flows of the constantly available solar and gravitational energy.

- For example, the energy value of biomass is derived from the sunlight used by plants during their growth.

- Fig. 1.2 gives a schematic illustration of renewable versus non-renewable energy, and primary versus secondary energy.

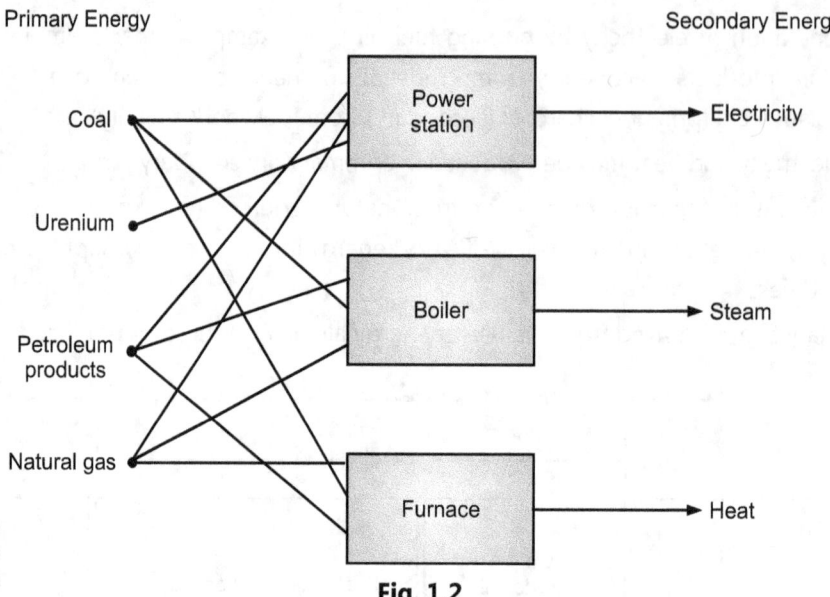

Fig. 1.2

1.1.2 Commercial Energy

• The energy sources that are available in the market for a definite price are known as commercial energy. By far the most important forms of commercial energy are electricity, coal and refined petroleum products.

• Commercial energy forms the basis of industrial, agricultural, transport and commercial development in the modern world. In the industrialized countries, commercialized fuels are predominant source not only for economic production, but also for many household tasks of general population.

Examples: Electricity, lignite, coal, oil, natural gas etc.

1.1.3 Non-Commercial Energy

• The energy sources that are not available in the commercial market for a price are classified as non-commercial energy.

• Non-commercial energy sources include fuels such as firewood, cattle dung and agricultural wastes, which are traditionally gathered, and not bought at a price used especially in rural households.

• These are also called traditional fuels. Non-commercial energy is often ignored in energy accounting.

Examples: Firewood, agro waste in rural areas; solar energy for water heating, electricity generation, for drying grain, fish and fruits; animal power for transport, threshing, lifting water for irrigation, crushing sugarcane; wind energy for lifting water and electricity generation.

1.2 GLOBAL ENERGY SCENARIO
WORLD'S PRIMARY ENERGY SOURCE

- In 2005, total worldwide energy consumption was 500 EJ (= 5×10^{20} J) with 86.5% derived from the combustion of fossil fuels. This is equivalent to 15 TW (= 1.5×10^{13} W) of power.

- Most of the world energy resources are from the sun's rays hitting earth - some of that energy has been preserved as fossil energy, some is directly or indirectly usable e.g. via wind, hydro or wave power.

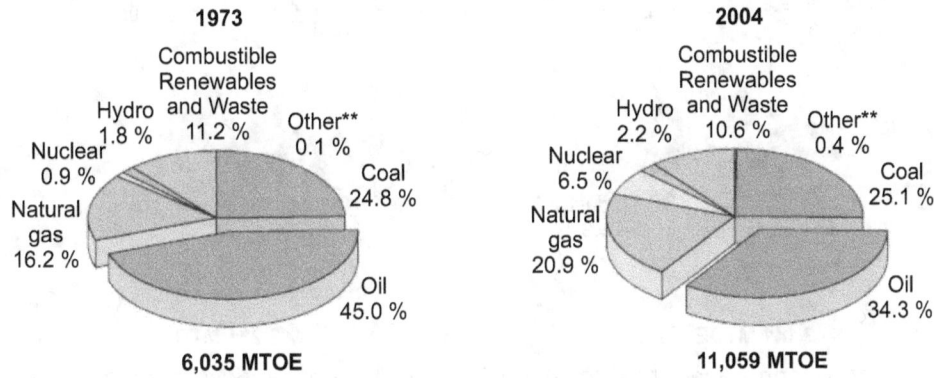

Fig. 1.3: World total primary energy supply in 1973 and 2004

1.2.1 Oil

- The global proven oil reserve was estimated to be 1147 billion barrels by the end of 2003.
- Saudi Arabia had the largest share of the reserve with almost 23%. (One barrel of oil is approximately 160 litres).

Table 1.1: Oil producing countries in the world

Country	Oil (Million tonnes)	% of World Reservoirs
USA	3700	2.5
Venezuela	11500	6.6
Kazakstan	5500	3.3
Russian Federation	10900	6.6
Iran	18900	11.4
Iraq	15500	9.5
Kuwait	14500	8.4
Qutar	2000	1.3
Saudi Arabia	36300	21.9

Contd...

UAE	13000	8.1
Libya	5400	3.4
Nigeria	4900	3.0
China	2200	1.3
India	800	0.5
World	**146500**	**100**

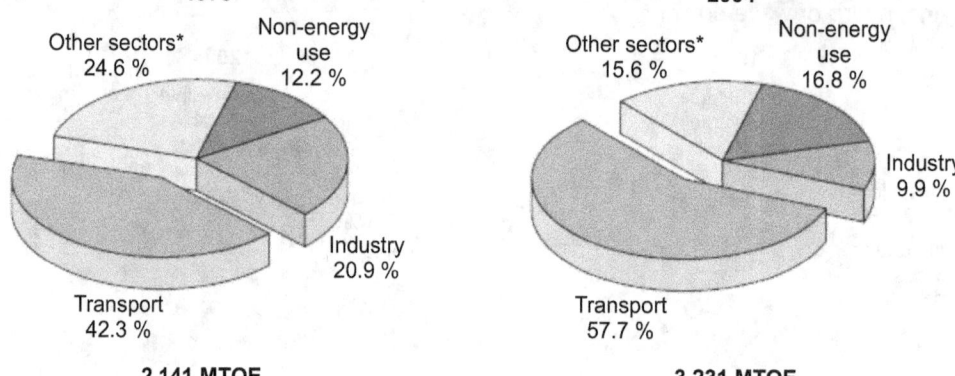

*Other sectors comprise agriculture, commercial and public service, residential and non-specified

Fig. 1.4: World oil consumption

1.2.2 Coal

- The proven global coal reserve was estimated to be 9,84,453 million tonnes by end of 2003.
- The USA had the largest share of the global reserve (25.4%) followed by Russia (15.9%), China (11.6%). India was 4th in the list with 8.6%.

Table 1.2: Coal producing countries in the world

Country	Coal (Million tonnes)	% of World Reservoirs
USA	246643	27.1
Brazil	10113	1.1
Kazakstan	31279	3.4
Russian Federation	157010	17.3
Ukraine	34153	3.8
South Africa	48750	5.4
Australia	78500	8.6

Contd...

China	114500	12.6
India	92445	10.2
World	**909064**	**100**

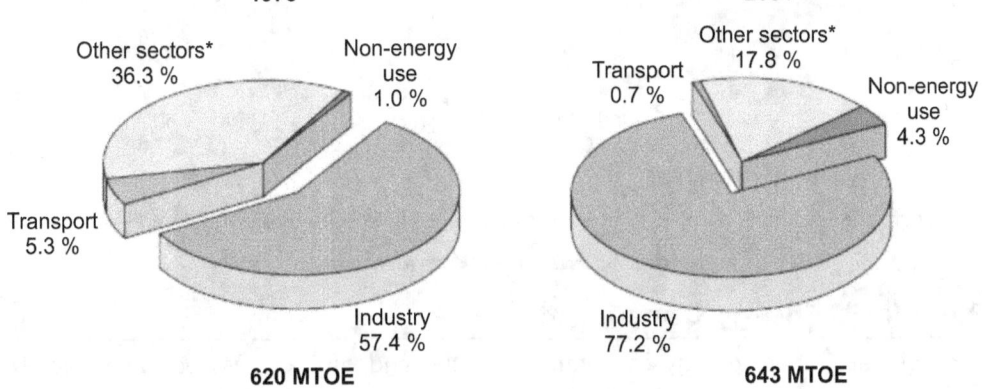

*Other sectors comprise agriculture, commercial and public service, residential and non-specified

Fig. 1.5: World coal consumption

1.2.3 Gas

- The global proven gas reserve was estimated to be 176 trillion cubic metres by the end of 2003.
- The Russian Federation had the largest share of the reserve with almost 27%.

Table 1.3: Gas producing countries in the world

Country	Natural Gas (TCM)	% of World Reservoirs
USA	5.90	3.3
Venezuela	4.32	2.4
Russian Federation	47.65	26.3
Iran	28.13	15.5
Qutar	25.36	14.0
Soudi Arabia	7.07	3.9
UAE	6.06	3.3
Algeria	4.50	2.5
Nigeria	5.21	2.9
China	2.45	1.3
India	1.08	0.6
World	**181.46**	**100**

TCM: Trillion cubic meter

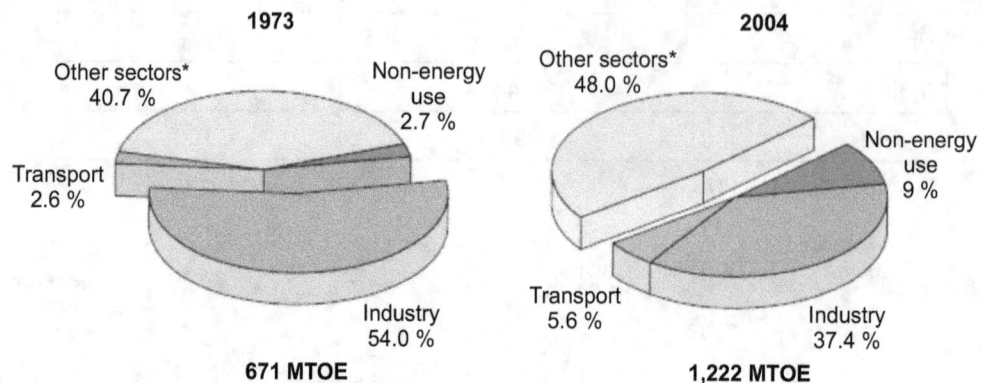

*Other sectors comprise agriculture, commercial and public service, residential and non-specified

Fig. 1.6: World gas consumption

1.2.4 World Energy Consumption

- The global primary energy consumption at the end of 2003 was equivalent to 9741 million tonnes of oil equivalent (MTOE). Table 1.4 shows in what proportions the sources mentioned above contributed to this global figure.

- The primary energy consumption for few of the developed and developing countries are shown in Table 1.4.

- It may be seen that India's absolute primary energy consumption is only 1/29th of the world, 1/7th of USA, 1/1.6[th] time of Japan but 1.1, 1.3, 1.5 times that of Canada, France and UK respectively.

Table 1.4: World's Total Energy Consumption

Country	Oil (MTOE)	Gas (MTOE)	Coal (MTOE)
USA	938.8	566.9	567.3
Canada	98.8	87.0	35.0
France	92.8	40.6	13.1
Russian Federation	128.5	388.9	112.3
UK	82.2	81.7	43.8
China	349.8	50.0	1191.3
India	120.3	35.8	237.7
Japan	235.0	76.1	119.1
Singapore	44.0	5.9	0.0
Pakistan	18.4	27.6	4.0
Australia	40.3	25.8	51.1
Germany	123.5	78.5	82.4
World	**3889.9**	**2574.9**	**3090.1**

MTOE - Million tonnes of oil equivalent

1.2.5 Energy Scenario in India   (S-12, S-13)

- Energy is the prime mover of economic growth and is vital to the sustenance of a modern economy.
- Future economic growth crucially depends on the long-term availability of energy from sources that are affordable, accessible and environmentally friendly.
- India ranks sixth in the world in total energy consumption and needs to accelerate the development of the sector to meet its growth aspirations. The country, though rich in coal and abundantly endowed with renewable energy in the form of solar, wind, hydro and bio-energy has very small hydrocarbon reserves (0.4% of the world's reserve).
- India, like many other developing countries, is a net importer of energy, more than 25 per cent of primary energy needs being met through imports mainly in the form of crude oil and natural gas.
- The rising oil import bill has been the focus of serious concerns due to the pressure it has placed on scarce foreign exchange resources and is also largely responsible for energy supply shortages.
- The sub-optimal consumption of commercial energy adversely affects the productive sectors, which in turn hampers economic growth.
- If we look at the pattern of energy production, coal and oil account for 54 per cent and 34 per cent respectively with natural gas, hydro and nuclear contributing to the balance.
- In the power generation front, nearly 62 per cent of power generation is from coal-fired thermal power plants and 70 per cent of the coal produced every year in India has been used for thermal generation.
- The distribution of primary commercial energy resources in India is quite skewed. 70 per cent of the total hydro potential is located in the Northern and Northeastern regions, whereas the Eastern region accounts for nearly 70 per cent of the total coal reserves in the country.
- The Southern region, which has only 6 per cent of the total coal reserves and 10 per cent of the total hydro potential, has most of the lignite deposits occurring in the country.
- On the consumption front, the **industrial sector** in India is a major energy user accounting for about 52 per cent of commercial energy consumption. **Per capita energy consumption** in India is one of the lowest in the world.
- But, **energy intensity**, which is energy consumption per unit of GDP, is one of the highest in comparison to other developed and developing countries.
- For example, it is 3.7 times that of Japan, 1.55 times that of the United States, 1.47 times that of Asia and 1.5 times that of the world average. Thus, there is a huge scope for energy conservation in the country.

Coal Supply:

- Coal has been recognized as the most important source of energy for electricity generation in India.
- About 75% of the coal in the country is consumed in the power sector. In addition, other industries like steel, cement, fertilizers, chemicals, paper and thousands of medium and small-scale industries are also dependent on coal for their process and energy requirements.
- In the transport sector, though direct consumption of coal by the Railways is going down on account of phasing out of steam locomotives, the energy requirement for electric traction is still dependent on coal converted into electric power.
- The Department of Coal is engaged in developing coal resources of this country in a manner to meet the requirements of coal of different consuming sectors. Performance of coal sector in this respect has been impressive.

Table 1.5: Coal resources in India

State	Coal Resources in Million Tonnes			
	Proved	**Indicated**	**Inferred**	**Total**
Andhra Pradesh	8403	6158	2584	17145
Arunachal Pradesh	31	40	19	90
Assam	315	27	34	376
Bihar	0	0	160	160
Chhattisgarh	9570	27433	4439	41442
Jharkhand	36148	31411	6339	73898
Madhya Pradesh	7565	9258	2935	19758
Maharashtra	4653	2432	1992	9077
Meghalaya	117	41	301	459
Nagaland	4	1	15	20
Orissa	16911	30793	14295	61999
Uttar Pradesh	766	296	0	1062
West Bengal	11383	11879	4553	27815
Total	**95866**	**119769**	**37666**	**253301**

Oil Supply:

- Oil accounts for about 36 per cent of India's total energy consumption. India today is one of the top ten oil-guzzling nations in the world and will soon overtake Korea as the third largest consumer of oil in Asia after China and Japan.
- The country's annual crude oil production is peaked at about 32 million tonne as against the current peak demand of about 110 million tonne.
- In the current scenario, India's oil consumption by the end of 2007 is expected to reach 136 million tonne (MT), of which domestic production will be only 34 MT.
- India will have to pay an oil bill of roughly $50 billion, assuming a weighted average price of $50 per barrel of crude.
- In 2003-04, against total export of $64 billion, oil imports accounted for $21 billion. India imports 70% of its crude needs mainly from gulf nations.
- The majority of India's roughly 5.4 billion barrels in oil reserves are located in the Bombay High, upper Assam, Cambay, Krishna-Godavari.
- In terms of sector-wise petroleum product consumption, transport accounts for 42% followed by domestic and industry with 24% and 24% respectively.
- India spent more than ₹ 1,10,000 crore on oil imports at the end of 2004.

Gas Supply:

- Natural gas accounts for about 8.9 per cent of energy consumption in the country.
- The current demand for natural gas is about 96 million cubic metres per day (mcmd) as against availability of 67 mcmd. By 2007, the demand is expected to be around 200 mcmd.
- Natural gas reserves are estimated at 660 billion cubic metres.

Electric Energy Supply:

- Harnessed energy has become a symbol of growth and instrument for development. Electric power particularly the hydro is among the cleanest and renewable energy input for economic activity, domestic and civic conveniences, climate control, communication and technology.
- Power generation in India began more than a century ago in 1898 when the first hydro power unit was set up at Darjeeling. When India achieved freedom in 1947, the country had an installed capacity of 1,360 MW.
- The present installed generating capacity in the country is 1,07,973 MW. The share of hydro with 26,910 MW capacity is about 25%.
- Thermal accounts for maximum share of 71% with 76,607 MW. It comprises of 63,801 MW from Coal, 11,633 MW from Gas and 1,173 MW from Diesel. The share of Nuclear is about 2.5% with 2,720 MW while Wind accounts for the balance 1,736 MW. The attainment is significant.

Table 1.6: Total Installed Capacity

Sector	MW	Percentage
State Sector	74,829.36	52.5
Central Sector	48,470.99	34.0
Private Sector	20010.66	13.5
Total	**1,43,311.01**	

Table 1.7: Percentage of various sources for Power Generation

Fuel		MW	Percentage
Total Thermal		92,156.84	64.6
	Coal	76,298.88	53.3
	Gas	14,656.21	10.5
	Oil	1,201.75	0.9
Hydro (Renewable)		35,908.76	24.7
Nuclear		4,120.00	2.9
RES** (MNRE)		11125.41	7.7
Total		**1,43,311.01**	

**Renewable Energy Sources (RES) include SHP, BG, U&I and Wind Energy.

1.3 ENERGY SECURITY　　　　　　(S-12, W-13)

- The basic aim of energy security for a nation is to reduce its dependency on the imported energy sources for its economic growth.
- India will continue to experience an energy supply shortfall throughout the forecast period. This gap has widened since 1985, when the country became a net importer of coal.
- India has been unable to raise its oil production substantially in the 1990s. Rising oil demand of close to 10 per cent per year has led to sizable oil import bills.
- In addition, the government subsidises refined oil product prices, thus compounding the overall monetary loss to the government.
- Imports of oil and coal have been increasing at rates of 7% and 16% per annum respectively during the period 1991 – 99. The dependence on energy imports is projected to increase in the future.

- Estimates indicate that oil imports will meet 75% of total oil consumption requirements and coal imports will meet 22% of total coal consumption requirements in 2006.
- The imports of gas and LNG (liquefied natural gas) are likely to increase in the coming years.
- This energy import dependence implies vulnerability to external price stocks and supply fluctuations, which threaten the energy security of the country.
- Increasing dependence on oil imports means reliance on imports from the Middle East, a region susceptible to disturbances and consequent disruptions of oil supplies.
- This calls for diversification of sources of oil imports. The need to deal with oil price fluctuations also necessitates measures to be taken to reduce the oil dependence of the economy, possibly through renewable energy.
- Some of the strategies that can be used to meet future challenges to their energy security are
  - Building stockpiles
  - Diversification of energy supply sources
  - Increased capacity of fuel switching
  - Demand restraint
  - Development of renewable energy sources
  - Energy efficiency
  - Sustainable development
- Although all these options are feasible, their implementation will take time. Also, for countries like India, reliance on stockpiles would tend to be slow because of resource constraints.
- Besides, the market is not sophisticated enough or the monitoring agencies experienced enough to predict the supply situation in time to take necessary action.
- Insufficient storage capacity is another cause for worry and needs to be augmented, if India has to increase its energy stockpile.
- However, out of all these options, the simplest and the most easily attainable is reducing demand through persistent energy conservation efforts.

1.4 ENERGY CONSERVATION　(S-12, W-13)

- Energy cost is a significant factor in economic activity, on par with factors of production like capital, land and labor.
- During the last four decades, the induction of energy efficient technologies has lead to dramatic reduction in energy usage in chemical process industries.
- Due to compulsions from global competition to be highly cost competitive and the awareness thereof, companies are on a drive to reduce costs.
- Energy consumption in Chemical Process Industries (CPI) is dependent on the products manufactured and process employed.

- Energy cost in caustic chlorine plant is around 60% of the manufacturing cost. But on an average the energy cost in CPI lies between 10-12% of the total manufacturing cost.
- Therefore, energy cost reduction can play a significant role in increasing the profitability of any CPI. On an average the net profit of a company is around 3% of revenue.
- For companies having utility cost as 10% of revenue, a saving of 20% in utility consumption can result in an increase of profit by 66%.

Table 1.8: Percentage Cost of energy to various Industries

Industry	Energy Cost as % gross output
Organic Chemicals	5.8
Inorganic Chemicals	10.3
Pharmaceuticals	1.6
Paper	7.5
Cement	20
Glass	8.3
Fibre	3.8
Steel Industry	12
Aluminium	3.8
Plastic and Rubber	3.5
Car Manufacturing	1.4
Electrical Appliances	1.7
Pottery	6.5
Food Processing	1.6

- Energy conservation is many times understood as a cut in energy consumption but actually it is a cut in the misuse/waste of energy.
- Successful firms concentrate on efficiency first, products second, and then on marketing and sales.
- Revenue expansion based on efficient operations results in severe operating losses.
- Successful companies reduce cost to watch existing revenue levels. Unsuccessful companies attempt to increase revenue to cover existing costs.
- Countries economical condition is dependent upon price of crude oil. Our country is importer of crude oil and amount accounts of thousands of crore rupees.
- In the world market, price of crude oil is continuously increasing. The imperatives of energy shortage call for energy conservation measures, which essentially mean using less energy for the same level of activity.

- Energy conservation is the deliberate practice or an attempt to save electricity, fuel oil or gas or any other combustible material, to be able to put to additional use for additional productivity without spending any additional resources or money.
- Energy is a scarce commodity. Energy in any form is a scarce commodity and an expensive resource. However, if we look at the predicted future human pollution figures and consider the probability that the individual life expectation will increase, we see that energy could, in the future, be in short supply.
- Unless that supply is increased it will be a source of friction in human affairs.

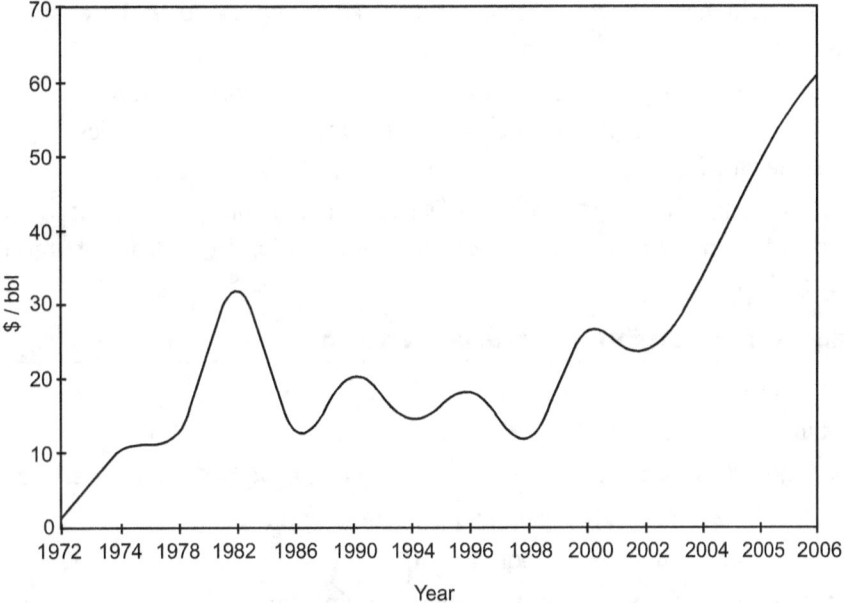

Fig. 1.7: Crude oil price in US dollar/barrel

1.4.1 Energy Conservation Objectives

- Broadly, energy conservation program initiated at micro or macro level will have the following objectives of manufactured goods (either lower process or increased) availability and profitability, and in consequence raise the standard of living both of the workers in industry and of those who buy the products.

  (a) To reduce imports of energy and reduce the drain on foreign exchange.

  (b) To improve exports of manufactured goods (either lower process or increased availability helping sales) or of energy, or both.

  (c) To reduce environmental pollution per unit of industrial output - as carbon dioxide, smoke, sulphur dioxide, dust, grit or as coal mine discard for example.

  (d) Thus, reducing the costs that pollution incurs either directly as damage, or as needing, special measures to combat it once pollutants are produced.

  (e) Generally to relieve shortage and improve development.

1.4.2 Energy Efficiency

- Energy efficiency means using less energy to perform the same function. It is achieved when energy intensity in a specific product, process or area of production or consumption is reduced without effecting output, consumption or comfort levels.

- Promotion of energy efficiency will contribute to energy conservation and is therefore an integral part of energy conservation promotional policies.

- Energy efficiency is often viewed as a resource option like coil, oil or natural gas. It provides additional economic value by preserving the resource base and reducing pollution.

- For example, replacing traditional light bulbs with Compact Fluorescent Lamps (CFLs) means you will use only $1/4^{th}$ of the energy to light a room. Pollution levels also reduce by the same amount.

- Nature sets some basic limits on how efficiently energy can be used, but in most cases our products and manufacturing processes are still a long way from operating at this theoretical limit.

1.4.3 Measures for Energy Conservation   (S-12)

Short Term Measures:

(Potential savings of 5 to 10%).

(a) Meeting operational improvements requiring nil/negligible capital investment.

(b) Improved fuel storage, handling and preparation practices.

(c) Insulation of steam lines and equipment.

(d) House keeping and scheduling of process equipment.

(e) Minimizing radiation losses through opening.

(f) Improved load factor.

Medium Term Measures:

(Potential savings of 15 to 20%).

(a) Waste heat recovery devices and modifications and design of equipment, needing moderate capital investment with payback period of around three years.

(b) Installation of waste heat recovery devices.

(c) Reducing wall losses in the furnaces with better insulating materials.

(d) Instrumentation of furnace and process house.

(e) Change of grate design and firing system.

(f) Incorporation of condensate recovery system.

(g) Power factor improvement.

(h) Optimization.

Long Term Measures:

(Potential savings of 20 to 25%).

(a) Fuel substitution, modernization of equipment, process as well as utilities and capital intensive heat recovery devices with payback period of 5 to 6 years.

(b) Replacement of old inefficient boilers / equipments.

(c) Substitution of fuel oil to coal in boilers and thermic fuel heater or other equipments.

(d) Modernization of inefficient drives.

(e) Replacement of furnaces with modern efficient ones.

(f) Standardization.

(g) Use of correct size of motors.

(h) Optimization.

(Total savings through all measures = 20% to 30%).

1.4.4 Environment and Energy

- The usage of energy resources in industry leads to environmental damages by polluting the atmosphere.

- Few of examples of air pollution are sulphur dioxide (SO_2), nitrous oxide (NO_x) and carbon monoxide (CO) emissions from boilers and furnaces, chloro-fluro carbons (CFC) emissions from refrigerants use, etc.

- In chemical and fertilizers industries, toxic gases are released. Cement plants and power plants spew out particulate matter.

- A variety of air pollutants have known or suspected harmful effects on human health and the environment.

- These air pollutants are basically the products of combustion from fossil fuel use.

- Air pollutants from these sources may not only create problems near to these sources but also can cause problems far away.

- Air pollutants can travel long distances, chemically react in the atmosphere to produce secondary pollutants such as acid rain or ozone.

- Greenhouse gases makeup only 1 per cent of the atmosphere, but they act as a blanket around the earth, or like a glass roof of a greenhouse and keep the earth 30 degrees warmer than it would be otherwise - without greenhouse gases, earth would be too cold to live.

- Human activities that are responsible for making the greenhouse layer thicker are emissions of carbon dioxide from the combustion of coal, oil and natural gas; by additional methane and nitrous oxide from farming activities and changes in land use; and by several man made gases that have a long life in the atmosphere.

- The increase in greenhouse gases is happening at an alarming rate. If greenhouse gases emissions continue to grow at current rates, it is almost certain that the atmospheric levels of carbon dioxide will increase twice or thrice from pre-industrial levels during the 21st century.

- Even a small increase in earth's temperature will be accompanied by changes in climate- such as cloud cover, precipitation, wind patterns and duration of seasons.

- In an already highly crowded and stressed earth, millions of people depend on weather patterns, such as monsoon rains, to continue as they have in the past. Even minimum changes will be disruptive and difficult.

- Carbon dioxide is responsible for 60 per cent of the "enhanced greenhouse effect". Humans are burning coal, oil and natural gas at a rate that is much faster than the rate at which these fossil fuels were created.

- This is releasing the carbon stored in the fuels into the atmosphere and upsetting the carbon cycle (a precise balanced system by which carbon is exchanged between the air, the oceans and land vegetation taking place over millions of years). Currently, carbon dioxide levels in the atmosphere are rising by over 10 per cent every 20 years.

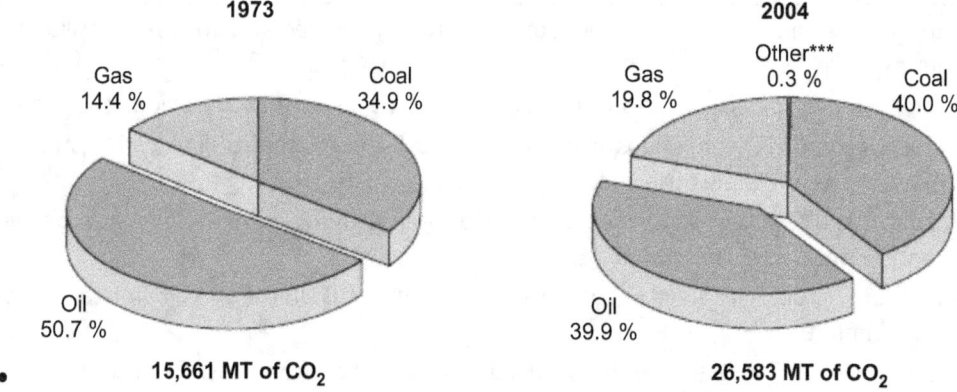

-       **15,661 MT of CO$_2$**   **26,583 MT of CO$_2$**

* World includes international aviation and international marine bunkers.

** Calculated using IEA's Energy balance Tables and the Revised 1996 IPCC Guidelines. CO$_2$ emissions are from fuel combustion only.

*** Other includes industries waste and non-renewable municipal waste.

Fig. 1.8: Total CO$_2$ emission in world

1.5 ENERGY CONSERVATION ACT

- Considering the vast potential of energy savings and benefits of energy efficiency, the Government of India enacted the Energy Conservation Act, 2001.

- The Act provides for the legal framework, institutional arrangement and a regulatory mechanism at the Central and State level to embark upon energy efficiency drive in the country.

1.5.1 Salient Features of the Energy Conservation Act 2001

(S-12, S-13)

The Act empowers the Central Government and, in some instances, State Governments to:

- specify energy consumption standards for notified equipment and appliances;
- direct mandatory display of label on notified equipment and appliances;
- prohibit manufacture, sale, purchase and import of notified equipment and appliances not conforming to energy consumption standards;
- notify energy intensive industries, other establishments, and commercial buildings as designated consumers;
- establish and prescribe energy consumption norms and standards for designated consumers;
- prescribe energy conservation building codes for efficient use of energy and its conservation in new commercial buildings having a connected load of 500 kW or a contract demand of 600 kVA and above;
- direct designated consumers to:
  - designate or appoint certified energy manager in charge of activities for efficient use of energy and its conservation;
  - get an energy audit conducted by an accredited energy auditor in the specified manner and interval of time;
  - furnish information with regard to energy consumed and action taken on the recommendation of the accredited energy auditor to the designed agency;
  - comply with energy consumption norms and standards;
  - prepare and implement schemes for efficient use of energy and its conservation if the prescribed energy consumption norms and standards are not fulfilled;
    - get energy audit of the building conducted by an accredited energy auditor in this specified manner and intervals of time;
- State Governments may :
  - amend the energy conservation building codes prepared by the Central Government to suit regional and local climatic conditions;
  - direct every owners or occupier of a new commercial building or building complex being a designated consumer to comply with the provisions of energy conservation building codes;
  - direct, if considered necessary for efficient use of energy and its conservation, any designated consumer to get energy audit conducted by an accredited energy auditor in such manner and at such intervals of time as may be specified.

1.5.2 Establishment of Bureau of Energy Efficiency

- Under the previsions of the Act, Bureau of Energy Efficiency has been established with effect from 1st March, 2002 by merging the erstwhile Energy Management Centre, a society under the Ministry of Power.
- The Bureau would be responsible for spearheading the improvement of energy efficiency of the economy through various regulatory and promotional instruments.
- The mission of the Bureau of Energy Efficiency is to develop policy and strategies with a thrust on self-regulation and market principles, within the overall framework of the Energy Conservation Act, 2001 with the primary objective of reducing energy intensity of the Indian economy.
- This will be achieved with active participation of all stake holders, resulting in accelerated and sustained adoption of energy efficiency in all sectors of the economy.
- The primary objective of BEE is to reduce energy intensity in the Indian economy through adoption of result oriented approach.
- The broad objectives of the BEE are:
  o to assume leadership and provide policy framework and direction to national energy efficiency and conservation efforts and programmes;
  o to co-ordinate policies and programmes on efficient use of energy and its conservation with the involvement of stakeholders;
  o to establish systems and procedures to measure, monitor and verify energy efficiency results in individual sectors as well as at national level;
  o to leverage multi-lateral, bi-lateral and private sector support in implementation of the Energy Conservation Act and programmes for efficient use of energy and its conservation;
  o to demonstrate energy efficiency delivery mechanisms, through private-public partnership;
  o to plan, manage and implement energy conservation programmes as envisaged in the Energy Conservation Act.
- The Director-General is the chief executive officer of the Bureau of Energy Efficiency.
- The general superintendence, direction and management of the affairs of BEE is vested in the Governing Council having upto 26 members.
- The Governing Council is headed by Union Minister of Power and consists of Secretaries of various line Ministries, heads of various technical agencies under the Ministries, members representing industry, equipment and appliance manufacturers, architects and consumers, and members from each of the five power regions representing the states of the region.
- The Director-General of the Bureau is the ex-officio member-secretary of the Governing Council.
- BEE has been given a corpus fund of ₹ 50 Crore for setting up of the Central Energy Conservation Fund for meeting the expenses relating to the salaries, allowances and

other remuneration of the officers and employees of the Bureau and to meet the expenses of the Bureau in discharge of its functions as well as on objects and for purposes authorized by the Act.

- It has also been authorized to collect appropriate fees in discharge of functions assigned to it and raise funds from other sources. BEE may become self-sufficient in a period of 5-7 years.

1.5.3 Functions of BEE   (S-12)

- The functions of BEE can be classified as regulatory functions being recommendatory body to the Central Government in implementing the provisions of the Energy Conservation Act and facilitation, market development and market transformation functions such as:
  - o arrange and organize training of personnel and specialists in the techniques for efficient uses of energy and its conservation;
  - o develop testing and certification procedures and promote testing facilities;
  - o strengthen consultancy services;
  - o create awareness and disseminate information;
  - o promote research and development;
  - o formulate and facilitate implementation of pilot projects and demonstration projects;
  - o promote use of energy efficient processes, equipment, devices and systems;
  - o take steps to encourage preferential treatment for use of energy efficient equipment or appliances;
  - o promote innovative financing of energy efficiency projects;
  - o give financial assistance to institutions for promoting efficient use of energy and its conservation;
  - o prepare educational curriculum on efficient use of energy and its conservation and
  - o implement international co-operation programmes relating to efficient use of energy and its conservation.

SOME IMPORTANT CONVERSION FACTORS

Table 1.9: General conversion factors for energy

From \ To	TJ	Gcal	Mtoe	MBtu	GWh
	Multiply by:				
TJ	1	238.8	2.388×10^{-5}	947.8	0.2778
Gcal	4.1868×10^{-3}	1	10^{-7}	3.968	1.163×10^{-3}
Mtoe	4.1868×10^{4}	10^{7}	1	3.968×10^{7}	11630
MBtu	1.0551×10^{-3}	0.252	2.52×10^{-8}	1	2.931×10^{-4}
GWh	3.6	860	8.6×10^{-5}	3412	1

Table 1.10: General conversion factors for mass

To From	kg	t	lt	st	lb
	Multiply by:				
Kilogram (kg)	1	0.001	9.84×10^{-4}	1.102×10^{-3}	2.2046
tonne (t)	1000	1	0.984	1.1023	2204.6
long ton (lt)	1016	1.016	1	1.120	2240.0
short ton (st)	907.2	0.9072	0.893	1	2000.0
pound (lb)	0.454	4.54×10^{-4}	4.46×10^{-4}	5.0×10^{-4}	1

Table 1.11: General conversion factors for volume

To From	gal U.S.	gal U.K.	bbl	ft^3	l	m^3
	Multiply by:					
U.S. Gallon (gal)	1	0.8327	0.02381	0.1337	3.785	0.0038
U.K. Gallon (gal)	1.201	1	0.02859	0.1605	4.546	0.0045
Barrel (bbl)	42.0	34.97	1	5.615	159.0	0.159
Cubic foot (ft^3)	7.48	6.229	0.1781	1	28.3	0.0283
Litre (l)	0.2642	0.220	0.0063	0.0353	1	0.001
Cubic metre (m^3)	264.2	220.0	6.289	35.3147	1000.0	1

Practice Questions

1. Define the following terms:
   (a) Primary and secondary energy.
   (b) Commercial and non-commercial energy.
   (c) Renewable and non-renewable energy.
2. List at least five states where coal deposits are concentrated in India.
3. How much percentage of our country's oil consumption is imported and how much does it cost (approximately) per year ?
4. Name any three places of oil reserves located in India.
5. What is the hydropower generation potential available in India and how much is exploited so far.
6. What are the percentage shares of commercial energy consumption in industrial and agricultural sector ?

7. How is economic growth linked to energy consumption ?

8. What do you think of strategies required for long term management of energy in India ?

9. Differentiate between energy conservation and energy efficiency.

10. Name any three main provisions of the EC act 2001 as applicable to the designated consumers.

11. What do you understand by the word Energy Security.

12. Give importance of energy conservation.

MSBTE Questions and Answers (As Per 'E' Scheme)

Summer 2012

1. Write any four salient features of energy conservation Act 2001.

Ans. Please refer to Section 1.5.1.

2. How is energy conservation? State its importance in industry. How energy conservation cell will catalyse energy conservation activities in industry?

Ans. Please refer to Section 1.4.

3. State any four energy conservation measures in a pump.

Ans. Please refer to Section 1.4.3.

4. What is BEE? State its role in energy conservation Act 2001.

Ans. Please refer to Section 1.5.3.

5. How energy conservation measures are classified according to type of investment?

Ans. Please refer to Section 1.4.3.

6. Why energy security is important for our nation?

Ans. Please refer to Section 1.3.

7. Explain Indian energy scenario w.r.t. petroleum fuels and electricity production. Why our crude oil import bill is increasing day by day?

Ans. Please refer to Section 1.2.5.

Winter 2013

1. How are energy classified? State any two objectives of energy management?

Ans. Please refer to Section 1.1.1.

2. Write any four energy conservation Act 2001.

Ans. Please refer to Section 1.5.3.

3. Explain the importance of energy conservation. Also state the stages of Indian energy scenario.

Ans. Please refer to Sections 1.4 and 1.2.5.

4. What are the factors to be considered for energy security.

Ans. Please refer to Section 1.3.

❑❑❑

Chapter 2

BASICS OF ENERGY

Objectives

Students will study and understand the following:

- Give examples of modes of heat transfer
- Calculate energy content in fuel
- Calculate power factor

2.1 BASICS OF ENERGY

- Energy is important because it provides the ability to do work. Work is done when one or more forces move an object over a distance.
- The objects being moved can be very small, such as molecules, atoms, electrons, or protons, or they can be much larger objects.
- When forces act on objects and do work, energy is converted from one form to another. In later periods, we will learn how forces act on objects to do work. All forces can be related to one or more of the four fundamental forces of nature.
- As energy is converted from one form into another, the Law of Conservation of Energy requires that no energy can be lost.
- The total amount of energy put into a conversion process must equal the total amount of energy out. However, during each energy conversion, some energy is converted into a form other than the form you desire. Energy converted into an undesirable form is called wasted energy.
- Many energy conversion processes require multiple steps, such as the steps involved when coal is converted into electrical energy. Each step in the process converts some energy into a form other than that needed for the next step.
- Because of this wasted energy, the amount of electrical energy obtained is less than the amount of energy in the coal burned to produce the electricity.
- The energy wasted at each step makes the overall process less efficient than the efficiency of any step.
- Electrical energy is measured in an energy unit, kilowatt-hour (kWh). Quantities of heat in steam flows are calculated from measurements of the pressure and temperature of the steam and may be expressed in calories or joules.
- Apart from the measurements to derive the heat content of steam, heat flows are rarely measured but inferred from the fuel used to produce them.

(2.1)

2.1.1 Various Forms of Energy

- Although there are many ways to classify energy, the first three forms of energy are related to the energy of motion associated with moving objects, atoms, and molecules.

    (1) Mechanical Energy of Motion: Moving objects exhibit mechanical energy of motion, also called kinetic energy. A ball thrown through the air or a car travelling down a road has mechanical energy of motion.

    (2) Thermal Energy: Energy of motion occurs within an object as its atoms and molecules vibrate randomly. Thermal energy is the unorganized energy of motion of vibrating objects too small to see. The faster the atoms and molecules in a substance vibrate, the more thermal energy the substance has and the higher its temperature.

    (3) Sound Energy: When atoms and molecules vibrate in an organized manner, their vibrations may travel as a wave. Sound is the transmission of vibrations through a solid, liquid, or gas by vibrating atoms or molecules. When sound waves reach our eardrums, the energy in the sound waves causes our eardrums to vibrate. Our brains interpret the vibrations as sounds.

    Matter contains positive and negative charges. Forms of energy that result from the forces between these charges are called electromagnetic energy. We can distinguish three forms of electromagnetic energy.

    (4) Electrical Energy: Electrical energy results from the forces between charged particles. These electrical forces exist between charged particles at rest and in motion.

    (5) Magnetic Energy: Charges moving within some types of materials produce magnetic forces. These magnetic forces are in addition to the electrical forces between moving charges. Magnetic materials are called magnets and attract or repel one another due to their magnetic forces. A coil of wire with charges moving through it acts like a magnet and is called an electromagnet.

    (6) Radiant Energy: While vibrations of matter produce thermal and sound energy, radiant energy results from vibrations of charges. Radiant energy is another name for waves of electromagnetic energy. For example, the sun's energy is transported to Earth as waves of radiant energy. Radio waves, microwaves, infrared radiation, light waves, X-rays and cosmic rays are all waves of radiant energy.

    Stored energy, which can be used to do work, is called potential energy. We consider five types of potential energy.

    (7) Gravitational Potential Energy: When a rock is raised above the Earth and released, the gravitational attraction between the rock and the Earth causes the rock to fall to the ground. A raised object has gravitational potential energy.

    (8) Strain Potential Energy: If we stretch or compress a spring and release it, the spring moves back toward its original length. The stretched or compressed spring has strain potential energy because it has the potential to move.

(9) **Chemical Potential Energy:** Chemical potential energy exists because atoms and molecules can take in or give off energy when their chemical bonds are formed or broken.

(10) **Electrical Potential Energy:** Electrical potential energy is stored when positive and negative electric charges are separated. The amount of stored energy depends on the number of separated charges and the distance they are separated.

(11) **Nuclear Energy:** In nuclear reactions, energy is given off or taken in by atomic nuclei. Energy is available from the nuclei of atoms that are radioactive and undergo nuclear changes.

2.1.2 Energy Conversions

- Often the form of energy most readily available is not the most useful form.
- Coal can be burned to provide heat, but converting the chemical energy stored in coal into electrical energy requires a series of intermediate steps.
- In each step of the conversion process, some energy is wasted.

Electrical Energy to Mechanical Energy of Motion:

- The model electric train illustrates the conversion of electrical energy into mechanical energy of motion.
- Electrical energy, which operates the train, is generated at a power plant. The electric motor in the train's engine transforms that electrical energy into mechanical energy of motion.
- Since electrical energy is delivered to the train at a nearly constant rate, the train slows down as it climbs an incline because energy is required to lift the train up as well as to move it forward.
- As the train climbs the incline, some of its mechanical energy of motion is converted into gravitational potential energy.

Mechanical Energy to Motion Electrical Energy:

- Although we cannot easily store large amounts of electrical energy, electricity can be continuously transferred to us from a generating plant.
- In class, you will use hand-cranked generators to convert the mechanical energy of motion of your arm into electrical energy.
- In future periods we will learn more about the power plant generators that provide electricity for our homes and businesses.

Electrical Energy to Thermal Energy:

- The conversion of electrical energy into thermal energy is the most common energy conversion in our household appliances. Many appliances, such as toasters, hair dryers, and electric heaters, convert electrical energy into useful thermal energy.
- Appliances designed for purposes other than providing heat waste energy by converting some of their electrical energy into undesirable thermal energy, giving the warmth you feel when you touch an operating television or computer.

Thermal Energy to Mechanical Energy of Motion:

- Appliances, such as toasters and hair dryers, contain thermostats to regulate their temperature.
- Some thermostats illustrate the conversion of thermal energy into mechanical energy of motion.
- In class you will see a demonstration of how thermostats with bimetallic strips work.
- A bimetallic strip consists of two layers of different metals, which react differently when they are heated. The metal in one layer of the strip expands more when heated than does the metal in the other layer, causing the strip to bend.
- When a bimetallic strip is heated to a critical temperature, the strip bends until it opens a switch, which interrupts the flow of electric current and turns off the appliance.

Radiant Energy to Electrical Energy:

- Solar cells convert radiant energy from the sun into electrical energy. In class, we will use solar cells to light a flashlight bulb, run a toy car, and operate a small motor.

Chemical Potential to Electrical Energy:

- Perhaps the most common energy storage device is the battery. Batteries store chemical potential energy, which is converted into electrical energy when the battery operates.

Chemical Potential to Thermal Energy:

- When substances burn, their stored chemical energy is converted into thermal energy and into visible and invisible radiant energy.
- Burning natural gas, coal, and petroleum products is one of our most economically important energy conversion processes.
- We will explore the economic and environmental consequences of this energy conversion.

2.1.3 Basics of Electric Energy

- Electric current is divided into two types: Directional Current (DC) and Alternating Current (AC).

Directional (Direct) Current:

- A non-varying, unidirectional electric current (e.g.: Current produced by batteries).

Characteristics:

- Direction of the flow of positive and negative charges does not change with time.
- Direction of current (direction of flow for positive charges) is constant with time.
- Potential difference (voltage) between two points of the circuit does not change polarity with time.

Alternating Current:

- A current which reverses in regularly recurring intervals of time and which has alternately positive and negative values, and occurring a specified number of times per second. (e.g. household electricity produced by generators, electricity supplied by utilities.)

Characteristics:

- Direction of the current reverses periodically with time.
- Voltage (tension) between two points of the circuit changes polarity with time.
- In 50 cycle AC, current reverses direction 100 times a second (two times during one cycle).

Ampere (A):

- Current is the rate of flow of charge. The ampere is the basic unit of electric current. It is that current which produces a specified force between two parallel wires, which are 1 metre apart in a vacuum.

Voltage (V):

- The volt is the International System of Units (SI) measure of electric potential or electromotive force. A potential of one volt appears across a resistance of one ohm when a current of one ampere flows through that resistance.

Resistance:

The unit of resistance is ohm (Ω).

$$\text{Resistance} = \frac{\text{Voltage}}{\text{Current}}$$

Frequency:

- The supply frequency tells us the cycles at which alternating current changes. The unit of frequency is hertz (**Hz:** cycles per second).

  kW is Working Power (also called Actual Power or Active Power or Real Power). It is the power that actually powers the equipment and performs useful work.

  kVAr is Reactive Power. It is the power that magnetic equipment (transformer, motor and relay) needs to produce the magnetizing flux.

  kVA is Apparent Power. It is the vectorial summation of kVAr and kW.

For single-phase power supply,

$$\text{Apparent power (kVA)} = \frac{\text{Voltage} \times \text{Amperes}}{1000}$$

$$\text{Power (kW)} = \frac{\text{Voltage} \times \text{Amperes} \times \text{Power factor}}{1000}$$

For three-phase power supply,

$$\text{Apparent power (kVA)} = \frac{\sqrt{3} \times \text{Voltage} \times \text{Amperes}}{1000}$$

$$\text{Power (kW)} = \frac{1.732 \times \text{Voltage} \times \text{Amperes} \times \text{Power factor}}{1000}$$

Power Factor:

- Power Factor (PF) is the ratio between the active power (kW) and apparent power (kVA).

$$\text{Power factor } (\cos \phi) \;=\; \frac{\text{Active power (kW)}}{\text{Apparent power (kVA)}} \;=\; \frac{kW}{\sqrt{(kW)^2 + (kVAr)^2}}$$

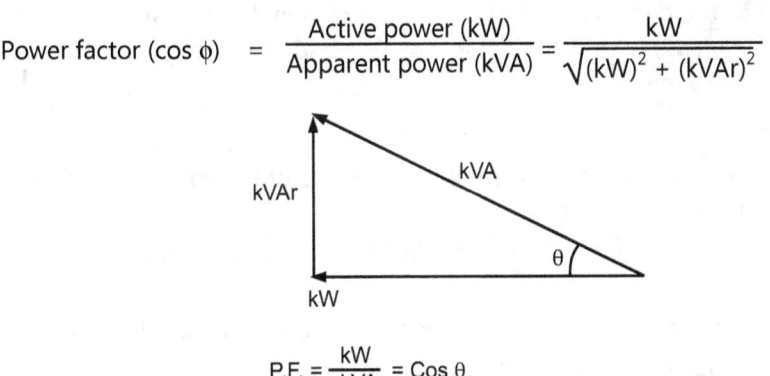

$$P.F. = \frac{kW}{kVA} = \cos \theta$$

Fig. 2.1: The power triangle

- When current lags the voltage like in inductive loads, it is called lagging power factor and when current leads the voltage like in capacitive loads, it is called leading power factor.
- Inductive loads such as induction motors, transformers, discharge lamp, etc. absorb comparatively more lagging reactive power (kVAr) and hence, their power factor is poor.
- Lower the power factor; electrical network is loaded with more current. It would be advisable to have highest power factor (close to 1) so that network carries only active power which does real work.
- Power factor improvement is done by installing capacitors near the load centres, which improve power factor from the point of installation back to the generating station.

Kilowatt-hour (kWh):

- Standard unit of electricity or consumption equal to 1000 watts over one hour, and equivalent to about 3412 British thermal units (Btu) or 860 kilocalories.
- It is most commonly used to express amounts of energy delivered by electric utilities, and it appears on electric meters and bills in some countries.

Electricity Tariff:

Calculation of Electric Bill for a Company:

- Electrical utility or power supplying companies charge industrial customers not only based on the amount of energy used (kWh) but also on the peak demand (kVA) for each month.

Contract Demand:

- Contract demand is the amount of electric power that a customer demands from utility in a specified interval. Unit used is kVA or kW. It is the amount of electric power that the consumer agreed upon with the utility. This would mean that utility has to plan for the specified capacity.

Maximum Demand:

- Maximum demand is the highest average kVA recorded during any one-demand interval within the month. The demand interval is normally 30 minutes, but may vary from utility to utility from 15 minutes to 60 minutes. The demand is measured using a tri-vector meter / digital energy meter.

Prediction of Load:

- While considering the methods of load prediction, some of the terms used in connection with power supply must be appreciated.

  Connected Load: It is the nameplate rating (in kW or kVA) of the apparatus installed on a consumer's premises.

  Demand Factor: It is the ratio of maximum demand to the connected load.

  Load Factor: The ratio of average load to maximum load.

$$\text{Load factor} \ = \ \frac{\text{Average load}}{\text{Maximum load}}$$

- The load factor can also be defined as the ratio of the energy consumed during a given period to the energy, which would have been used if the maximum load had been maintained throughout that period. For example, load factor for a day (24 hours) will be given by,

$$\text{Load factor} \ = \ \frac{\text{Energy consumed during 24 hours}}{\text{Maximum load recorded} \times 24 \text{ hours}}$$

2.2 BASICS OF THERMAL ENERGY

Temperature:

- Temperature is a physical property of a system that underlies the common notions of hot and cold; something that is hotter generally has the greater temperature. Specifically, temperature is a property of matter.

- Temperature is one of the principal parameters of thermodynamics. On the microscopic scale, temperature is defined as the average energy of microscopic motions of a single particle in the system per degree of freedom.

- On the macroscopic scale, temperature is the unique physical property that determines the direction of heat flow between two objects placed in thermal contact.

- If no heat flow occurs, the two objects have the same temperature; otherwise heat flows from the hotter object to the colder object.

- It can be measured in various units like °C, K or °F.

$$°C \ = \ (°F - 32) \times 5/9$$

Pressure:

- Pressure is defined as force per unit area. It is usually more convenient to use pressure rather than force to describe the influences upon fluid behaviour.

- The standard unit for pressure is the Pascal, which is a Newton per square metre.

- For an object sitting on a surface, the force pressing on the surface is the weight of the object, but in different orientations it might have a different area in contact with the surface and therefore exert a different pressure.

Heat: **(W-13)**

- Heat may be defined as energy in transit from a high temperature object to a lower temperature object. An object does not possess "heat"; the appropriate term for the microscopic energy in an object is the internal energy.

- The internal energy may be increased by transferring energy to the object from a higher temperature (hotter) object - this is properly called heating.

- Calorie is the unit for measuring the quantity of heat. It is the quantity of heat, which can raise the temperature of 1 g of water by 1°C.

- Calorie is too small unit for many purposes. Therefore, a bigger unit kilocalorie (1 kilocalorie = 1000 calories) is used to measure heat. 1 kilocalorie can raise the temperature of 1000 g (i.e. 1 kg) of water by 1°C.

- However, nowadays, generally joule as the unit of heat energy is used. It is the internationally accepted unit. Its relationship with calorie is as follows:

$$1 \text{ calorie} = 4.187 \text{ J}$$

- The quantity of heat is given by

$$Q = \text{mass} \times \text{specific heat} \times \text{increase in temperature}$$
$$Q = m \times C_p \times \Delta t$$

Specific Heat:

- Specific heat capacity, also known simply as specific heat, is the measure of the heat energy required to increase the temperature of a unit quantity of a substance by a certain temperature interval.

- Consider the specific heat of copper as 0.385 J/g °C. What this means is that it takes 0.385 joules of heat to raise 1 gram of copper 1°C.

- Thus, if we take 1 gram of copper at 25°C and add 1 joule of heat to it, we will find that the temperature of the copper will have risen to 26°C.

- We can then ask: How much heat will it take to raise by 1°C 2g of copper ? Clearly the answer is 0.385 J for each gram or 2 × 0.385 J = 0.770 J.

Sensible Heat:

- Sensible heat is the potential energy in the form of thermal energy or heat. The thermal body must have a temperature higher than its surroundings (also see latent heat).

- The thermal energy can be transported via conduction, convection, radiation or by a combination thereof.

- The quantity or magnitude of sensible heat is the product of the body's mass, its specific heat capacity and its temperature above a reference temperature.

Latent Heat:

- In thermochemistry, latent heat is the amount of energy in the form of heat released or absorbed by a substance during a change of phase (i.e. solid, liquid, or gas) – also called a phase transition.

- Two latent heats (or enthalpies) are typically described latent heat of fusion (melting) and latent heat of vaporization (boiling).

- The names describe the direction of heat flow from one phase to the next:
  - solid → liquid → gas.

- The change is endothermic, i.e. the system absorbs energy, when the change is from solid to liquid to gas.

- It is exothermic (the process releases energy) when it is in the opposite direction. For example, in the atmosphere, when a molecule of water evaporates from the surface of any body of water, *energy* is transported by the water molecule into a lower temperature air parcel that contains more water vapour than its surroundings.

- Because energy is needed to overcome the molecular forces of attraction between water particles, the process of transition from a parcel of water to a parcel of vapour requires the input of energy causing a drop in temperature in its surroundings.

- If the water vapour condenses back to a liquid or solid phase onto a surface, the latent energy absorbed during evaporation is released as sensible heat onto the surface.

- The large value of the enthalpy of condensation of water vapour is the reason that steam is a far more effective heating medium than boiling water, and is more hazardous.

- The **enthalpy of vaporization**, (symbol ΔH_v), also known as the **heat of vaporization** or **heat of evaporation**, is the energy required to transform a given quantity of a substance into a gas.

- It is measured at the normal boiling point of the substance, although tabulated values are usually corrected to 298 K: the correction is small, and is often smaller than the uncertainty in the measured value.

- Values are usually quoted in kJ/mol, although kJ/kg, kcal/mol, cal/g and Btu/lb are also possible, among others.

- The **enthalpy of condensation** (or **heat of condensation**) is numerically exactly equal to the enthalpy of vaporization, but has the opposite sign: enthalpy changes of vaporization are always positive (heat is absorbed by the substance), whereas enthalpy changes of condensation are always negative (heat is released by the substance).

- The **standard enthalpy of fusion** (symbol ΔH_{fus}), also known as the **heat of fusion** or **specific melting heat**, is the amount of thermal energy which must be absorbed or evolved for 1 mole of a substance to change states from a solid to a liquid or vice versa.

- It is also called the **latent heat of fusion** or the **enthalpy change of fusion**, and the temperature at which it occurs is called the melting point.

- When you withdraw thermal energy from a liquid or solid, the temperature falls. When you add heat energy the temperature rises.
- However, at the transition point between solid and liquid (the melting point), extra energy is required (the heat of fusion).
- To go from liquid to solid, the molecules of a substance must become more ordered.
- For them to maintain the order of a solid, extra heat must be withdrawn. In the other direction, to create the disorder from the solid crystal to liquid, extra heat must be added.

Humidity:

- The moisture content of air is referred to as humidity and may be expressed in two ways: specific humidity and relative humidity.

Specific Humidity:

- It is the actual weight of water vapour mixed in a kg of dry air.

Humidity Factor:

- Humidity factor = kg of water per kg of dry air (kg/kg).

Relative Humidity (RH) :

- It is the measure of degree of saturation of the air at any dry-bulb (DB) temperature.
- Relative humidity given as a percentage is the actual water content of the air divided by the moisture content of fully saturated air at the existing temperature.

Dew Point:

- It is the temperature at which condensation of water vapour from the air begins as the temperature of the air-water vapour mixture falls.

Dry-bulb Temperature:

- It is an indication of the sensible heat content of air-water vapour mixtures.

Wet-bulb Temperature:

- It is a measure of total heat content or enthalpy. It is the temperature approached by the dry bulb and the dew point as saturation occurs.

Calorific value:

- The heating value of fuel is the measure of the heat released during the complete combustion of unit weight of fuel.
- It is expressed as Gross Calorific Value (GCV) or Net Calorific Value (NCV). The difference between GCV and NCV is the heat of vaporization of the moisture and atomic hydrogen (conversion to water vapour) in the fuel.
- Typical GCV and NCV for heavy fuel oil are 10,500 kcal/kg and 9,800 kcal/kg.

Difference between Gross and Net Calorific Value:

- Most fuels are mixtures of carbon and hydrogen and these are the main heating agents. There may be other elements which do not contribute, or contribute only slightly, to the calorific value of the fuel.

- Both the carbon and the hydrogen combine with oxygen during combustion and the reactions provide the heat.

- When the hydrogen combines with oxygen, it forms water in a gaseous or vapour state at the high temperature of the combustion.

- The water is therefore almost always carried away with the other products of combustion in the exhaust gases from the apparatus in which the combustion takes place (boiler, engine, furnace, etc.).

- When the exhaust gases cool, the water will condense into a liquid state and release heat, known as latent heat, which is wasted in the atmosphere.

- The heating value of a fuel may, therefore, be expressed as a gross value or a net value. The gross value includes all of the heat released from the fuel, including any heat carried away in the water formed during combustion.

- The net value excludes the latent heat of the water formed during combustion. It is important when obtaining a calorific value to check whether it is net or gross.

- The differences between net and gross are typically about 5% to 6% of the gross value for solid and liquid fuels, and about 10% for natural gas.

- There are few fuels which contain no, or very little hydrogen (for example blast furnace gas, high-temperature cokes and some petroleum cokes).

- In these cases, there will be negligible differences between net and gross calorific values. The derivation of net calorific values for solid fuels is further complicated because they often contain water trapped within the fuel in addition to the water which will be formed from the hydrogen they contain.

- The reduction in net calorific value as a result of the additional water is uncertain because the dampness of the fuel may vary according to weather and storage conditions.

- In summary, the net calorific value of a fuel is the total heat produced by burning it, minus the heat needed to evaporate the water present in the fuel or produced during its combustion.

- Major users of solid fuels, such as power stations, should be able to provide net calorific values based on the monitoring of the electricity generation.

2.2.1 Heat Transfer (W-13)

- Heat transfer is the passage of thermal energy from a hot to a colder body. When a physical body, e.g. an object or fluid, is at a different temperature than its surroundings or another body, transfer *of thermal energy*, also known as heat transfer, or *heat exchange*, occurs in such a way that the body and the surroundings reach thermal equilibrium.

- Heat transfer always occurs from a hot body to a cold one, a result of the second law of thermodynamics.

- Where there is a temperature difference between objects in proximity, heat transfer between them can never be stopped; it can only be slowed down.

Heat is transferred by three primary modes:

- Conduction (Energy transfer in a solid)
- Convection (Energy transfer in a fluid)
- Radiation (Does not need a material to travel through)

Conduction:

- Conduction is the transfer of thermal energy from a region of higher temperature to a region of lower temperature through direct molecular communication within a medium or between mediums in direct physical contact without a flow of the material medium.
- The transfer of energy could be primarily by elastic impact as in fluids or by free electron diffusion as predominant in metals or phonon vibration as predominant in insulators.
- In other words, heat is transferred by conduction when adjacent atoms vibrate against one another, or as electrons move from atom to atom.
- Conduction is greater in solids, where atoms are in constant contact.
- In liquids (except liquid metals) and gases, the molecules are usually further apart, giving a lower chance of molecules colliding and passing on thermal energy.
- Heat conduction is directly analogous to diffusion of particles into a fluid, in the situation where there are no fluid currents.
- This type of heat diffusion differs from mass diffusion in behaviour, only in as much as it can occur in solids, whereas mass diffusion is limited to fluids.
- Metals (e.g. copper) are usually the best conductors of thermal energy.
- This is due to the way that metals are chemically bonded: metallic bonds (as opposed to covalent or ionic bonds) have free-moving electrons and form a crystalline structure, greatly aiding in the transfer of thermal energy.
- As density decreases so does conduction. Therefore, fluids (and especially gases) are less conductive.
- This is due to the large distance between atoms in a gas: fewer collisions between atoms means less conduction.
- Conductivity of gases increases with temperature but only slightly with pressure near and above atmospheric. Conduction does not occur at all in a perfect vacuum.
- To quantify the ease with which a particular medium conducts, engineers employ the *thermal conductivity*, also known as the *conductivity constant* or *conduction coefficient* k.
- In thermal conductivity, k is defined as "the quantity of heat, Q, transmitted in time (t) through a thickness (L), in a direction normal to a surface of area (A), due to a temperature difference (ΔT)".
- Thermal conductivity is a material *property* that is primarily dependent on the medium's phase, temperature, density, and molecular bonding.

Convection:

- Convection is a combination of conduction and the transfer of thermal energy by fluid circulation or movement of the hot particles in bulk to cooler areas in a material medium.

- Unlike the case of pure conduction, now *currents in fluids* are additionally involved in convection.
- This movement occurs into a fluid or within a fluid, and cannot happen in solids.
- In solids, molecules keep their relative position to such an extent that *bulk movement* or flow is prohibited, and therefore convection does not occur.
- In *natural convection*, a fluid surrounding a heat source receives heat, becomes less dense and rises. The surrounding, cooler fluid then moves to replace it.
- This cooler fluid is then heated and the process continues, forming a convection current.
- The driving force for natural convection is buoyancy, a result of differences in fluid density when gravity or any type of acceleration is present in the system.
- *Forced convection*, by contrast, occurs when pumps, fans or other means are used to propel the fluid and create an artificially induced convection current. Forced heat convection is sometimes referred to as heat advection.

Radiation:
- Radiation is the transfer of heat through electromagnetic radiation. Hot or cold, all objects radiate energy at a rate equal to their emissivity times the rate at which energy would radiate from them if they were a black body.
- No medium is necessary for radiation to occur; radiation works even in and through a perfect vacuum. The energy from the Sun travels through the vacuum of space before warming the earth. Also, the only way that energy can leave earth is by being radiated to space.
- Both *reflectivity* and *emissivity* of all bodies is wavelength dependent. The temperature determines the wavelength distribution of the electromagnetic radiation as limited in intensity by Planck's law of black-body radiation.
- For any body the reflectivity depends on the wavelength distribution of incoming electromagnetic radiation and therefore the temperature of the source of the radiation while the emissivity depends on the wavelength distribution and therefore the temperature of the body itself.
- For example, fresh snow, which is highly reflective to visible light (reflectivity about 0.90) appears white due to reflecting sunlight with a peak energy wavelength of about 0.5 micrometres.
- Its emissivity, however, at a temperature of about –5°C, peak energy wavelength of about 12 micrometres, is 0.99.
- Gases absorb and emit energy in characteristic wavelength patterns that are different for each gas.
- Visible light is simply another form of electromagnetic radiation with a shorter wavelength (and therefore a higher frequency) than infrared radiation.
- The difference between visible light and the radiation from objects at conventional temperatures is a factor of about 20 in frequency and wavelength; the two kinds of emission are simply different "colours" of electromagnetic radiation.

SOLVED PROBLEMS

Problem 2.1:

A 250 W sodium vapour lamp is installed on a street. The supply voltage for a street light is 230 V and it operates for around 12 hours in a day. Considering the current of 2 amps and power factor 0.85, calculate the energy consumption per day.

Solution:

$$\text{Energy consumption} = V \times I \times \cos\theta \times \text{Number of hours}$$
$$= 230 \times 2 \times 0.85 \times 12$$
$$= 4692 \text{ watt hours}$$
$$= 4.692 \text{ kWh}$$

Problem 2.2:

A three-phase induction 75 kW motor operates at 55 kW. The measured voltage is 415 V, current is 80 amperes. Calculate the power factor of the motor.

Solution:

$$\text{Power consumption} = 3 \times V \times I \times \cos\theta$$
$$(55 \times 1000) = 3 \times 415 \times 80 \times \cos\theta$$
$$\text{Power factor } (\cos\theta) = (55 \times 1000)/(3 \times 415 \times 80)$$
$$= 0.96$$

Problem 2.3:

An electric heater of 230 V, 5 kW rating is used for hot water generation in an industry. Find electricity consumption per hour (a) at the rated voltage, (b) at 200 V.

Solution:

(a) Electricity consumption (kWh) at rated voltage = 5 kW × 1 hour
$$= 5 \text{ kWh.}$$

(b) Electricity consumption at 200 V (kWh) = (200 / 230) 2 × 5 kW × 1 hour
$$= 3.78 \text{ kWh.}$$

Problem 2.4:

A substance of mass 25 kg @ 25°C is heated to 75°C. If the specific heat of the substance is 0.25 kcal/kg °C, calculate the quantity of heat added in the substance.

Solution:

$$\text{Quantity of heat} = m \times C_p \times \Delta T$$
$$= 25 \times 0.25 \times (75 - 25)$$
$$= 312.5 \text{ kcal}$$

Units and Conversions:

Various units are used for energy, mass and volume worldwide. In India, we are following SI unit system. Following Table 2.1 shows various conversion systems.

Table 2.1

1 MW	1,000 kW
1 kW	1,000 watts
1 kWh	3,412 Btu
1 kWh	1,340 Hp hours
1,000 Btu	0.293 kWh
1 Therm	100,000 Btu (British Thermal Units)
1 Million Btu	293.1 kilowatt hours
100,000 Btu	1 Therm
1 watt	3.412 Btu per hour
1 Horsepower	746 watts or 0.746 kilo watts
1 Horsepower hr.	2,545 Btu
1 kJ	0.239005 kilocalories
1 calorie	4.187 joules
1 kcal/kg	1.8 Btus/lb
1 Million Btu	252 Mega calories
1 Btu	252 carlories
1 Btu	1,055 joules
1 Btu/lb	2.3260 kJ/kg
1 Btu/lb	0.5559 kilocalories/kg

Table 2.2: Power (Energy Rate) Equivalents

1 kilowatt (kW)	1 kilo joule/second (kJ/s)
1 kilowatt (kW)	3413 BTU/hour (Btu/hr.)
1 horsepower (hp)	746 watts (0.746 kW)
1 Ton of refrigeration	12000 Btu/hr

Table 2.3: Fuel to kWh (Approximate conversion)

Natural gas	$m^3 \times 10.6$	kWh
	$Ft^3 \times 0.3$	kWh
	therms $\times$ 29.3	kWh
LPG (propane)	$m^3 \times 25$	kWh
Coal	kg $\times$ 8.05	kWh
Coke	kg $\times$ 10.0	kWh
Gas oil	litres $\times$ 12.5	kWh
Light fuel oil	litres $\times$ 12.9	kWh
Medium fuel oil	litres $\times$ 13.1	kWh
Heavy fuel oil	litres $\times$ 13.3	kWh

Practice Questions

1. Describe various forms of energy.
2. Define the following terms:
  (a) Temperature
  (b) Pressure
  (c) Heat
  (d) Specific heat
  (e) Sensible heat
  (f) Latent heat
3. Differentiate between gross and net calorific value.
4. What are modes of heat transfer ?
5. Give classification of basic electric energy with their units.
6. Define power factor and its units.
7. Define the term load factor.
8. Why a cube of ice at 0°C is more effective in cooling than the same quantity of water at 0°C ?
9. 10 kg of steam at 100°C with latent heat of vaporization 2260 kJ is cooled to 50°C. If the specific heat of water is 4200 J/kg°C, find the quantity of heat given out.

MSBTE Questions and Answers (As Per 'E' Scheme)

Summer 2012

1. A industrial unit consumes average 120 kWh power in a day. Tariff for 1 kWh is ₹ 10 from 7.00 a.m. to ₹ 10.00 a.m. ₹ 8 from 10.00 a.m. to 5.00 p.m., ₹ 11 from 5.00 p.m. to 10.00 p.m. to 7.00 a.m. Calculate electricity bill of industrial unit in the month of January. (Fixed charges are ₹ 150 per month and fuel surcharge is ₹ 50 per month)

Winter 2013

1. A mild steel tank of wall thickness 12 mm contains water at 95°C. The thermal conductivity of mild steel is 50 W/m°C, and the heat transfer coefficients for the inside and outside the tank are 2850 and 10 W/m^2 °C respectively. If the atmospheric temperature is 15°C. Calculate:
  (i) The rate of heat loss per m^2 of the tank surface area.
  (ii) The temperature of the outside surface of the tank.
2. Define heat. State its types.
Ans. Please refer to Section 2.2.
3. State the advantages of liquid fuels.
4. What is DC and AC current? State the modes of heat transfer.
Ans. Please refer to Section 2.1.3 and 2.2.1.

❑❑❑

$$\boxed{\textit{Chapter } \textbf{3}}$$

ENERGY AUDIT

Objectives

Students will study and understand the following:

- State necessity of energy audit
- Compare energy utilization for given product
- Suggest ENCON recommondation

3.1 ENERGY MANAGEMENT

Introduction:

- With rising fuel costs and the opening of electricity and gas markets to alternate suppliers and climate change, the need to monitor and reduce energy consumption is receiving greater attention than ever before.
- The process of managing energy is not new. Energy should be regarded as a business cost similar to other costs like raw material and labour.
- The efforts required to manage energy effectively will vary between companies and depend on the company size, energy costs and energy intensity.
- Energy costs are expressed as a percentage of total company costs. It is not unreasonable for a company, starting out in energy management, to achieve a reduction of 20% or more in their energy bills with just a few simple measures and close monitoring.
- Hence, it is imperative to incorporate a structured energy management system in an organization.
- A structured approach with clear sequence of events is the essence of any efforts for conservation of energy.
- Any organization, whether introducing energy management for the first time or upgrading its existing efforts, needs to be aware of this and adapt its activities accordingly.

Definition of Energy Management:

- Energy management is defined as:

  "The judicious use of energy to maximize profits (minimize cost) and enhance competitive positions".

(3.1)

- Therefore, any management activity that affects the use of energy falls under this definition. This rather broad definition covers many operations from product and equipment design through product delivery.
- Waste disposal also presents many opportunities for efficient management energy.
- The primary objective of energy management is to maximize profit and minimize costs. Some desirable sub-objectives of energy management programs include:
  - Conserving energy, thereby reducing cost.
  - Cultivating good communications on energy matters.
  - Developing and maintaining effective monitoring, reporting, and management strategies for efficient energy usage.
  - Finding new and better ways to increase returns from energy investments through research and development.
  - Developing interest in and dedication to energy management program from all employees.

Need for Energy Management:

- It is estimated that industrial energy use in developing countries constitutes about 45-50% of the total commercial energy consumption.
- Much of this energy is converted from imported oil, the price of which has increased tremendously.
- So much so that most of the developing countries spend more than 50% of their foreign exchange earnings on oil imports.
- Not withstanding these fiscal constraints, developing countries need to expand their industrial base so as to generate the resources to improve the quality of life of its people. The expansion of industrial base does require additional energy inputs.
- India is a developing nation and has very low per capita energy consumption. To achieve economic growth, we need to increase the pace of development and increase the manufacturing of goods in quality and volume, which requires energy.
- In any industry, the main operating costs are, energy (both electrical and thermal), labour, and material. If one were to assess manageability of the costs or potential cost savings in each of the above components, energy would invariably emerge as the top ranker.
- Thus, energy management function constitutes a strategic area for cost reduction.
- Energy cost savings of 5-15% are usually obtained quickly without any capital expenditure, when aggressive energy management program is launched.
- Thus, energy management is one of the most promising profit improvements, cost reduction programs available today.

Designing an Energy Management Program:

- Fundamental to the effective implementation of energy efficiency is good management. Like any resource that an organization employs, energy will only be used efficiently if it is managed properly.

- Good energy management, in itself saves energy.

  Energy management can be broken down into a number of key areas:
  - Preparation of Policy Statement
  - Appointment of Energy Manager
  - Planning and organizing
  - Monitoring and control
  - Conducting an Energy Audit
  - Motivating People
  - Reporting and review
  - Formalized and Energy Management Policy Statement
- All these steps are necessary for effective energy management.
- However, the extent of criticality and type of approach would depend on the nature and size of the organization.
- Energy management is a highly cost-effective tool requiring very little capital.
- Nonetheless effective application needs total commitment from the top management, allocation of requisite time and patience.

Energy Management Cell:

- All energy intensive industries should have a dedicated energy management cell with a full time 'Energy Manager' who will be responsible for overseeing its operations.
- The energy management cell should provide necessary structure and formalise the process of energy conservation thereby enhancing its efficacy with full support from top management.
- Besides energy manager, the cell should also have skilled persons in different disciplines.
- The cell should interact with manufacturing and other divisions like production, engineering, maintenance, utilities, and even finance.
- This will help in carrying out its activities like planned internal and external energy audits, conceptualisation and implementation of projects in close co-ordination with respective departments/divisions, carrying out educational campaigns etc.
- Thus, the cell will become the focal point for effective energy management in the plant.
- This dedicated working will also bring to the force the energy issues in the minds of personnel working in different areas and will influence their decision-making.

  The objectives of Energy Management Cell are:
  1. To carry out energy management studies, analysis, recommendations and implementations of useful studies for energy conservation.
  2. To accelerate the energy management activities in the Industry.
  3. **Regular maintenance:** From an energy perspective, regular maintenance is important because it can ensure that systems are operated as they were intended. Systems consume energy, and over time their efficiency may drop because of

various factors. A decrease in efficiency results in an increase in consumption, therefore incorporating energy efficiency measures in maintenance activities can prevent excessive energy consumption.

4. **Conduct an Energy Audit:** An energy audit is a systematic gathering and analysis of energy use information within a business. Once the data has been analysed, the information can then be used to promote energy efficient practices in the areas of the business where they will prove to be most effective. Progress of any initiatives that are put in place can then be accurately monitored.

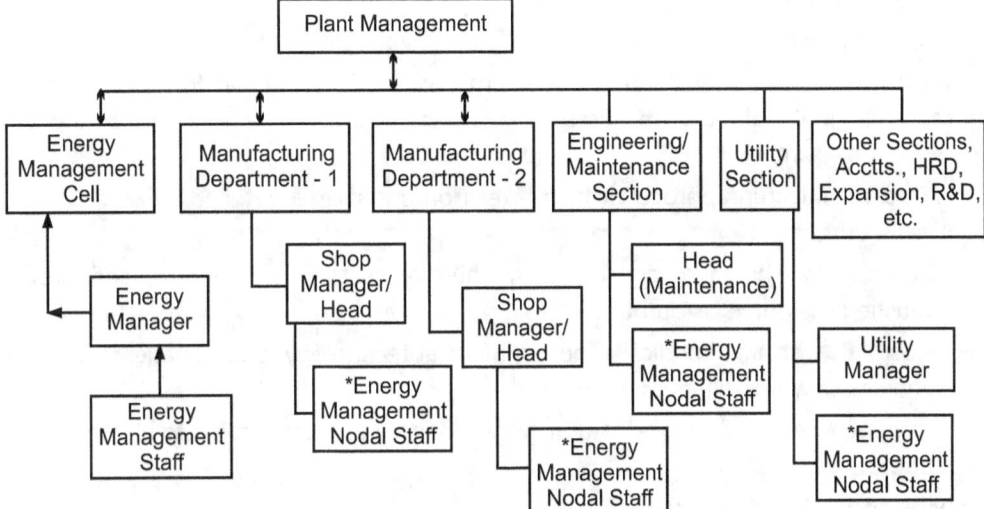

Fig. 3.1: Energy Management Cell in organization

3.1.1 Energy Audit

Introduction :

- An Energy Audit solves the measurement problem.
- Auditing for energy purchases, use, conversion, and waste is the first step in managing your energy consumption.
- For maximum effectiveness, it is essential to focus on the essentials. This is best done through the Pareto Principle (80% of the effect is caused by 20% of the factors).
- During an **Energy Audit**, a broad, comprehensive approach, then progressively zooms in on the specific issues and opportunities that deserve further investigation. The Energy Audit report can be used as the starting point for Feasibility Studies, Energy Management Plans, Retrofitting Existing Systems, and Design of new Energy Efficient Processes.
- With each Energy Audit, you get a detailed report on your current situation, and professional recommendations for more detailed study.
- Typical costs for an Energy Audit range from $500 (small, partial audits) to $20,000 for comprehensive studies on large buildings or industrial processes. Typical audits are $3,000 to 5,000 for 80% of the initial Energy Audits done.

Why is an Energy Audit Important?

- Energy supplies and its consumption are the fundamental tools for our life and standard of living. Canada is the *most inefficient nation* in the industrialized world.

- It is predicted that *Energy* will become the primary economic driving force in the 2010 decade. Everyone must do their part to ensure long term, sustainable benefits for mankind.

Who Needs an Energy Audit?

- Process Owners
- Building Owners

Process owners are concerned about energy use and conversion for their processes. A process has inputs, outputs, and uses conversions and transformations to turn inputs to outputs. Examples are:

- Steel manufacturing process which takes iron ore as an input, and make steel ingots as an output.

- Restaurants who take raw foods and hungry customers as inputs, and produce satisfied customers as outputs.

- Hospitals who take medical supplies, medical technology, and ill patients as inputs, and create well patients as the outputs.

- Power converters who take natural gas as an input and convert it into electricity as an output.

Synonyms and Related Terms:

- Energy Efficiency
- Green House Gasses (GHG)
- Global Warming
- Climate Change
- Gross Domestic Product (GDP)
- Electricity
- Fuel
- Energy Supply
- Consumption
- Sustainable Development
- Green Energy
- Alternative Fuels

Details About Energy Audits:

Generally, there are three types of Energy Audits. Each one goes into greater depth, is more specific to your particular circumstances, and is therefore more expensive. The three types are:

- **Historical Data Analysis:** Preliminary audits that gather and analyse data on your facility's average energy consumption. This frequently includes statistical analysis of your energy purchases, calculation of your energy efficiency indices, and benchmarking against similar operations.

- **Walk-through audits** involve a review of your facility's energy use profiles, overall assessments of energy-consuming systems and equipment, collection of on-site data on building conditions, process equipment, and conditions (temperatures, pressures, flows, leaks, horse powers etc.).

- **Technical or Engineering audits** and *feasibility studies* are the most complex energy use studies. These can provide detailed analyses of your facility's energy use profiles, as well as full descriptions of building systems, operations, levels of performance and potential for savings. They explain not only what energy is being used, by why it is so high, and what changes could be achieved to reduce the energy consumption. These studies can include detailed heat loss calculations, computer simulations and other technical analysis. Technologies that can be assessed are wind, solar PV (photo-voltaic), hot water heating, solar heating (passive and active), CHP (Combined Heat Power), CHCP (Combined Heat Cool Power), refrigeration (mechanical and absorption), heat pumps, HVAC, high efficiency electric motors, biomass, and small hydro-electric.

Typical Uses:

An Energy Audit can be used to analyze one or more of the following:

- Historic energy supplies and uses (oil, coal, wood, natural gas, electricity, wind, solar etc.)
- Historic energy consumption (BTU/hr, kW-hrs/month etc.).
- Energy trends and projections (cost, sources, availability etc.).
- Available technologies (domestic water heaters, space heaters, glazing, insulation, vapour barriers etc.).
- Energy efficiency and waste (heat losses, conversion efficiency, waste by-products, risks, costs etc.).
- Environmental impact (Greenhouse gasses, global warming, sustainable development etc.).
- Cost Reduction (energy supply contracts, retrofits, best technology, ROI, payback etc.).
- Legislation and regulations (approvals, certificates, recommended practices etc.).
- Identifying air leakage through the building envelope (usually 25% - 40% of space heating costs are caused by air leakage).

Typical Results Achieved:

An Energy Audit report that:

- Defines the data collected.

- Provides analysis of the raw data.
- Gives interpretation of the data for significance to the organization that commissioned the report (e.g. Why is this important?).
- Presents conclusions based on excellent technical analysis of the situation.
- Propose solutions as to available options, pros and cons, risks, costs, sequence, and optimum plan for the future.
- Offer Recommendations on the best course of action.

Typical Symptoms:

You know you need an Energy Audit if:

- Your security and/or reliability of future energy supplies is in doubt (electricity outages, natural gas supplies etc.)
- Your energy costs are increasing.
- Peak load, demand charges and variation in consumption are creating premium costs and charge rates.
- The "degree of Green" and Sustainability has become an issue to your Customers and/or Stakeholders.
- Government regulations on emissions are hindering your business, or limiting your growth.
- You are unable to continue using the same past methods and processes (i.e. obsolete technology etc.).
- You need a faster rate of improvement and/or cost reduction.
- Stakeholders complain about cold drafts, indoor temperature/humidity swings, indoor condensation on walls, windows etc.
- You are implementing or registered to ISO 14001 International Standard for Environmental Management.

Typical Problems Encountered:

- Audit and/or Auditor has a fore-gone conclusion/outcome to sell a particular product or service, whether it is needed or not.
- Audit lacks historical basis to see trends into the future.
- Audit is narrow focused on a few, easy issues (not comprehensive).
- Audit has numerous assumptions and/or lacks scientific foundation.
- Auditor lacks the credentials and experience in the client's specific industry.
- Insufficient, inaccurate, un-calibrated, or poorly placed measuring devices.
- Undetected mistakes are made in the data collection or analysis.
- Audit is not focussed on the organization's specific needs (i.e. one size fits all).
- Audit concentrates on traditional solutions and technologies, ignoring recent improvements.
- Poor value for the money and effort expended.

- Audit doesn't consider transitory peak consumption rates and premium charge rates.
- Energy reliability, outages, and poor quality of supply are not considered.

Things to Consider before Implementing an Energy Audit:

1. Why do you want to do an Energy Audit?
2. How does energy and energy efficiency rank on your organization's overall priority list today? 20 years from today?
3. Why is energy and energy efficiency a significant competitive factor for your business?
4. Why do you want to do an Energy Audit now?
5. What are competitors and industry leaders doing about energy efficiency and supply?
6. How do your customers and stakeholders feel about green energy, energy efficiency, green house gasses, and sustainable development?
7. What specific actions will you take once you receive your Energy Audit report?
8. Would you still do an Energy Audit, even if government subsidies were not available?
9. How will you find the best person to do your Energy Audit?
10. What is your budget for doing an Energy Audit (minimum $, maximum $, ideal $)?

Features of Energy Audit:

Energy Audit systems typically include one or more of the following features:

- Energy Audit is custom designed to each organization's specific needs. One-size Energy Audit doesn't fit all.
- Statistical analysis of historical energy consumption rates and energy efficiency indices.
- Energy Audit is designed to be a tool for improving each of the organization's internal and external processes (linked to your 21 Success Factors).
- Energy Audit data is linked to the nine Competitive Factors (the nine reasons why customers buy from you instead of your competitors).
- Web-based Energy Audit data entry software system is open 24/7/365 for collecting Energy Audit data from all source (all personnel, suppliers, customers, and other stakeholders), where and when it occurs.
- Customer and supplier satisfaction and loyalty survey is linked to Energy Audit data for generating objective Energy Audit data for the "Soft Energy Audit costs".
- Project analysis templates for analysis of implementation cost, savings, cash flow, and ROI (Return on Investment).
- Energy Audit assessment, consulting, coaching, feasibility studies, detailed design, project management, and implementation assistance to ensure effective implementation at all stages of your energy efficiency improvement project.

- During project stage, energy saving devices are implemented to the extent possible.
- Any energy saving equipment will increase the cost of the project and make it unviable. Thus, there is some restriction on implementing all energy saving systems and these are deferred to a future date for incorporation.
- Apart from this, after commissioning of a project, technological developments and innovative ideas bring about feasible solutions to bring down energy consumption.
- It becomes an attractive investment for a plant to implement these feasible solutions.
- The unforeseen market forces such as drop in product prices and rise in energy costs etc. also force the plant to look for additional potential areas of energy saving to retain the profitability of the operations.
- Energy audit involves looking at plant process and operations from energy angle. It exposes the points ignored/ undermined or missing from energy saving point of view.
- The plant operational data is obtained with the help of an elaborate questionnaire and the data is analysed.
- Energy audit of an old and inefficient plant is easier, whereas it is tougher to audit an already improved and efficient plant.
- It is the first step to know and understand where the energy is being consumed. Specific energy consumption in various sections of the plant.
- Energy monitoring system to give break-up details of energy consumption for each section is implemented through either by kWh meters or kW transducers, which are calibrated at regular intervals.
- Energy monitoring and reporting shall be implemented through central control room.
- The break-up details of energy consumption are then compared with other similar size energy efficient plants.
- The additional consumption is studied. The inefficient processes and energy wastages are identified.

Broad approaches for energy audit:

- In-depth study of the processes where possibly with a modified scheme, may help to minimize energy wastages and thereby improve energy efficiency.
- Nominating an Energy Manage to conduct internal energy audit and implement energy conservation measures.
- Engaging an External Consultant to carry out energy audit and suggest further measures for energy conservation.
- Establishing the techno-conservation measures and evaluating the results.
- Setting of benchmark for each year and taking steps to achieve the targets.
- Training of personnel through seminars on energy conservation.
- Keeping up-to-date on developments in technology and innovative ideas for energy conservation.

Types of Energy Audit:

- The term energy audit is commonly used to describe a broad spectrum of energy studies ranging from a quick walk-through of a facility to identify major problem areas to a comprehensive analysis of the implications of alternative energy efficiency measures sufficient to satisfy the financial criteria of sophisticated investors.

- Three common audit programs are described in more detail below, although the actual tasks performed and level of effort may vary with the consultant providing services under these broad headings. The only way to insure that a proposed audit will meet your specific needs is to spell out those requirements in a detailed scope of work.

- Taking the time to prepare a formal solicitation will also assure the building owner of receiving competitive and comparable proposals.

(a) Preliminary Audit:

- The preliminary audit alternatively called a simple audit, screening audit or walk-through audit, is the simplest and quickest type of audit.

- It involves minimal interviews with site operating personnel, a brief review of facility utility bills and other operating data, and a walk-through of the facility to become familiar with the building operation and identify glaring areas of energy waste or inefficiency.

- Typically, only major problem areas will be uncovered during this type of audit. Corrective measures are briefly described, and quick estimates of implementation cost, potential operating cost savings, and simple payback periods are provided.

- This level of detail, while not sufficient for reaching a final decision on implementing a proposed measures, is adequate to prioritize energy efficiency projects and determine the need for a more detailed audit.

(b) General Audit:

- The general audit alternatively called a mini-audit, site energy audit or complete site energy audit expands on the preliminary audit described above by collecting more detailed information about facility operation and performing a more detailed evaluation of energy conservation measures identified.

- Utility bills are collected for a 12 to 36 month period to allow the auditor to evaluate the facility's energy/demand rate structures, and energy usage profiles.

- Additional metering of specific energy-consuming systems is often performed to supplement utility data.

- In-depth interviews with facility operating personnel are conducted to provide a better understanding of major energy consuming systems as well as insight into variations in daily and annual energy consumption and demand.

- This type of audit will be able to identify all energy conservation measures appropriate for the facility given its operating parameters.

- A detailed financial analysis is performed for each measure based on detailed implementation cost estimates, site-specific operating cost savings, and the customer's investment criteria. Sufficient detail is provided to justify project implementation.

(c) Investment-Grade Audit:

- In most corporate settings, upgrades to a facility's energy infrastructure must compete with non-energy related investments for capital funding. Both energy and non-energy investments are rated on a single set of financial criteria that generally stress the expected return on investment (ROI).

- The projected operating savings from the implementation of energy projects must be developed such that they provide a high level of confidence. In fact, investors often demand guaranteed savings.

- The investment-grader audit alternatively called a comprehensive audit, detailed audit, maxi audit, or technical analysis audit, expands on the general audit described above by providing a dynamic model of energy use characteristics of both the existing. facility and all energy conservation measures identified.

- The building model is calibrated against actual utility data to provide a realistic baseline against which to compute operating savings for proposed measures. Extensive attention is given to understanding not only the. operating characteristics of all energy consuming systems; but also situations that cause load profile variations on both an annual and daily basis. Existing utility data is supplemented with submetering of major energy consuming systems and monitoring of system operating characteristics.

Detailed Energy Audit:

- A comprehensive audit provides a detailed energy project implementation plan for a facility, since it evaluates all major energy using systems.

- This type of audit offers the most accurate estimate of energy savings and cost. It considers the interactive effects of all projects, accounts for the energy use of all major equipment, and includes detailed energy cost saving calculations and project cost.

- In a comprehensive audit, one of the key elements is the energy balance.

- This is based on an inventory of energy using systems, assumptions of current operating conditions and calculations of energy use.

- This estimated use is then compared to utility bill charges.

  Detailed energy auditing is carried out in three phases: Phase I, II and III.

  Phase I - Pre Audit Phase

  Phase II - Audit Phase

  Phase III - Post Audit Phase

It involves

- Detailed Mass and Energy Balance of Major Energy Consuming Equipments.
- Evaluation of system efficiencies.
- Identification of various measures for improving the End Use of Energy Efficiently.
- Proposals for major Retrofitting/Replacement/Modifications providing cost-benefit analysis.

The information to be collected during the detailed audit includes:

1. Energy consumption by type of energy, by department, by major items of process equipment, by end-use.

2. Material balance data (raw materials, intermediate and final products, recycled materials, use of scrap or waste products, production of by-products for re-use in other industries, etc.)

3. Energy cost and tariff data.

4. Process and material flow diagrams.

5. Generation and distribution of site services (e.g. compressed air, steam).

6. Sources of energy supply (e.g. electricity from the grid or self-generation).

7. Potential for fuel substitution, process modifications, and the use of co-generation systems (combined heat and power generation).

8. Energy Management procedures and energy awareness training programs within the establishment.

- Existing baseline information and reports are useful to get consumption pattern, production cost and productivity levels in terms of product per raw material inputs. The audit team should collect the following baseline data:

  - Technology, processes used and equipment details
  - Capacity utilisation
  - Amount and type of input materials used
  - Water consumption
  - Fuel consumption
  - Electrical energy consumption
  - Steam consumption
  - Other inputs such as compressed air, cooling water etc.
  - Quantity and type of wastes generated
  - Percentage rejection / reprocessing
  - Efficiencies / yield

3.1.2 Identification of Energy Conservation Opportunities

Fuel substitution: Identifying the appropriate fuel for efficient energy conversion

Energy generation: Identifying Efficiency opportunities in energy conversion equipment/utility such as captive power generation, steam generation in boilers, thermic fluid heating, optimal loading of DG sets, minimum excess air combustion with boilers/thermic fluid heating, optimising existing efficiencies, efficient energy conversion equipment, biomass gasifiers, cogeneration, high efficiency DG sets etc.

Energy distribution: Identifying Efficiency opportunities network such as transformers, cables, switchgears and power factor improvement in electrical systems and chilled water, cooling water, hot water, compressed air, etc.

Energy usage by processes: This is where the major opportunity for improvement and many of them are hidden. Process analysis is useful tool for process integration measures.

Technical and Economic feasibility:

The technical feasibility should address the following issues:

- Technology availability, space, skilled manpower, reliability, service etc.
- The impact of energy efficiency measure on safety, quality, production or process.
- The maintenance requirements and spares availability.
- The economic viability often becomes the key parameter for the management acceptance. The economic analysis can be conducted by using a variety of methods. Example: Pay back method, Internal Rate of Return method, Net Present Value method etc. For low investment short duration measures, which have attractive economic viability, simplest of the methods, payback is usually sufficient.

Classification of Energy Conservation Measures:

- Based on energy audit and analyses of the plant, a number of potential energy saving projects may be identified.
- These may be classified into three categories:
    1. Low cost-high return;
    2. Medium cost-medium return;
    3. High cost-high return.
- Normally, the low cost-high return projects receive priority. Other projects have to be analyzed, engineered and budgeted for implementation in a phased manner.
- Projects relating to energy cascading and process changes almost always involve high costs coupled with high returns, and may require careful scrutiny before funds can be committed.
- These projects are generally complex and may require long lead times before they can be implemented.

3.1.3 Energy Audit Report (S-12)

- After successfully carrying out energy audit, energy manager/energy auditor should report to the top management for effective communication and implementation.

- A typical energy audit reporting contents and format are given below. The following format is applicable for most of the industries.

- However the format can be suitably modified for specific requirement applicable for a particular type of industry.

Report on

DETAILED ENERGY AUDIT

TABLE OF CONTENTS

(i) Acknowledgement

(ii) Executive Summary

     Energy Audit Options at a glance and Recommendations

1.0 Introduction about the plant

     1.1 General Plant details and descriptions

     1.2 Energy Audit Team

     1.3 Component of production cost (Raw materials, energy, chemicals, manpower, overhead, others)

     1.4 Major Energy use and Areas

2.0 Production Process Description

     2.1 Brief description of manufacturing process

     2.2 Process flow diagram and Major Unit operations

     2.3 Major Raw material Inputs, Quantity and Costs

3.0 Energy and Utility System Description

     3.1 List of Utilities

     3.2 Brief Description of each utility

          3.2.1 Electricity

          3.2.2 Steam

          3.2.3 Water

          3.2.4 Compressed air

          3.2.5 Chilled water

          3.2.6 Cooling water

- The following Worksheets can be used as guidance for energy audit assessment and reporting.

Table 3.1: Summary of Energy Saving Recommendations

Sr. No.	Energy Saving Recommendations	Annual Energy (Fuel and Electricity) Savings (kWh/MT (or) kl/MT)	Annual Savings (₹ Lakhs)	Capital Investment (₹ Lakhs)	Simple Payback Period
1.					
2.					
3.					
4.					
Total					

Table 3.2: Types and Priority of Energy Saving Measures

	Types of Energy Saving Options	Annual Electricity / Fuel Savings	Annual Savings	Priority
		kWh/MT (or) kl/MT	(₹ Lakhs)	
A	No investment (immediate) – Operational improvement – Housekeeping			
B	Low investment (Short to medium term) – Controls – Equipments modification – Process change			
C	High investment (Long term) – Energy efficient devices – Product modification – Technology change			

- Following Table 3.3 shows potential of energy saving in India after energy auditing of various industries/units.

Table 3.3

Year	No. of participating units	Savings in ₹ Crores	Investment in ₹ Crores	Electrical Energy Saving		Furnace oil savings in lakhs kl	Coal savings in lakh metric tonnes	Gas savings in lakh cubic metres
				Million kWh	Equivalent avoided capacity in MW			
2005	311	989	1316	1316	250	2.40	7.58	13122
2004	297	763	1364	814	155	2.49	5.37	18585
2003	191	539	1071	542	103	2.21	12.65	73181
2002	174	594	691	641	122	1.7	7.4	35588
2001	157	587	659	485	90	2.21	4.79	3929
2000	120	366	630	524	100	1.327	0.64	707
1999	123	205	940	205	45	1.62	2.15	2444
Total 7 years		4,043	6,671	4,527	865	13.957	40.58	1475,56

Instruments used for Energy Audit:

1.　**Electrical Measuring Instruments:** These are instruments for measuring major electrical parameters such as kVA, kW, PF, Hertz, kVAr, Amps and Volts. In addition some of these instruments also measure harmonics. These instruments are applied on-line i.e. on running motors without any need to stop the motor. Instant measurements can be taken with hand-held meters, while more advanced ones facilitate cumulative readings with print outs at specified intervals.

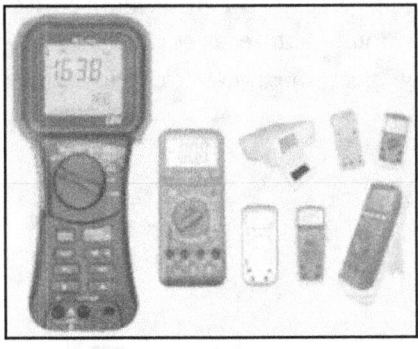

Fig. 3.2

2.   Combustion Analyzer: This instrument has in-built chemical cells which measure various gases such as O_2, CO, NO_x and SO_x.

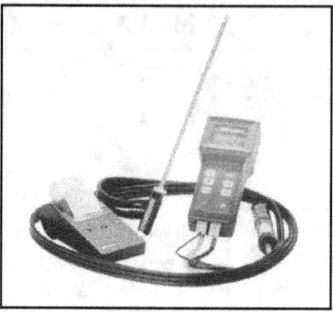

Fig. 3.3

3.   Thermometer: *Contact thermometer:* These are thermocouples which measure, for example, flue gas, hot air, hot water temperatures by insertion of probe into the stream. For surface temperature, a leaf type probe is used with the same instrument.

Infrared Thermometer: This is a non-contact type measurement which when directed at a heat source directly gives the temperature read out. This instrument is useful for measuring hot spots in furnaces, surface temperatures etc.

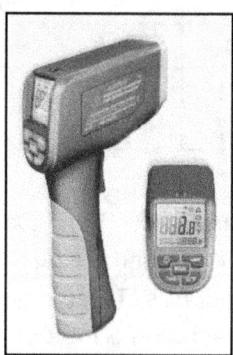

Fig. 3.4

4.   Flow Meter: This non-contact flow measuring device using Doppler effect/Ultra sonic principle. There is a transmitter and receiver which are positioned on opposite sides of the pipe. The meter directly gives the flow. Water and other fluid flows can be easily measured with this meter.

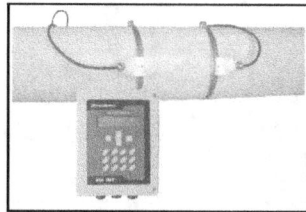

Fig. 3.5: Dynameters fixed transit-time ultrasonics flowmeter

5.   Leak Detector: Ultrasonic instruments are available which can be used to detect leaks of compressed air and other gases which are normally not possible to detect with human abilities.

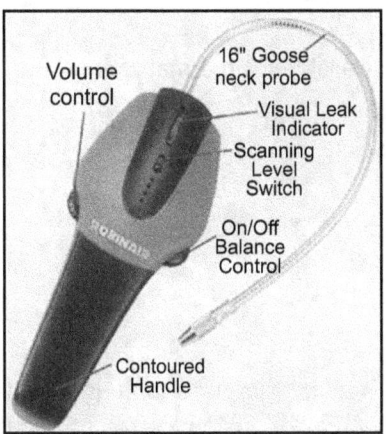

Fig. 3.6

6.   Lux Meter: Illumination levels are measured with a lux meter. It consists of a photo cell which senses the light output, converts to electrical impulses which are calibrated as lux.

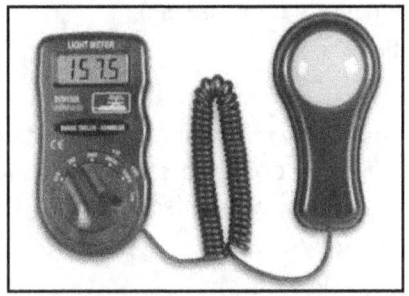

Fig. 3.7

3.2 UNDERSTANDING ENERGY COSTS   (S-12; W-13)

- Understanding energy cost is vital factor for awareness creation and saving calculation. In many industries, sufficient meters may not be available to measure all the energy used. In such cases, invoices for fuels and electricity will be useful.
- The annual company balance sheet is the other sources where fuel cost and power are given with production related information.
- Energy invoices can be used for the following purposes:
  o   They provide a record of energy purchased in a given year, which gives a base-line for future reference.
  o   Energy invoices may indicate the potential for savings when related to production requirements or to air conditioning requirements/space heating etc.
  o   When electricity is purchased on the basis of maximum demand tariff.

- o They can suggest where savings are most likely to be made.
- o In later years invoices can be used to quantify the energy and cost savings made through energy conservation measures.

Fuel Costs:

- A wide variety of fuels are available for thermal energy supply. Few are listed below:
  - o Fuel oil
  - o Low Sulphur Heavy Stock (LSHS)
  - o Light Diesel Oil (LDO)
  - o Liquefied Petroleum Gas (LPG)
  - o Coal
  - o Lignite
  - o Wood, etc.
- Understanding fuel cost is fairly simple and it is purchased in tonnes or kilolitres. Availability, cost and quality are the main three factors that should be considered while purchasing. The following factors should be taken into account during procurement of fuels for energy efficiency and economics.
  - o Price at source, transport charge, type of transport
  - o Quality of fuel (contaminations, moisture etc)
  - o Energy content (calorific value)

Power Costs:

- Electricity price in India not only varies from State to State, but also city to city and consumer to consumer though it does the same work everywhere. Many factors are involved in deciding final cost of purchased electricity such as:
  - o Maximum demand charges, kVA

    (i.e. **How fast** the electricity is used ?)

    Energy charges, kWh (i.e., **How much** electricity is consumed ?)
  - o TOD charges, Peak/Non-peak period

    (i.e. **When** electricity is utilized ?)
  - o Power factor charge, P.F.

    (i.e., **Real power use versus Apparent power use factor**)
  - o Other incentives and penalties applied from time to time
  - o High tension tariff and low tension tariff rate changes
  - o Slab rate cost and its variation
  - o Type of tariff clause and rate for various categories such as commercial, residential, industrial, Government, agricultural, etc.
  - o Tariff rate for developed and underdeveloped area/States
  - o Tax holiday for new projects

- Unfortunately the different forms of energy are sold in different units e.g. kWh of electricity, litres of fuel oil, tonne of coal. To allow comparison of energy quantities, these must be converted to a common unit of energy such as kWh, Giga joules, kcals etc.

Electricity (1 kWh) = 860 kcal/kWh (0.0036 GJ)

Heavy fuel oil (Gross calorific value, GCV) =10000 kcal/litre (0.0411 GJ/litre)

Coal (Gross calorific value, GCV) = 4000 kcal/kg (28 GJ/ton)

3.3 BENCHMARKING AND ENERGY PERFORMANCE (S-12; W-13)

3.3.1 Approach to Benchmarking

- One of the major critiques of using a benchmark to evaluate industrial projects is that there is a rarely a homogenous output to use as the basis for measuring the intensity of energy use (Lazarus et al).

- In electricity generation, it is common to think of energy intensity in terms of energy use per kilowatt-hour of electricity generated. There is basically one output commodity in electricity generation, so this metric makes sense. For industrial manufacturing, output is generally much more heterogeneous.

- Some commodities appear to be fairly homogenous, such as steel, but a close look shows that steel output includes diverse products such as ingots, slabs, wire, and sheets, and the processes used can vary.

- For example, steel can be made starting with iron ore and coking coal, or can be made from recycled steel. Each of these differences translates into different energy requirements.

- In the process step approach, the key energy consuming steps for a manufacturing process are identified, and a facility is evaluated according to how well it performed at each of these key steps.

- If it is designed well, a process step evaluation tool can be used to compare a number of different· facilities, even if their production methods and outputs vary.

- There are four key steps to setting up the process step approach:

Step 1:

- **Understand the Industrial Processes:** The process step approach begins with an understanding of the production processes used in an industry. Often, there are a number of pathways that lead to the production of the one central product, such as liquid steel in the steel industry, or clinker in the cement industry.

- The production of this product encompasses the most energy intensive production steps. There are then more pathways that lead from the central intermediate product to a number of final products such as a wide range of steel products or various grades of cement.

- An understanding of the production pathways and key products is needed to correctly set up a benchmarking system.

Step 2:

- **Set the Boundaries of the Analysis:** After the key process steps are understood, a decision is required about which process steps are included in the analysis for an industry and which will be outside the analysis boundary.

- This decision is somewhat subjective, but is based on a combination of factors. The most energy intensive steps should always be included, and steps with lower energy intensity can be excluded, particularly if the data required for accurate evaluation are difficult to acquire.

- It is important that all potentially substitutable steps fall on the same side of the analysis boundary, whether that is inside or outside of the analysis. Setting up boundaries like this helps to make sure that all projects are evaluated fairly, and also helps to limit the data requirements by focusing the analysis as much as possible.

- Each of these steps must have some sort of measurable physical throughput that can be used as the basis of an intensity measure.

Step 3:

- **Define the Benchmark Energy Categories:** Once the process steps that will be used in the analysis have been set, there remains a decision about how to treat the benchmark categories.

- There are a few factors that are considered at this point. For example, is it necessary to include all of the energy sources in the analysis, or can focusing on the main energy sources help to simplify the analysis while still capturing the important information?

- Also, special consideration is needed for secondary energy carriers, including electricity and steam, to determine the primary energy savings associated with saving one unit of each of these.

Step 4:

- **Determine Values for the Benchmarks:** The final step is to establish benchmark intensities for each process step.

- There are two major approaches to determining the benchmark values. The first approach is to compile performance information from existing plants or plants that are under construction and to base the benchmark value on this data.

- The benchmark might be set as the average performance weighted by output, or it might be set to the top 10 or 25 per cent of performance.

- A more sophisticated approach would be to estimate a trend in the data to look for improving performance that would indicate how future plants would be expected to perform.

- In practice, existing data are often not complete enough to do a thorough analysis of this sort.

- In any approach that determines a benchmark from a set of existing plants, there needs to be a decision about which plants are included when making the evaluation.

- Some parameter might be set, such as all plants built in the past ten years, or the most recent 10 plants built, to define which plants belong in the evaluation set.

- The second major approach for determining benchmark values is to use data that represents 'best practice' performance, which could be derived from either observations at highly efficient plants or from scholarly publications that study the industry.

- This approach is much less data intensive than basing the benchmark of a set of existing plants, but these 'best practice' values may not be good indicator of the types of projects going on in individual countries.

3.3.2 Benchmarking in the Cement Industry

- Cement production is an energy intensive process in which a combination of raw materials is chemically altered through intense heat to form a compound with binding properties.

- Raw materials, including limestone, chalk, and clay, are mined or quarried, usually at a site close to the cement mill. These materials are then ground to a fine powder in the proper proportions needed for the cement.

- These can be ground as a dry mixture or combined with water to form a slurry.

- The addition of water at this stage has important implications for the production process and for the energy demands during production. Production is often categorized as dry process and wet process. Additionally, equipment can be added to remove some water from the slurry after grinding; the process is then called semi-wet or semi-dry.

- This mixture of raw materials enters the clinker production stage. During this stage the mixture is passed through a kiln (and possibly a preheater system) and exposed to increasingly intense heat, up to 1400 °C.

- This process drives off all moisture, dissociates carbon dioxide from calcium, carbonate, and transforms the raw materials into new compounds.

- The output from this process, called clinker, must be cooled rapidly to prevent further chemical changes.

- Finally, the clinker is blended with certain additives and ground into a powder to make cement.

- Following this cement grinding step, the cement is bagged and transported for sale, or and transported in bulk.

- Fig. 3.8 shows an overview of the key production steps in cement making. The box on this figure indicated where we choose to set a system boundary for this benchmarking analysis. The most energy intensive stage of the process is clinker production, which accounts for up to 90 per cent of the total energy use.

- The grinding of raw materials and of the cement mixture both are electricity intensive steps and account for much of the remaining energy use in cement production.

- For each of the process steps within the boundary, we focus on the major energy use at step; for example, in clinker production we just include the combustion of fuel to generate the heat required, not the electricity used to rotate the kiln. Thereby, we are left with three benchmark categories :

  1. Electricity use for raw material preparation,

  2. Fossil fuel use for clinker production, and

  3. Electricity use for cement grinding (or finish grinding).

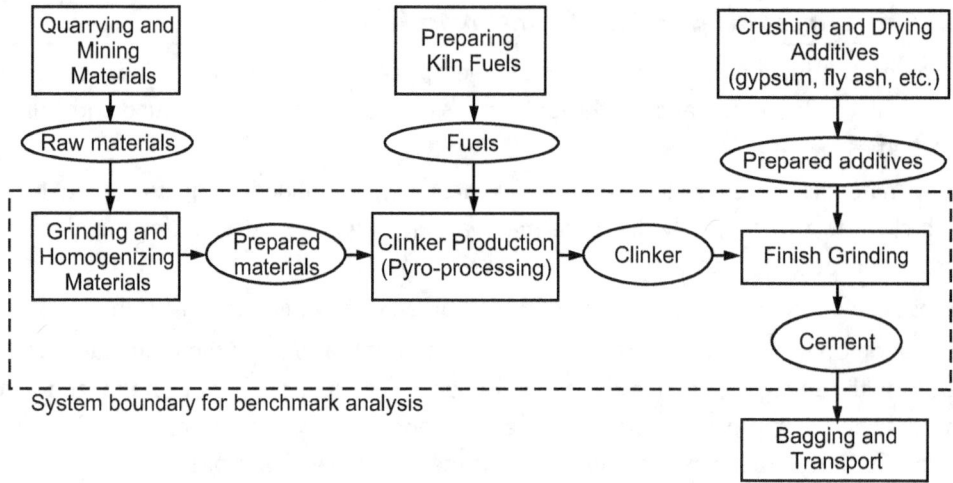

Fig. 3.8: The cement production process

- Table 3.4 provides energy consumption values for the three cement-making process steps included in the system boundary.

- The first three rows of the table present "best practice" estimates of energy use in cement plants taken from two sources that survey the available technologies for cement manufacturing (Cembureau 1997, Conroy 1994).

- For raw material preparation and cement grinding, the main energy demand is electricity to power grinding mills, so these estimates are given in terms of kWh per ton of material throughput. Energy requirements for cement grinding are roughly double those for raw material preparation because the cement is harder and need to be ground more finely than the raw materials.

**Table 3.4: Energy Use Data for Three Cement Making Process Steps,
"Best Practice" and Actual Performance**

Plant		Raw Material Preparation	Clinker Production		Cement Grinding	
		Energy use (kWh/t raw metal)	Fuel used	Energy use (kJ/kg clinker)	Product fineness (cm²/g)	Energy use (kWh/t cement)
Technical Publications	Cembureau – Dry	13.20	n/a	2900-3200	3500	24.5-36.5
	Cembureau – Wet	5-13	n/a	Upto 6000		
	Conroy's "Modern Plant Design"	10-11	Coal	2990-3010	3600	25.0
Actual Plant Performance Data	Lampang, Thailand	21.4	Lignite	3014	3300	41.76
	Bernburg, Germany	n/a	Lignite	3008-3100	n/a	22.8
	Rajshree Cement, India	17-20	Coal	2931 (expected)	3000	31.25
	Tepeaca, Mexico	n/a	Fuel oil	3030	n/a	n/a

Sources : Cembureau, 1997, Conroy, 1994, Philipp et. al., 1997, Seigert et. al., 1998, Somani et. al., 1997, Turley, 1995.

- An important issue when considering "best practice" energy requirements for grinding is that energy use is related to the hardness of the raw materials and the additives included before cement grinding as well as the desired fineness of the finished product.

- These features can vary, so it is important to specify the fineness and composition of the product when discussing energy use. In this table we have included information on the fineness of the final product expressed tenns of cm^2 per gram of product.

- Clinker production accounts for a majority of the energy use in the cement making process. Multi-stage preheaters and precalciners, which begin the clinker production process by eliminating water and bound carbon dioxide from the raw materials before they are sent to the kiln are part of any "best practice" cement plant.

- Using these technologies energy use is around 3,000 kJ per kilogram of clinker produced.

- Wet process cement making uses much more energy, and even under "best practice" can consume up to 6,000 kJ per kilogram of clinker.

- The second half of Table 3.4 provides examples from actual plant experience worldwide. Data on clinker production, the most energy intensive step, are generally given, while grinding energy data are less commonly available.

- The four examples shown all use multi-stage preheaters and precalciners, and all show energy consumption around what is expected from the "best practice" information.

- In general, the energy use for grinding appears to be higher than the "best practice" estimates, although for cement grinding comparison is difficult because the final products vary.

- Benchmarking of energy consumption internally (historical/trend analysis) and externally (across similar industries) are two powerful tools for performance assessment and logical evolution of avenues for improvement.

- Historical data well documented helps to bring out energy consumption and cost trends month-wise/day-wise.

- Trend analysis of energy consumption, cost, relevant production features, specific energy consumption, help to understand effects of capacity utilization on energy use efficiency and costs on a broader scale.

- External benchmarking relates to inter-unit comparison across a group of similar units. However, it would be important to ascertain similarities, as otherwise findings can be grossly misleading.

- Few comparative factors, which need to be looked into while benchmarking externally are:
  - Scale of operation
  - Vintage of technology
  - Raw material specifications and quality
  - Product specifications and quality

Benchmarking energy performance permits:

  - Quantification of fixed and variable energy consumption trends vis-à-vis production levels.
  - Comparison of the industry energy performance with respect to various production levels (capacity utilization).
  - Identification of best practices (based on the external benchmarking data).
  - Scope and margin available for energy consumption and cost reduction.
  - Basis for monitoring and target setting exercises.

The benchmark parameters can be:

  - **Gross production related**

    e.g. kWh/MT clinker or cement produced (cement plant)

    e.g. kWh/kg yarn produced (Textile unit)

    e.g. kWh/MT, kcal/kg, paper produced (Paper plant)

e.g. kcal/kWh Power produced (Heat rate of a power plant)

e.g. Million kilocals/MT Urea or Ammonia (Fertilizer plant)

e.g. kWh/MT of liquid metal output (in a foundry)

- **Equipment / utility related**

e.g. kW/ton of refrigeration (on Air conditioning plant)

e.g. % thermal efficiency of a boiler plant

e.g. % cooling tower effectiveness in a cooling tower

e.g. kWh/Nm^3 of compressed air generated

e.g. kWh/litre in a diesel power generation plant.

- While such benchmarks are referred to, related crucial process parameters need mentioning for meaningful comparison among peers. For instance, in the above case:

  - For a cement plant – type of cement, blaine number (fineness) i.e. Portland and process used (wet/dry) are to be reported alongside kWh/MT figure.

  - For a textile unit – average count, type of yarn i.e. polyester/cotton, is to be reported along side kWh/square meter.

  - For a paper plant – paper type, raw material (recycling extent), GSM quality is some important factors to be reported along with kWh/MT, kcal/kg figures.

  - For a power plant / cogeneration plant – plant % loading, condenser vacuum, inlet cooling water temperature, would be important factors to be mentioned alongside heat rate (kcal/kWh).

  - For a fertilizer plant – capacity utilization (%) and on-stream factor are two inputs worth comparing while mentioning specific energy consumption.

  - For a foundry unit – melt output, furnace type, composition (mild steel, high carbon steel/cast iron etc.) raw material mix, number or power trips could be some useful operating parameters to be reported while mentioning specific energy consumption data.

  - For an Air conditioning (A/c) plant – Chilled water temperature level and refrigeration load (TR) are crucial for comparing kW/TR.

  - For a boiler plant – fuel quality, type, steam pressure, temperature, flow, are useful comparators alongside thermal efficiency and more importantly, whether thermal efficiency is on gross calorific value basis or net calorific value basis or whether the computation is by direct method or indirect heat loss method, may mean a lot in benchmarking exercise for meaningful comparison.

  - Cooling tower effectiveness – ambient air wet/dry bulb temperature, relative humidity, air and circulating water flows are required to be reported to make meaningful sense.

- Compressed air specific power consumption – is to be compared at similar inlet air temperature and pressure of generation.
- Diesel power plant performance – is to be compared at similar loading %, steady run condition etc.

3.4 ENERGY MONITORING AND TARGETING

3.4.1 Definition

- Energy monitoring and targeting is primarily a management technique that uses energy information as a basis to eliminate waste, reduce and control current level of energy use and improve the existing operating procedures.
- It builds on the principle **"you can't manage what you don't measure"**.
- It essentially combines the principles of energy use and statistics.
- While, monitoring is essentially aimed at establishing the existing pattern of energy consumption, targeting is the identification of energy consumption level which is desirable as a management goal to work towards energy conservation.
- Monitoring and Targeting is a management technique in which all plant and building utilities such as fuel, steam, refrigeration, compressed air, water, effluent, and electricity are managed as controllable resources in the same way that raw materials, finished product inventory, building occupancy, personnel and capital are managed.
- It involves a systematic, disciplined division of the facility into Energy Cost Centers. The utilities used in each centre are closely monitored, and the energy used is compared with production volume or any other suitable measure of operation.
- Once this information is available on a regular basis, targets can be set, variances can be spotted and interpreted, and remedial actions can be taken and implemented.
- The Monitoring and Targeting programs have been so effective that they show typical reductions in annual energy costs in various industrial sectors between 5 and 20%.

3.4.2 Elements of Monitoring and Targeting System

The essential elements of monitoring and targeting system are:

- **Recording :** Measuring and recording energy consumption.
- **Analysing :** Correlating energy consumption to a measured output, such as production quantity.
- **Comparing :** Comparing energy consumption to an appropriate standard or benchmark.
- **Setting Targets :** Setting targets to reduce or control energy consumption.
- **Monitoring :** Comparing energy consumption to the set target on a regular basis.
- **Reporting :** Reporting the results including any variances from the targets which have been set.

- **Controlling :** Implementing management measures to correct any variances, which may have occurred.

Particularly monitoring and targeting system will involve the following:

- **Checking** the accuracy of energy invoices.
- **Allocating** energy costs to specific departments (Energy Accounting Centres).
- **Determining** energy performance/efficiency.
- **Recording** energy use, so that projects intended to improve energy efficiency can be checked.
- **Highlighting** performance problems in equipment or systems.

3.4.3 A Rationale for Monitoring, Targeting and Reporting

The energy used by any business varies with production processes, volumes and input. Determining the relationship of energy use to key performance indicators will allow you to determine :

- Whether your current energy is better or worse than before.
- Trends in energy consumption that reflects seasonal, weekly, and other operational parameters.
- How much your future energy use is likely to vary if you change aspects of your business?
- Specific areas of wasted energy.
- Comparison with other business with similar characteristics. This "benchmarking" process will provide valuable indications of effectiveness of your operations as well as energy use.
- How much your business has reacted to changes in the past?
- How to develop performance targets for an energy management program?

Information related to energy use may be obtained from the following sources :

- Plant level information can be derived from financial accounting systems, utilities cost centre.
- Plant department level information can be found in comparative energy consumption data for a group of similar facilities, service entrance meter readings etc.
- System level (for example, boiler plant) performance data can be determined from submetering data.
- Equipment level information can be obtained from name plate data, run-time and schedule information, sub-metered data on specific energy consuming equipment.

The important point to be made here is that all of these data are useful and can be processed to yield information about facility performance.

Practice Questions

1. List out objectives of energy management.

2. What are the managerial functions involved in energy management ?

3. What are the various steps in the implementation of energy management in an organization.

4. State importance of energy policy for industries.

5. What is an energy audit ?

6. What are the benefits of benchmarking energy consumption ?

7. Give general tips for energy monitoring.

MSBTE Questions and Answers (As Per 'E' Scheme)

Summer 2012

1. Write names of any four energy audit instruments. Which parameter is found out by these instruments ? State their units.

Ans. Please refer to Section 3.1.3.

2. Explain monitoring and targeting. List benefits that are derived from effective monitoring and targeting.

Ans. Please refer to Section 3.4.

3. State with reason the need of energy audit in industry.

Ans. Please refer to Section 3.1.1.

4. What are the types of energy audit? Write down the points which should be included in energy audit report.

Ans. Please refer to Sections 3.1.1 and 3.1.3.

5. What is the purpose of knowing energy cost in energy audit?

Ans. Please refer to Section 3.2.

6. Explain methodology of detailed energy audit. What are the post-audit activities?

Ans. Please refer to Section 3.1.1.

7. What is benchmarking? Write any four benchmarking parameters used in industry.

Ans. Please refer to Section 3.3.

Winter 2013

1. What are the different types of energy audit? State the uses of energy audit.

Ans. Please refer to Section 3.1.1.

2. State with reasons why energy audit is used in any industry.

Ans. Please refer to Section 3.1.1.

3. What are the parameter to be considered while determining energy cost.

Ans. Please refer to Section 3.2.

4. Write any four benchmarking parameters used in industrial equipment/utilities.

Ans. Please refer to Section 3.3.

5. Define energy monitoring and targetting. List the benefits of effective monitoring and targetting system.

Ans. Please refer to Section 3.4.

Chapter 4

ENERGY EFFICIENCY IN ELECTRICAL AND THERMAL UTILITIES

Objectives

Students will study and understand the following:

- Calculate efficiency of boiler by direct method
- Describe steps for efficiency calculation
- Calculate specified power for pump

4.1 INTRODUCTION

- Pumping systems account for nearly 20% of the world's electrical energy demand and range from 25-50% of the energy usage.

- Pumps have two main purposes:

  o Transfer of liquid from one place to another place (e.g. water from an underground aquifer into a water storage tank).

  o Circulate liquid around a system (e.g. cooling water or lubricants through machines and equipment) in certain industrial plant operations.

4.1.1 Types of Pumps

- This section describes the various types of pumps. Pumps come in a variety of sizes for a wide range of applications.

- They can be classified according to their basic operating principle as dynamic or positive displacement pumps.

- In principle, any liquid can be handled by any of the pump designs. Where different pump designs could be used, the centrifugal pump is generally the most economical followed by rotary and reciprocating pumps.

- Although, positive displacement pumps are generally more efficient than centrifugal pumps, the benefit of higher efficiency tends to be offset by increased maintenance costs.

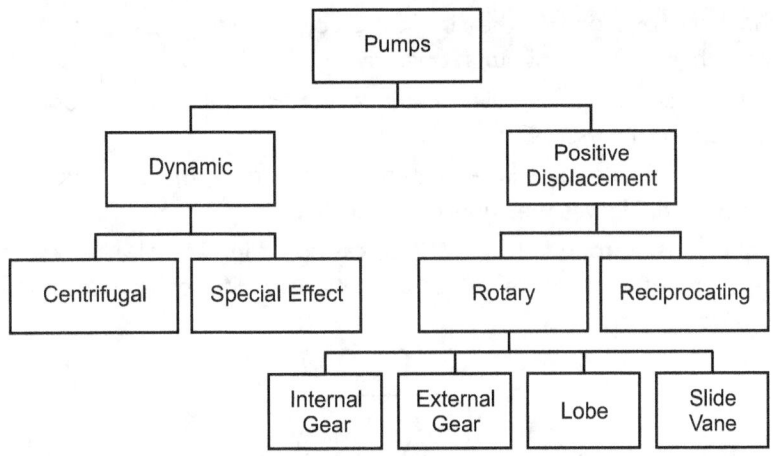

4.1.2 Positive Displacement Pumps

(W-13)

- Positive displacement pumps are distinguished by the way they operate: liquid is taken from one end and positively discharged at the other end for every revolution.
- Positive displacement pumps are widely used for pumping fluids other than water, mostly viscous fluids.
- Positive displacement pumps are further classified based upon the mode of displacement:

Reciprocating pump: If the displacement is by reciprocation of a piston plunger. Reciprocating pumps are used only for pumping viscous liquids and oil wells.

Rotary pumps: If the displacement is by rotary action of a gear, cam or vanes in a chamber of diaphragm in a fixed casing. Rotary pumps are further classified such as internal gear, external gear, lobe and slide vane etc. These pumps are used for special services with particular conditions existing in industrial sites. In all positive displacement type pumps, a fixed quantity of liquid is pumped after each revolution. So if the delivery pipe is blocked, the pressure rises to a very high value, which can damage the pump.

4.1.3 Dynamic Pumps

(S-12; W-13)

- Dynamic pumps are also characterized by their mode of operation: a rotating impeller converts kinetic energy into pressure or velocity that is needed to pump the fluid.
- There are two types of dynamic pumps:

Centrifugal pumps are the most common pumps used for pumping water in industrial applications. Typically, more than 75% of the pumps installed in an industry are centrifugal pumps. For this reason, this pump is further described below.

Special effect pumps are particularly used for specialized conditions at an industrial site.

Centrifugal Pump:

- How a centrifugal pump works ?

- A centrifugal pump is one of the simplest pieces of equipment in any process plant. Fig. 4.1 shows how this type of pump operates:
  - o Liquid is forced into an impeller either by atmospheric pressure, or in case of a jet pump by artificial pressure.
  - o The vanes of impeller pass kinetic energy to the liquid, thereby causing the liquid to rotate. The liquid leaves the impeller at high velocity.
  - o The impeller is surrounded by a volute casing or in case of a turbine pump and a stationary diffuser ring. The volute or stationary diffuser ring converts the kinetic energy into pressure energy.

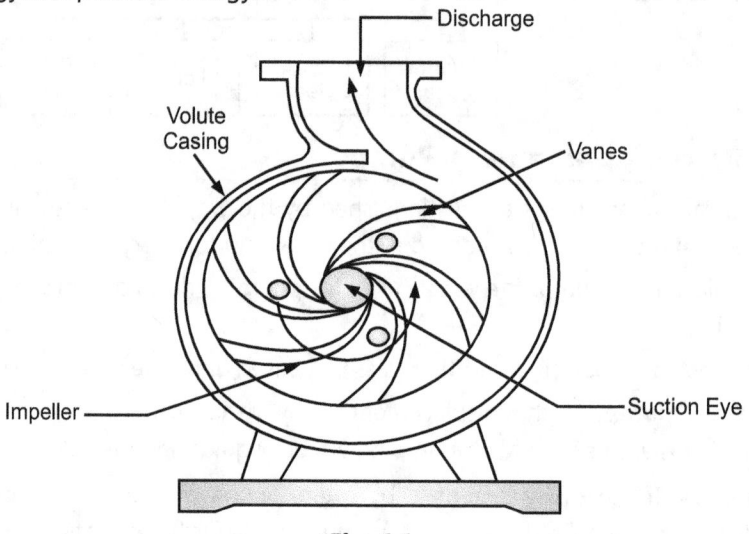

Fig. 4.1

(a) **Impeller:** An impeller is a circular metallic disc with a built-in passage for the flow of fluid. Impellers are generally made of bronze, polycarbonate, cast iron or stainless steel, but other materials are also used. As the performance of the pump depends on the type of impeller, it is important to select a suitable design and to maintain the impeller in good condition. The number of impellers determines the number of stages of the pump. A single stage pump has one impeller and is best suited for low head (= pressure) service. A two-stage pump has two impellers in series for medium head service. A multi-stage pump has three or more impellers in series for high head service.

(b) **Shaft:** The shaft transfers the torque from the motor to the impeller during the startup and operation of the pump.

(c) **Casing:** The main function of casing is to enclose the impeller at suction and delivery ends and thereby form a pressure vessel. The pressure at suction end may be as little as one-tenth of atmospheric pressure and at delivery end may be twenty times the atmospheric pressure in a single-stage pump. For multi-stage pumps the pressure difference is much higher. The casing is designed to withstand at least twice this pressure to ensure a large enough safety margin. A second function of casing is to provide a supporting and bearing medium for the shaft and impeller. Therefore the pump casing should be designed to:

- Provide easy access to all parts of pump for inspection, maintenance and repair.
- Make the casing leak-proof by providing stuffing boxes.
- Connect the suction and delivery pipes directly to the flanges.
- Be coupled easily to its prime mover (i.e. electric motor) without any power loss.

4.1.4 NPSH (S-12)

- The value, by which the pressure in the pump suction exceeds the liquid vapour pressure, is expressed as a head of liquid and referred to as Net Positive Suction Head Available (NPSHA).
- This is a characteristic of the system design.
- The value of NPSH needed at the pump suction to prevent the pump from cavitation is known as NPSH Required (NPSHR). This is a characteristic of the pump design.
- If the incoming liquid is at a pressure with insufficient margin above its vapour pressure, then vapour cavities or bubbles appear along the impeller vanes just behind the inlet edges. This phenomenon is known as cavitation.
- The undesirable effects of cavitation on pumping systems are
  - o Formation of cavitational bubbles leading to erosion of the vane surface.
  - o Noise and vibration.
  - o Partially choking of impeller passage and thereby reduction of pump performance.

4.1.5 Pump Performance (W-13)

- The work performed by a pump is a function of the total head and of the weight of the liquid pumped in a given time period.
- Pump shaft power (P_s) is the actual horsepower delivered to the pump shaft, and can be calculated as follows:

Pump shaft power, P_s = Hydraulic power, h_p/Pump efficiency η_{pump}.

or

Pump efficiency η_{pump} = Hydraulic power/Pump shaft power

- Pump output, water horsepower or hydraulic horsepower (h_p) is the liquid horsepower delivered by the pump, and can be calculated as follows:

$$\boxed{\text{Hydraulic power } h_p = Q(m^3/s) \times (h_d - h_s \text{ in m}) \times \rho \ (kg/m^3) \times g \ (m/s^2)/1000}$$

where,

Q = Flow rate

H_d = Discharge head

h_s = Suction head

ρ = Density of the fluid

g = Acceleration due to gravity

Power required for pump is

$$P = H \times Q \times g \times \text{Specific gravity} / \eta_{pump} \times \eta_{motor}$$

where,

P = Power in kW

H = Head in m

g = Gravity due to acceleration = 9.8 m/s^2

η_{pump} = Efficiency of pump

η_{motor} = Efficiency of motor

Pump performance curve:

- The pressure (head) that a pump will develop is in direct relationship to the impeller diameter, the number of impellers, the size of impeller eye, and shaft speed. Capacity is determined by the exit width of the impeller.

- The head and capacity are the main factors, which affect the horsepower size of the motor to be used.

- The more the quantity of water to be pumped, the more energy is required.

- A centrifugal pump is not positive acting; it will not pump the same volume always. The greater the depth of the water, the lesser is the flow from the pump.

- Also, when it pumps against increasing pressure, the less it will pump. For these reasons it is important to select a centrifugal pump that is designed to do a particular job.

- Since the pump is a dynamic device, it is convenient to consider the pressure in terms of head i.e. meters of liquid column.

- The pump generates the same head of liquid whatever the density of the liquid being pumped.

- The actual contours of the hydraulic passages of the impeller and the casing are extremely important, in order to attain the highest efficiency possible.

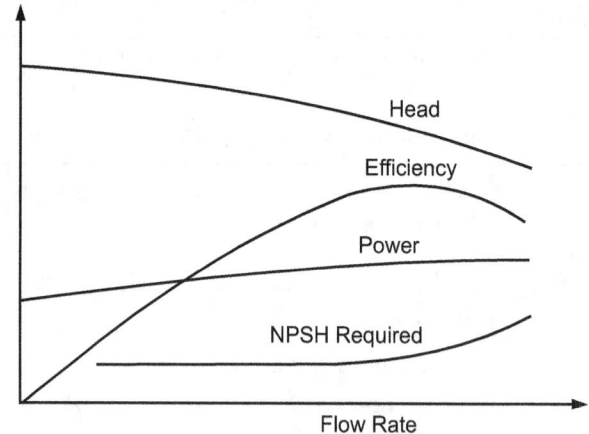

Fig. 4.2: Pump performance curve

- The standard convention for centrifugal pump is to draw the pump performance curves showing Flow on the horizontal axis and Head generated on the vertical axis.
- Efficiency, Power and NPSH Required (described later), are also all conventionally shown on the vertical axis, plotted against Flow, as illustrated in Fig. 4.2.

Parameters affecting pump system curves:

- The system curve is basically a plot of system resistance i.e. head to be overcome by the pump versus various flow rates.
- The system curves change with the physical configuration of the system; for example, the system curves depend upon height or elevation, diameter and length of piping, number and type of fittings and pressure drops across various equipment - say a heat exchanger.

4.1.6 Energy Efficiency Opportunities   (W-12)

- This section includes main areas for improving pumps and pumping systems. The main areas for energy conservation include:
  - Selecting the right pump
  - Controlling the flow rate by speed variation
  - Pumps in parallel to meet varying demand
  - Eliminating flow control valve
  - Eliminating by-pass control
  - Start/stop control of pump
  - Impeller trimming

Energy loss in throttling: (W-13)

- Consider a case (see Fig. 4.3) where we need to pump 68 m³/hr. of water at 47 m head. The pump characteristic curves (A...E) for a range of pumps are given in Fig. 4.3.

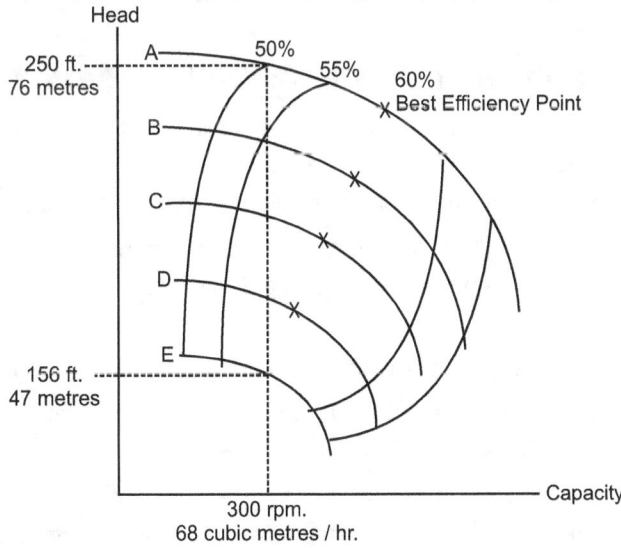

Fig. 4.3

- If we select E, then the pump efficiency is 60%.

$$\text{Hydraulic power} = Q \ (m^3/s) \times \text{Total head,}$$
$$h_d - h_s \ (m) \times \rho \ (kg/m^3) \times g \ (m/s^2)/1000$$
$$= \frac{(68/3600) \times 47 \times 1000 \times 9.81}{1000}$$
$$= 8.7 \ kW$$

Shaft power – 8.7/0.60   =   14.5 kW

Motor power – 14.5/0.9   =   16.1 kW (considering motor efficiency of 90%).

- If we select A, then the pump efficiency is 50% (drop from earlier 60%).
- Obviously, this is an oversize pump. Hence, the pump has to be throttled to achieve the desired flow. Throttling increases the head to be overcome by the pump. In this case, head is 76 metres.

$$\text{Hydraulic power} = Q \ (m^3/s) \times \text{Total head,}$$
$$h_d - h_s \ (m) \times \rho \ (kg/m^3) \times g \ (m/s^2)/1000$$
$$= \frac{(68/3600) \times 76 \times 1000 \times 9.81}{1000}$$
$$= 14 \ kW$$

Shaft power – 14/0.50   =   28 kW

Motor power – 28/0.9   =   31 kW (considering a motor efficiency of 90%)

- Hence, additional power drawn by A over E is 31 – 16.1 = 14.9 kW.

Extra energy used   =   8760 hrs/year × 14.9 = 1,30,524 kWh/annum
   =   ₹ 5,22,096/annum

- In this example, the extra cost of the electricity is more than the cost of purchasing a new pump.

4.2 EFFICIENT PUMPING SYSTEM OPERATION

- To understand a pumping system, one must realize that all of its components are interdependent. When examining or designing a pump system, the process demands must first be established and most energy efficiency solution introduced.
- For example, does the flow rate have to be regulated continuously or in steps ? Can on-off batch pumping be used ? What are the flow rates needed and how are they distributed in time ?
- The first step to achieve energy efficiency in pumping system is to target the end-use.
- A plant water balance would establish usage pattern and highlight areas where water consumption can be reduced or optimized.
- Good water conservation measures, alone, may eliminate the need for some pumps. Once flow requirements are optimized, then the pumping system can be analysed for energy conservation opportunities.

- Basically, this means matching the pump to requirements by adopting proper flow control strategies. Common symptoms that indicate opportunities for energy efficiency in pumps are given in the Table 4.1.

Table 4.1: Symptoms that indicate potential opportunity for energy savings

Symptom	Likely Reason	Best Solutions
Throttle valve-controlled systems	Oversized pump	Trim impeller, smaller impeller, variable speed drive, two speed drive, lower rpm.
Bypass line (partially or completely) open	Oversized pump	Trim impeller, smaller impeller, variable speed drive, two speed drive, lower rpm.
Multiple parallel pump system with the same number of pumps always operating.	Pump use not monitored or controlled.	Install controls.
Constant pump operation in a batch environment.	Wrong system design.	On-off controls.
High maintenance cost (seals, bearings).	Pump operating far away from BEP.	Match pump capacity with system requirement.

Effect of Speed Variation:

- As stated above, a centrifugal pump is a dynamic device with the head generated from a rotating impeller. There is therefore a relationship between impeller peripheral velocity and generated head.
- Peripheral velocity is directly related to shaft rotational speed, for a fixed impeller diameter and so varying the rotational speed has a direct effect on the performance of the pump.
- All the parameters shown in Fig. 4.3 will change if the speed is varied and it is important to have an appreciation of how these parameters vary in order to safely control a pump at different speeds.
- The equations relating rotodynamic pump performance parameters of flow, head and power absorbed, to speed are known as the *Affinity Laws:*

$$Q \propto N$$
$$H \propto N^2$$
$$P \propto N^3$$

where,

Q = Flow rate, H = Head

P = Power absorbed N = Rotating speed

Efficiency is essentially independent of speed.

Flow: Flow is proportional to the speed

$$Q_1/Q_2 = N_1/N_2$$

Example: $100/Q_2 = 1750/3500$

$$Q_2 = 200 \text{ m}^3/\text{hr}$$

Head: Head is proportional to the square of speed.

$$H_1/H_2 = (N_1^2)/(N_2^2)$$

Example: $100/H_2 = 1750^2/3500^2$

$$H_2 = 400 \text{ m}$$

Power (kW): Power is proportional to the cube of speed.

$$kW_1/kW_2 = (N_1^3)/(N_2^3)$$

Example: $5/kW_2 = 1750^3/3500^3$

$$kW_2 = 40$$

- As can be seen from the above laws, doubling the speed of the centrifugal pump will increase the power consumption by 8 times. Conversely a small reduction in speed will result in drastic reduction in power consumption. This forms the basis for energy conservation in centrifugal pumps with varying flow requirements.
- The most commonly used method to reduce pump speed is Variable Speed Drive (VSD).
- VSDs allow pump speed adjustments over a continuous range, avoiding the need to jump from speed to speed as with multiple-speed pumps. VSDs control pump speeds use two types of systems:
  - Mechanical VSDs include hydraulic clutches, fluid couplings, and adjustable belts and pulleys.
  - Electrical VSDs include eddy current clutches, wound-rotor motor controllers, and variable frequency drives (VFDs). VFDs are the most popular and adjust the electrical frequency of the power supplied to a motor to change the motor's rotational speed.

Impeller trimming:

- Changing the impeller diameter gives a proportional change in the impeller's peripheral velocity. Similar to the affinity laws, the following equations apply to the impeller diameter D:

$$Q \propto D$$
$$H \propto D^2$$
$$P \propto D^3$$

- Changing the impeller diameter is an energy efficient way to control the pump flow rate. However, for this option, the following should be considered:
  - This option cannot be used where varying flow patterns exist.
  - The impeller should not be trimmed more than 25% of the original impeller size, otherwise it leads to vibration due to cavitation and therefore decrease the pump efficiency.

o   The balance of the pump has to be maintained, i.e. the impeller trimming should be the same on all sides.

- Changing the impeller itself is a better option than trimming the impeller, but is also more expensive and sometimes the smaller impeller is too small.

Comparison of different energy conservation options in pumps:

Parameter	Change control valve	Trim impeller	VFD
Impeller diameter	430 mm	375 mm	430 mm
Pump head	71.7 m	42 m	34.5 m
Pump efficiency	75.1%	72.1%	77%
Rate of flow	80 m^3/hr	80 m^3/hr	80 m^3/hr
Power consumed	23.1 kW	14 kW	11.6 kW

4.3 ENERGY CONSERVATION OPPORTUNITIES IN PUMPING SYSTEMS

- Ensure adequate NPSH at site of installation.
- Ensure availability of basic instruments at pumps like pressure gauges, flow meters.
- Operate pumps near best efficiency point.
- Modify pumping system and pumps losses to minimize throttling.
- Adapt to wide load variation with variable speed drives or sequenced control of multiple units.
- Stop running multiple pumps - add an auto-start for an on-line spare or add a booster pump in the problem area.
- Use booster pumps for small loads requiring higher pressures.
- Increase fluid temperature differentials to reduce pumping rates in case of heat exchangers.
- Repair seals and packing to minimize water loss by dripping.
- Balance the system to minimize flows and reduce pump power requirements.
- Avoid pumping head with a free-fall return (gravity); use siphon effect to advantage:
- Conduct water balance to minimize water consumption.
- Avoid cooling water re-circulation in DG sets, air compressors, refrigeration systems, cooling towers, feed water pumps, condenser pumps and process pumps.
- In multiple pump operations, carefully combine the operation of pumps to avoid throttling.
- Provide booster pump for few areas of higher head.
- Replace old pumps by energy efficient pumps.

- In the case of over designed pump, provide variable speed drive, or downsize / replace impeller or replace with correct sized pump for efficient operation.
- Optimise number of stages in multi-stage pump in case of head margins.
- Reduce system resistance by pressure drop assessment and pipe size optimization.

SOLVED PROBLEMS

Problem 4.1:

A cooling water pump in the plant is having the following specifications.

Q = 12.5 lps, H = 60 m, P = 13.4 kW

As per new requirement water flow should be 12.5 lps at 3.0 kg/cm^2. How much energy can be saved if new pump of 65% efficiency having H = 30 m and motor efficiency 90% is installed ?

Solution:

New pump power consumption:

$$Q \text{ (lps)} = 12.5$$
$$H \text{ (m)} = 30$$

Considering operating efficiency of pump as 65%, power consumption of new pump (motor efficiency as 90%).

$$P = \frac{12.5 \times 30 \times 9.81}{1000 \times 0.65 \times 0.9}$$

$$= 6.3 \text{ kW}$$

Reduction in power consumption = Present pump power – New proposed pump

$$= 13.4 - 6.3 = 7.1 \text{ kW}$$

Problem 4.2:

Estimate the reduction in power consumption of condensate transfer pump by reducing speed of the pump by 20% to the rated speed.

Q = 38 m^3/h, H = 65 m, P = 12.5 kW

Solution:

Running pump operating parameters at full speed (N),

$$Q_1 = 38 \text{ m}^3/\text{h}$$
$$H_1 = 65 \text{ m}$$
$$P_1 = 12.5 \text{ kW}$$

Power consumption at reduced speed (80% of full speed)

$$P_2 = P_1 \times \left(\frac{N_2}{N_1}\right)^3$$

$$P_2 = 12.5 \times \left(\frac{0.8\,N_1}{N_1}\right)^3 \quad [\because N_2 = 0.8\,N_1]$$

$$= 12.5 \times 0.512$$

$$= 6.4 \text{ kW}$$

4.4 COOLING TOWER   (S-12; W-13)

- A cooling tower is a heat rejection device, which extracts waste heat to the atmosphere though the cooling of a water stream to a lower temperature.

- The type of heat rejection in a cooling tower is termed "evaporative" in that it allows a small portion of the water being cooled to evaporate into a moving air stream to provide significant cooling to the rest of that water stream.

- The heat from the water stream transferred to the air stream raises the air's temperature and its relative humidity to 100%, and this air is discharged to the atmosphere.

- Evaporative heat rejection devices such as cooling towers are commonly used to provide significantly lower water temperatures than achievable with "air cooled" or "dry" heat rejection devices, like the radiator in a car, thereby achieving more cost-effective and energy efficient operation of systems in need of cooling.

- Think of the times you've seen something hot be rapidly cooled by putting water on it, which evaporates, cooling rapidly, such as an overheated car radiator.

- The cooling potential of a wet surface is much better than a dry one.

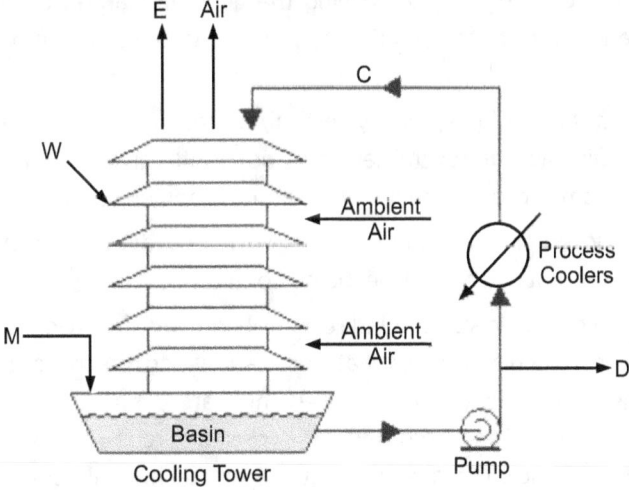

C = Circulating Cooling Water
E = Evaporated Water
W = Windage or Drift Loss
M = Makeup Water
D = Drawoff or Blowdown water

Fig. 4.4: Cooling tower

- Common applications for cooling towers are providing cooled water for air-conditioning, manufacturing and electric power generation.

- The smallest cooling towers are designed to handle water streams of only a few gallons of water per minute supplied in small pipes like those might seen in a residence, while the largest cool hundreds of thousands of gallons per minute supplied in pipes as much as 15 feet (about 5 metres) in diameter on a large power plant.

- The generic term "cooling tower" is used to describe both direct (open circuit) and indirect (closed circuit) heat rejection equipment.

- While most think of a "cooling tower" as an open direct contact heat rejection device, the indirect cooling tower, sometimes referred to as a "closed circuit cooling tower" is nonetheless also a cooling tower.

- A direct, or open circuit cooling tower is an enclosed structure with internal means to distribute the warm water fed to it over a labyrinth-like packing or "fill."

- The fill provides a vastly expanded air-water interface for heating of the air and evaporation to take place.

- The water is cooled as it descends through the fill by gravity while in direct contact with air that passes over it.

- The cooled water is then collected in a cold water basin below the fill from which it is pumped back through the process to absorb more heat.

- The heated and moisture laden air leaving the fill is discharged to the atmosphere at a point remote enough from the air inlets to prevent its being drawn back into the cooling tower.

- The fill may consist of multiple, mainly vertical, wetted surfaces upon which a thin film of water spreads (film fill), or several levels of horizontal splash elements which create a cascade of many small droplets that have a large combined surface area (splash fill).

- An indirect, or closed circuit cooling tower involves no direct contact of the air and the fluid, usually water or a glycol mixture, being cooled.

- Unlike the open cooling tower, the indirect cooling tower has two separate fluid circuits. One is an external circuit in which water is recirculated on the outside of the second circuit, which is tube bundles (closed coils) which are connected to the process for the hot fluid being cooled and returned in a closed circuit. Air is drawn through the recirculating water cascading over the outside of the hot tubes, providing evaporative cooling similar to an open cooling tower.

- In operation the heat flows from the internal fluid circuit, through the tube walls of the coils, to the external circuit and then by heating of the air and evaporation of some of the water, to the atmosphere. Operation of the indirect cooling towers is therefore very similar to the open cooling tower with one exception.

- The process fluid being cooled is contained in a "closed" circuit and is not directly exposed to the atmosphere or the recirculated external water.

- Some useful terms, commonly used in the cooling tower industry are:

    Drift: Water droplets that are carried out of the cooling tower with the exhaust air. Drift droplets have the same concentration of impurities as the water entering the tower. The drift rate is typically reduced by employing baffle-like devices, called drift eliminators, through which the air must travel after leaving the fill and spray zones of the tower.

    Blow-out: Water droplets blown out of the cooling tower by wind, generally at the air inlet openings. Water may also be lost, in the absence of wind, through splashing or misting. Devices such as wind screens, louvers, splash deflectors and water diverters are used to limit these losses.

    Plume: The stream of saturated exhaust air leaving the cooling tower. The plume is visible when water vapor it contains condenses in contact with cooler ambient air, like the saturated air in one's breath fogs on a cold day. Under certain conditions, a cooling tower plume may present fogging or icing hazards to its surroundings. Note that the water evaporated in the cooling process is "pure" water, in contrast to the very small percentage of drift droplets or water blown out of the air inlets.

    Blow-down: The portion of the circulating water flow that is removed in order to maintain the amount of dissolved solids and other impurities at an acceptable level.

    Leaching: The loss of wood preservative chemicals by the washing action of the water flowing through a wood structure cooling tower.

    Noise: Sound energy emitted by a cooling tower and heard (recorded) at a given distance and direction. The sound is generated by the impact of falling water, by the movement of air by fans, the fan blades moving in the structure, and the motors, gearboxes or drive belts.

4.4.1 Cooling Tower Efficiency

- The maximum cooling tower efficiency depends on the wet-bulb temperature of the air.

- Cooling towers use the principle of evaporative cooling in order to cool water. They can achieve water temperatures below the dry bulb temperature (t_{db}) of the air used to cool it, they are in general smaller and cheaper for the same cooling load than other cooling systems.

- Cooling towers are rated in terms of approach and range.

- The approach is the difference in temperature between the cooled-water temperature and the entering-air wet bulb (t_{wb}) temperature.

- The range is the temperature difference between the water inlet and exit states.

- Since the cooling towers are based on the principles of evaporative cooling, the maximum cooling tower efficiency depends on the wet bulb temperature (t_{wb}) of the air.

- The cooling tower efficiency can be expressed as:

$$\mu \;=\; \frac{(t_i - t_0)\,100}{(t_i - t_{wb})} \qquad\qquad \dots (1)$$

  where, μ = Cooling tower efficiency – Common range between 70 - 75%

  t_i = Inlet temperature of water to the tower (°C, °F)

  t_o = Outlet temperature of water from the tower (°C, °F)

  t_{wb} = Wet bulb temperature of air (°C, °F)

- The temperature difference between inlet and outlet water $(t_i - t_o)$ is normally in the range 10-15°C.

- The water consumption - the make up water - of a cooling tower is about 0.2-0.3 litre per minute and ton of refrigeration. Compared with using and wasting city water the water consumption is reduced with about 90-95%.

4.4.2 Types of Cooling Towers

- Cooling towers fall into two main sub-divisions: natural draft and mechanical draft. Natural draft designs use very large concrete chimneys to introduce air through the media.

- Due to the tremendous size of these towers (500 ft high and 400 ft in diameter at the base), they are generally used for water flow rates above 200,000 gal/min.

- Usually these types of towers are only used by utility power stations in the United States. Mechanical draft cooling towers are much more widely used.

- These towers utilize large fans to force air through circulated water.

- The water falls downward over fill surfaces which help to increase the contact time between the water and the air. This helps to maximize heat transfer between the two.

- Industrial cooling towers can be used to remove heat from various sources such as machinery or heated process material. The primary use of large, industrial cooling towers is to remove the heat absorbed in the circulating cooling water systems used in power plants, petroleum refineries, petrochemical plants, natural gas processing plants, food processing plants, semiconductor plants, and other industrial facilities.

- The circulation rate of cooling water in a typical 700 MW coal-fired power plant with a cooling tower amounts to about 71,600 cubic metres an hour (315,000 U.S. gallons per minute) and the circulating water requires a supply water make-up rate of perhaps 5 per cent (i.e. 3,600 cubic metres an hour).

- If that same plant had no cooling tower and used once-through cooling water, it would require about 100,000 cubic metres an hour and that amount of water would have to be continuously returned to the ocean, lake or river from which it was obtained and continuously resupplied to the plant.

- Furthermore, discharging large amounts of hot water may raise the temperature of the receiving river or lake to an unacceptable level for the local ecosystem.

- A cooling tower serves to dissipate the heat into the atmosphere instead and wind and air diffusion spreads the heat over a much larger area than hot water can distribute heat in a body of water.

- Cooling tower and water discharge of a nuclear power plant, some coal-fired and nuclear power plants located in coastal areas do make use of once-through ocean water.

- But even there, the offshore discharge water outlet requires very careful design to avoid environmental problems.

- Petroleum refineries also have very large cooling tower systems. A typical large refinery processing 40,000 metric tonnes of crude oil per day (300,000 barrels per day) circulates about 80,000 cubic metres of water per hour through its cooling tower system.

Heat Transfer Methods:

With respect to the **heat transfer** mechanism employed, the main types are:

o *Wet cooling towers* or simply *cooling towers* operate on the principle of **evaporation**.

o *Dry coolers* operate by **heat transfer** through a surface that separates the working fluid from ambient air, such as in a **heat exchanger**, utilizing convective heat transfer. They do not use evaporation.

o *Fluid coolers* are hybrids that pass the working fluid through a tube bundle, upon which clean water is sprayed and a fan-induced draft applied. The resulting heat transfer performance is much closer to that of a wet cooling tower, with the advantage provided by a dry cooler of protecting the working fluid from environmental exposure.

- In a wet cooling tower, the warm water can be cooled to a temperature lower than the ambient air dry-bulb temperature, if the air is relatively dry (see: **dew point** and **psychrometrics**).

- As ambient air is drawn past a flow of water, evaporation occurs.

- Evaporation results in saturated air conditions, lowering the temperature of the water to the **wet bulb** air temperature, which is lower than the ambient dry bulb air temperature, the difference determined by the humidity of the ambient air.

- To achieve better performance (more cooling), a media called *fill* is used to increase the surface area between the air and water flows.

- *Splash fill* consists of material placed to interrupt the water flow causing splashing. *Film fill* is composed of thin sheets of material upon which the water flows. Both methods create increased surface area.

Air flow generation methods:

With respect to drawing air through the tower, there are three types of cooling towers:

- *Natural draft*, which utilizes buoyancy via a tall chimney. Warm, moist air *naturally* rises due to the density differential to the dry, cooler outside air. Warm **moist air** is less dense than drier air at the same pressure. This moist air buoyancy produces a current of air through the tower.

- *Mechanical draft*, which uses power driven fan motors to force or draw air through the tower.

  - *Induced draft:* A mechanical draft tower with a fan at the discharge which pulls air through tower. The fan *induces* hot moist air out the discharge. This produces low entering and high exiting air velocities, reducing the possibility of *recirculation* in which discharged air flows back into the air intake. This fan/fill arrangement is also known as *draw-through*.

  - *Forced draft:* A mechanical draft tower with a blower type fan at the intake. The fan *forces* air into the tower, creating high entering and low exiting air velocities. The low exiting velocity is much more susceptible to recirculation. With the fan on the air intake, the fan is more susceptible to complications due to freezing conditions. Another disadvantage is that a forced draft design typically requires more motor horsepower than an equivalent induced draft design. The forced draft benefit is its ability to work with high static pressure. They can be installed in more confined spaces and even in some indoor situations. This fan/fill geometry is also known as *blow-through*.

  - Fan assisted natural draft. A hybrid type that appears like a natural draft though airflow is assisted by a fan.

- Hyperboloid (aka hyperbolic) cooling towers (Image 1) have become the design standard for all natural-draft cooling towers because of their structural strength and minimum usage of material.

- The hyperbolic form is popularly associated with **nuclear power plants**. However, this association is misleading, as the same kind of cooling towers are often used at large coal-fired power plants as well. Similarly, not all nuclear power plants have cooling towers.

Categorization by air-to-water flow:

Crossflow:

- Crossflow is a design in which the air flow is directed perpendicular to the water flow (see Fig. 4.5). Air flow enters one or more vertical faces of the cooling tower to meet the fill material. Water flows (perpendicular to the air) through the fill by gravity.

- The air continues through the fill and thus past the water flow into an open plenum area.

- A *distribution* or *hot water basin* consisting of a deep pan with holes or *nozzles* in the bottom is utilized in a crossflow tower. Gravity distributes the water through the nozzles uniformly across the fill material.

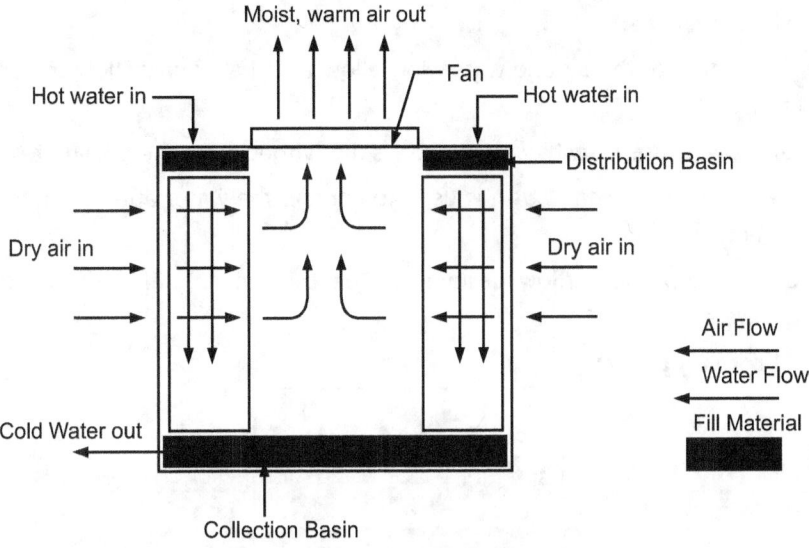

Fig. 4.5: Cross-flow type design

Counterflow:

- In a counterflow design, the air flow is directly opposite of the water flow (see Fig. 4.6). Air flow first enters an open area beneath the fill media and is then drawn up vertically.

- The water is sprayed through pressurized nozzles and flows downward through the fill, opposite to the air flow.

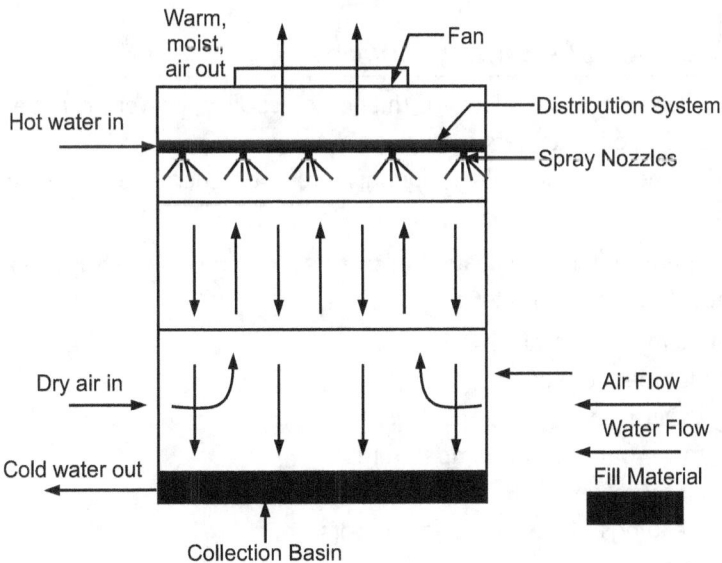

Fig. 4.6: Counterflow type basin

Common to both designs:

- The interaction of the air and water flow allow a partial equalization and evaporation of water.

- The air, now saturated with water vapor, is discharged from the cooling tower.

- A *collection* or *cold water basin* is used to contain the water after its interaction with the air flow.

Both crossflow and counterflow designs can be used in natural draft and mechanical draft cooling towers.

Natural draft cooling tower:

Fig. 4.7

4.4.3 Assessment of Cooling Towers

- This section describes how the performance of cooling powers can be assessed. The performance of cooling towers is evaluated to assess present levels of approach and range against their design values, identify areas of energy wastage and to suggest improvements.

- During the performance evaluation, portable monitoring instruments are used to measure the following parameters:
  - Wet bulb temperature of air
  - Dry bulb temperature of air
  - Cooling tower inlet water temperature
  - Cooling tower outlet water temperature
  - Exhaust air temperature
  - Electrical readings of pump and fan motors
  - Water flow rate
  - Air flow rate

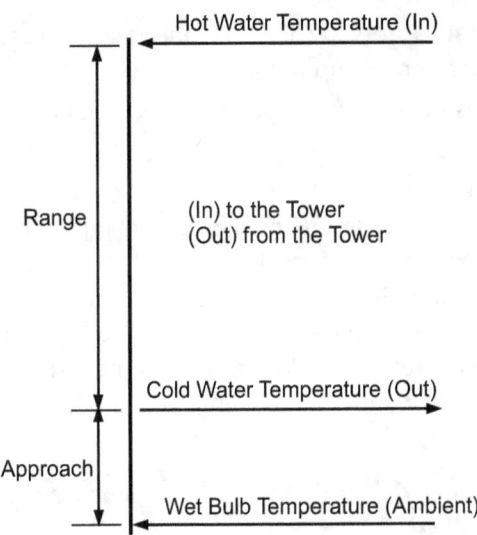

Fig. 4.8: Range and approach of cooling towers

- These measured parameters are then used to determine the cooling tower performance in several ways. (**Note:** CT = cooling tower; CW = cooling water). These are:

(a) **Range (see Fig. 4.8):** This is the difference between the cooling tower water inlet and outlet temperature. A high CT range means that the cooling tower has been able to reduce the water temperature effectively, and is thus performing well.

The formula is:

CT Range (°C) = [CW inlet temperature (°C) – CW outlet temperature (°C)]

(b) **Approach (see Fig. 4.8):** This is the difference between the cooling tower outlet cold water temperature and ambient wet bulb temperature. The lower the approach, the better the cooling tower performance. Although, both range and approach should be monitored, the 'Approach' is a better indicator of cooling tower performance.

CT Approach (°C) = [CW outlet temperature (°C) – Wet bulb temperature (°C)]

(c) **Effectiveness:** This is the ratio between the range and the ideal range (in percentage), i.e. difference between cooling water inlet temperature and ambient wet bulb temperature, or in other words it is = Range/(Range + Approach). The higher the ratio, the higher the cooling tower effectiveness.

CT Effectiveness (%) = 100 × (CW temp – CW out temp)/(CW in temp – WB temp)

(d) **Cooling capacity:** This is the heat rejected in kcal/hr or TR, given as product of mass flow rate of water, specific heat and temperature difference.

(e) **Evaporation loss:** This is the water quantity evaporated for cooling duty. Theoretically the evaporation quantity works out to 1.8 m³ for every 1,000,000 kcal heat rejected. The following formula can be used:

Evaporation loss (m³/hr) = 0.00085 × 1.8 × circulation rate (m³/hr) × (T_1 – T_2)

where T_1 – T_2 = temperature difference between inlet and outlet water

(f) Cycles of concentration (C.O.C): This is the ratio of dissolved solids in circulating water to the dissolved solids in make up water.

(g) Blow down losses depend upon cycles of concentration and the evaporation losses and is given by formula:

Blow down = Evaporation loss/(C.O.C. − 1)

(h) Liquid/Gas (L/G) ratio: The L/G ratio of a cooling tower is the ratio between the water and the air mass flow rates. Cooling towers have certain design values, but seasonal variations require adjustment and tuning of water and air flow rates to get the best cooling tower effectiveness. Adjustments can be made by water box loading changes or blade angle adjustments. Thermodynamic rules also dictate that the heat removed from the water must be equal to the heat absorbed by the surrounding air. Therefore, the following formulae can be used:

$$L(T_1 - T_2) = G(h_2 - h_1)$$
$$L/G = (h_2 - h_1)/(T_1 - T_2)$$

where,
L/G = Liquid to gas mass flow ratio (kg/kg)
T_1 = Hot-water temperature (°C)
T_2 = Cold-water temperature (°C)
h_2 = Enthalpy of air-water vapour mixture at exhaust wet-bulb temperature (same units as above)
h_1 = Enthalpy of air-water vapour mixture at inlet wet-bulb temperature (same units as above)

Wet bulb temperature:

- Wet bulb temperature is an important factor in performance of evaporative water cooling equipment, because it is the lowest temperature to which water can be cooled.
- For this reason, the wet bulb temperature of the air entering the cooling tower determines the minimum operating temperature level throughout the plant, process, or system.
- The following should be considered when pre-selecting a cooling tower based on the wet bulb temperature:
  - Theoretically, a cooling tower will cool water to the entering wet bulb temperature. In practice, however, water is cooled to a temperature higher than the wet bulb temperature because heat needs to be rejected from the cooling tower.
  - A pre-selection of towers based on the design wet bulb temperature must consider conditions at the tower site. The design wet bulb temperature also should not be exceeded for more than 5 per cent of the time. In general, the design temperature selected is close to the average maximum wet bulb temperature in summer.
  - Confirm whether the wet bulb temperature is specified as ambient (the temperature in the cooling tower area) or inlet (the temperature of the air entering the tower, which is often affected by discharge vapours recirculated into the tower). As the

impact of recirculation cannot be known in advance, the ambient wet bulb temperature is preferred.

o Confirm with the supplier if the cooling tower is able to deal with the effects of increased wet bulb temperatures.

o The cold-water temperature must be low enough to exchange heat or to condense vapours at the optimum temperature level. The quantity and temperature of heat exchanged can be considered when choosing the right size cooling tower and heat exchangers at the lowest costs.

4.4.4 Energy Saving Opportunities in Cooling Towers

- Follow manufacturer's recommended clearances around cooling towers and relocate or modify structures that interfere with the air intake or exhaust.
- Optimise cooling tower fan blade angle on a seasonal and/or load basis.
- Correct excessive and/or uneven fan blade tip clearance and poor fan balance.
- On old counter-flow cooling towers, replace old spray type nozzles with new square spray ABS practically non-clogging nozzles.
- Replace splash bars with self-extinguishing PVC cellular film fill.
- Install new nozzles to obtain a more uniform water pattern.
- Periodically clean plugged cooling tower distribution nozzles.
- Balance flow to cooling tower hot water basins.
- Cover hot water basins to minimize algae growth that contributes to fouling.
- Restrict flows through large loads to design values.
- Segregate high heat loads like furnaces, air compressors, DG sets, and isolate cooling towers for sensitive applications like A/C plants, condensers of captive power plant etc. A 1°C cooling water temperature increase may increase A/C compressor kW by 2.7%. A 1°C drop in cooling water temperature can give a heat rate saving of 5 kcal/kWh in a thermal power plant.
- Monitor L/G ratio, CW flow rates w.r.t. design as well as seasonal variations. It would help to increase water load during summer and times when approach is high and increase air flow during monsoon times and when approach is narrow.
- Monitor approach, effectiveness and cooling capacity for continuous optimization efforts, as per seasonal variations as well as load side variations.
- Consider energy efficient FRP blade adoption for fan energy savings.
- Consider possible improvements on CW pumps w.r.t. efficiency improvement.
- Control cooling tower fans based on leaving water temperatures especially in case of small units.
- Optimise process CW flow requirements, to save on pumping energy, cooling load, evaporation losses (directly proportional to circulation rate) and blow down losses.

4.5 FUELS AND COMBUSTION   (S-12)

4.5.1 Petroleum

- Petroleum is a complex mixture of liquid hydrocarbons, chemical compounds containing hydrogen and carbon, occurring naturally in underground reservoirs in sedimentary rock.

- Coming from the Latin petra, meaning rock, and oleum, meaning oil, the word "petroleum" is often interchanged with the word "oil".

- Broadly defined, it includes both primary (unrefined) and secondary (refined) products. Crude oil is the most important oil from which petroleum products are manufactured but several other feedstock oils are also used to make oil products.

- There is a wide range of petroleum products manufactured from crude oil. Many are for specific purposes, for example motor gasoline or lubricants; others are for general heat-raising needs, such as gas oil or fuel oil.

- The names of the petroleum products are those generally used in Western Europe and North America.

- They are commonly used in international trade but are not always identical to those employed in local markets. In addition to these oils, there are others which are "unfinished" oils and will be processed further in refineries or elsewhere.

- Oil supply and use in industrialised economies are complex and involve both energy use and non-energy use.

- Although oil supply continues to grow in absolute terms, its share in global total energy supply has been decreasing, from over 45% in 1973 to around 35% in recent years.

Table 4.2: Calorific value of petroleum products

Product	Density kg/m³	Litres per tonne	Gross calorific value (GJ/t)	Net calorific value (GJ/t)
Ethane	366.3	2730	51.90	47.51
Propane	507.6	1970	50.32	46.33
Butane	572.7	1746	49.51	45.72
LPG	522.2	1915	50.08	46.15
Naphtha	690.6	1448	47.73	45.34
Aviation gasoline	716.8	1395	47.40	45.03
Motor gasoline	740.7	1350	47.10	44.75
Aviation turbine fuel	802.6	1246	46.23	43.92
Other kerosene	802.6	1246	46.23	43.92
Gas/diesel oil	843.9	1185	45.66	43.38
Fuel oil, low-sulphur	925.1	1081	44.40	42.18
Fuel oil, high-sulphur	963.4	1038	43.76	41.57

4.5.2 Natural Gas

- Natural gas comprises several gases, but consists mainly of methane (CH_4). As its name suggests, natural gas is taken from natural underground reserves and is not a chemically unique product.

- When extracted from a gas field or in association with crude oil, it comprises a mixture of gases and liquids. Only after processing does it become one of the marketable gases among the original mixture.

- At this stage natural gas is still a mixture of gases but the methane content predominates (typically greater than 85%).

- Natural gas which is produced in association with oil is called associated gas, whereas production from a gas reservoir not associated with oil is non-associated gas.

- When mining for coal in underground mines, some gas can be released from the coal deposit.

- This gas is called colliery gas or colliery methane. This gas must be removed for safety reasons, and where this is collected and used as a fuel, the amounts involved should be included in marketed production. The terms wet and dry gas are also frequently used.

- When a gas contains an appreciable quantity of butane and heavier hydrocarbons (natural gas liquids – NGL), it is said to be a wet gas.

- Natural gas produced in association with oil – or associated gas – is usually wet gas. Dry gas consists mainly of methane with relatively small amounts of ethane, propane, etc.

- Non-associated gas, i.e. produced from a gas well not associated with oil, is usually dry gas. To facilitate transportation over long distances, natural gas may be converted to liquid form by reducing its temperature to –160°C under atmospheric pressure. When gas is liquefied, it is called liquefied natural gas (LNG).

- The extracted gas is dried and acid components removed before liquefaction. The cooling is achieved by one or several processes in which the gas is recirculated with successive extraction of the liquid component.

- Heavier saleable gases (ethane, propane, etc.) and inert gases are removed during the liquefaction stage.

- As a result, the composition of LNG is usually richer in methane (typically 95%) than marketable natural gas which has not been liquefied. Liquefaction is an energy-intensive process requiring electricity and heat.

- Both forms of energy are usually produced on site from the natural gas received by the liquefaction plant. Gas liquefaction changes only the physical state of natural gas from gas to liquid, it remains primarily methane.

- **Compressed natural gas (CNG)** is used increasingly as a clean fuel for road transport vehicles. Natural gas is compressed to a high pressure (typically 220 atmospheres) and stored in specially designed containers for use in the vehicles.

- The design and inspection of the containers are rigorous as they must withstand not only the high pressure but accident damage and fire. The costs of installation and inspection of CNG containers in smaller road vehicles is rarely economic when compared with conventional fuels.

- However, CNG use is often economic in public transport vehicles. There are plans for the transport of CNG by ship.

- Despite the difficult design problems, the high-pressure storage presents, such transport would permit the exploitation of "stranded" sources of natural gas which are too small to be economically exploited through liquefaction of the gas. Unlike LNG, no storage tanks are necessary.

- Natural gas supply and demand are growing fast. Natural gas now accounts for more than 21% of global total primary energy supply, compared to 16.2% in 1973.

- The calorific value of natural gas is usually expressed in MJ per cubic metre measured at specific temperature and pressure conditions set as a standard by the national gas industry or as specified in the sales contract.

- It is very unusual, in commercial gas trade, to find the calorific value of gaseous natural gas expressed in MJ per kg or gigajoule (GJ) per tonne. However, for reference, the calorific value of pure methane at 25°C is 55.52 GJ/tonne.

- Observed values will therefore be less than this.

LPG:

- LPG is a predominant mixture of Propane and Butane with a small percentage of unsaturates (Propylene and Butylene) and some lighter C_2 as well as heavier C_5 fractions.

- Included in the LPG range are Propane (C_3H_8), Propylene (C_3H_6), normal and iso-butane (C_4H_{10}) and Butylene (C_4H_8). LPG may be defined as those hydrocarbons, which are gaseous at normal atmospheric pressure, but may be condensed to the liquid state at normal temperature, by the application of moderate pressures.

- Although they are normally used as gases, they are stored and transported as liquids under pressure for convenience and ease of handling. Liquid LPG evaporates to produce about 250 times volume of gas.

- LPG vapour is denser than air: butane is about twice as heavy as air and propane about one and a half times as heavy as air. Consequently, the vapour may flow along the ground and into drains sinking to the lowest level of the surroundings and be ignited at a considerable distance from the source of leakage.

- In still air vapour will disperse slowly. Escape of even small quantities of the liquefied gas can give rise to large volumes of vapour / air mixture and thus cause considerable hazard.

- To aid in the detection of atmospheric leaks, all LPGs are required to be odorized. There should be adequate ground level ventilation where LPG is stored.

- For this very reason LPG cylinders should not be stored in cellars or basements, which have no ventilation at ground level.

Table 4.3: Calorific value of coal derived gases

Gas type	GCV (as used) MJ/m³	NCV (as used) MJ/m³	NCV (as used) MJ/kg	Carbon content (as used) kg/t
Coke-oven gas	19.01	16.90	37.54	464
Blast-furnace gas	2.89	2.89	2.24	179

4.5.3 Coal

- Primary coal is a fossil fuel, usually with the physical appearance of a black or brown rock, consisting of carbonised vegetal matter. The higher the carbon content of a coal, the higher its rank or quality.

- Coal types are distinguished by their physical and chemical characteristics. These characteristics determine the coal's price and suitability for various uses.

- All primary coal products covered in this chapter are solid fuels.

- The chapter also includes peat which is another primary fuel closely related to coal.

- There are three main categories of coal: hard coal, sub-bituminous coal and brown coal (also called lignite). Hard coal refers to coal of gross calorific value (GCV) greater than 23,865 kJ/kg, it includes two sub-categories: coking coal (used in blast furnaces), and other bituminous coal and anthracite used for space heating and raising steam (so the name of steam coal for this sub-category).

- Lignite or brown coal refers to non-agglomerating coal with a GCV less than 17,435 kJ/kg. Sub-bituminous coal includes non-agglomerating coal with a GCV comprised between those of the other two categories.

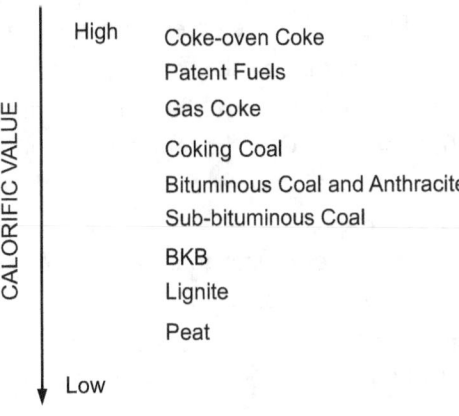

Table 4.4: Calorific value of coal

Hard coals	GCV (as used) MJ/kg	NCV (as used) MJ/kg	Carbon content (as used) kg/t	Moisture content (as used) %	Carbon content (dmmf) * kg/t
Anthracite	29.65 – 30.35	28.95 – 30.35	778 – 782	10 – 12	920 – 980
Coking coals	27.80 – 30.80	26.60 – 29.80	674 – 771	7 – 9	845 – 920
Other bituminous	23.85 – 26.75	22.60 – 25.50	590 – 657	13 – 18	810 - 845

*dmmf – dry mineral matter free.

- Liquefaction of coal covers the production of oils from coal, oil shale and tar sands. The process takes place above ground, so the operators of the plant should know the quantities entering the process.

- Ensure that in-situ (underground) coal liquefaction and in-situ extraction of oil from tar sands are excluded.

- The oil produced from in-situ processes is reported as indigenous production.

Characteristics of Coal:

- Coal is mainly composed of carbon. Coal also generates volatile matter when heated to decomposition temperatures.

- In addition, coal contains moisture and ash-forming mineral matter.

- Carbon, hydrogen, nitrogen, sulphur and oxygen are present in the coal matter. The combination of these elements and the shares of volatile matter, ash and water vary considerably from coal to coal.

- It is the fixed carbon content and associated volatile matter of coal that control its energy value and coking properties and make it a valuable mineral on world markets.

- Fixed carbon content generally influences the energy content of the coal. The higher the fixed carbon content, the higher the energy content of the coal.

High-temperature Coke:

- Coke is manufactured through coal pyrolysis. Coal pyrolysis means the heating of coal in an oxygen-free atmosphere to produce gases, liquids and a solid residue (char or coke).

- Coal pyrolysis at high temperature is called carbonization.

- During carbonization, several important changes take place. Moisture is released from the coal between 100°C and 150°C. In the temperature range of 400°C to 500°C, much of the volatile matter is released as gas. From 600°C to 1300°C, very little additional loss of volatile content occurs and weight loss is small.

- As the coal is heated it becomes plastic and porous during the release of gases. When it solidifies it has many fissures and pores.

- In the process, the temperature of the gases reaches 1,150°C to 1,350°C, indirectly heating the coal up to 1,000°C to 1,200°C for 14 to 24 hours.

- This produces blast-furnace and foundry cokes.

- Only certain coals with the right plastic properties (for example, bituminous coking or semi-soft coals) can be converted to coke.

- Several types of coal may be blended to improve blast furnace productivity, to extend coke battery life, etc. The coke is made in ovens comprising a battery of individual chambers upto 60 in number.

- The individual coke-oven chambers are separated by heating walls.

- These consist of a certain number of heating flues with nozzles for fuel supply, and one or more air inlet boxes, depending on the height of the coke-oven wall.

- The average nozzle-brick temperature, characterising heating flue operation, is usually set between 1150°C and 1350°C.

- Usually, cleaned coke-oven gas is used as a fuel, but other gases such as blast furnace gas enriched with natural gas, or straight natural gas can be used as well.

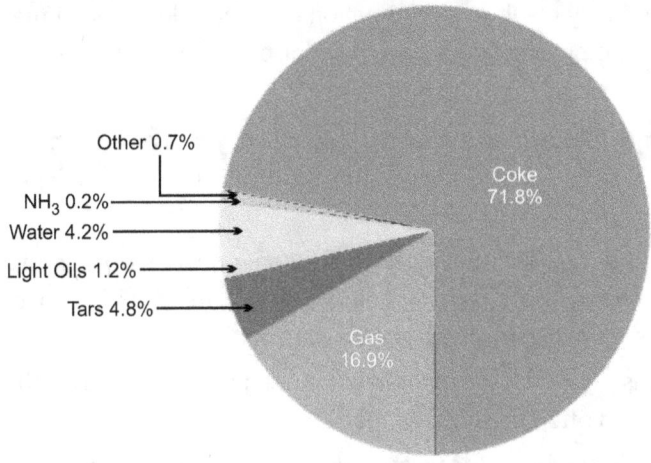

Fig. 4.9

4.5.4 Biofuels (W-13)

- Biofuels are derived from bio materials available in the nature. It may be gas, liquid or solid. e.g. Wood, agro residue, biodiesel, biogas.

- As fossil fuels are depleting world i.e. exploring new types of fuels which can be made indigenously.

- Biofuels cover bioethanol, biodiesel, biomethanol, biodimethyl ether, biooil. Liquid biofuels are mainly biodiesel and bioethanol/ETBE used as transport fuels.

- They can be made from new or used vegetable oils and may be blended with or replace petroleum-based fuels.

- The natural plant feedstock includes soya, sunflower and oil seed rape oils. Under some circumstances, used vegetable oils may also be used as feedstock for the process.

Properties of Fuel:

Viscosity:

- Viscosity is a measure of the **resistance** of a **fluid** which is being deformed by either **shear stress** or **extensional stress**. It is commonly perceived as "thickness", or resistance to flow.

- Viscosity describes a fluid's internal resistance to flow and may be thought of as a measure of fluid **friction**.

- Viscosity is the most important characteristic in the storage and use of fuel oil. It influences the degree of pre-heat required for handling, storage and satisfactory atomization.

- If the oil is too viscous, it may become difficult to pump, hard to light the burner, and tough to operate.

- Poor atomization may result in the formation of carbon deposits on the burner tips or on the walls. Therefore pre-heating is necessary for proper atomization.

Specific Gravity:

- **Specific gravity** is defined as the ratio of the **density** of a given substance to the density of **water**, when both are at the same temperature, it is therefore a dimensionless quantity (see below).

- Substances with a specific gravity greater than one are denser than water, and so (ignoring **surface tension** effects) will sink in it, and those with a specific gravity of less than one are less dense than water, and so will float in it.

- Specific gravity is a special case of, or in some usages synonymous with, **relative density**, with the latter term often preferred in modern scientific writing.

- The use of specific gravity is discouraged in technical use in scientific fields requiring high precision - actual density (in dimensions of mass per unit volume) is preferred.

  Specific gravity, SG, is expressed mathematically as:

$$SG = \frac{\rho_{substance}}{\rho_{H_2O}}$$

  where $\rho_{substance}$ is the density of the substance, and ρ_{H_2O} is the density of water.

- The **American Petroleum Institute** gravity, or **API gravity**, is a measure of how heavy or light a petroleum liquid is compared to water.

- If its API gravity is greater than 10, it is lighter and floats on water; if less than 10, it is heavier and sinks.

- API gravity is thus a measure of the relative density of a petroleum liquid and the density of water, but it is used to compare the relative densities of petroleum liquids.

- For example, if one petroleum liquid floats on another and is therefore less dense, it has a greater API gravity. Although mathematically API gravity has no units (see the formula below), it is nevertheless referred to as being in "degrees".

- API gravity is graduated in degrees on a *hydrometer instrument* and was designed so that most values would fall between 10 and 70 API gravity degrees.

Table 4.5: Specific gravity of various fuel oils

Fuel oil	L.D.O. Light Diesel Oil	Furnace oil	L.S.H.S. Low Sulphur Heavy Stock
Specific gravity	0.85 – 0.87	0.89 – 0.95	0.88 – 0.98

Calorific value:

- The **heating value** or **calorific value** of a *substance*, usually a *fuel* or *food*, is the amount of *heat* released during the combustion of a specified amount of it. The calorific value is a characteristic for each substance.

- It is measured in units of *energy* per unit of the substance, usually *mass*, such as kcal/kg, kJ/kg, J/mol, Btu/m³. Heating value is commonly determined by use of a bomb calorimeter.

Fuel Oil   Gross Calorific Value (kcal/kg)

Kerosene	–	11,100
Diesel oil	–	10,800
L.D.O.	–	10,700
Furnace Oil	–	10,500
LSHS	–	10,600

Flash Point and Fire Point:

- The **flash point** of a flammable liquid is the lowest *temperature* at which it can form an ignitable mixture in air. At this temperature the vapour may cease to burn when the source of ignition is removed.

- At slightly higher temperature, the *fire point* is defined as the temperature at which the vapour continues to burn after being ignited.

- Neither of these parameters are related to the temperatures of the ignition source or of the burning liquid, which are much higher.

- The flash point is often used as one descriptive characteristic of liquid *fuel*, but it is also used to describe liquids that are not used intentionally as fuels.

Table 4.6: Flash points of some fuels

Fuel	Flash point	Auto ignition temperature
Gasoline (petrol)	<−40°C (−40°F)	246°C (475°F)
Diesel	>62°C (143°F)	210°C (410°F)
Jet fuel	>38°C (100°F)	210°C (410°F)
Kerosene (paraffin oil)	>38–72°C (100–162°F)	220°C (428°F)
Vegetable oil (Canola)	327°C (620°F)	
Biodiesel	>130°C (266°F)	

Ash Content:
- The ash value is related to the inorganic material in the fuel oil. The ash levels of distillate fuels are negligible.
- Residual fuels have more of the ash-forming constituents.
- These salts may be compounds of sodium, vanadium, calcium, magnesium, silicon, iron, aluminium, nickel, etc.
- Typically, the ash value is in the range 0.03-0.07%. Excessive ash in liquid fuels can cause fouling deposits in the combustion equipment.
- Ash has erosive effect on the burner tips, causes damage to the refractories at high temperatures and gives rise to high temperature corrosion and fouling of equipments.

Water Content:
- Water content of furnace oil when supplied is normally very low as the product at refinery site is handled hot and maximum limit of 1% is specified in the standard.
- Water may be present in free or emulsified form and can cause damage to the inside furnace surfaces during combustion especially if it contains dissolved salts.
- It can also cause spluttering of the flame at the burner tip, possibly extinguishing the flame and reducing the flame temperature or lengthening the flame.

Table 4.7: Typical Specification of Fuel Oils

Properties	Fuel Oils		
	Furnace oil	L.S.H.S.	L.D.O.
Density (Approx. g/cc at 15°C)	0.89 – 0.95	0.88 – 0.98	0.85-0.87
Flash point (°C)	66	93	66
Pour point (°C)	20	72	18
G.C.V. (kcal/kg)	10,500	10,600	10,700
Sediment, % Wt. Max.	0.25	0.25	0.1
Sulphur Total, % Wt. Max.	Upto 4.0	Upto 0.5	Upto 1.8
Water Conent, % Vol. Max.	1.0	1.0	0.25
Ash % Wt. Max.	0.1	0.1	0.02

4.5.5 Combustion

- **Combustion** or **burning** is a complex sequence of *exothermic* chemical reactions between a *fuel* and an *oxidant* accompanied by the production of *heat* or both *heat* and *light* in the form of either a glow or *flames*.

- Combustion takes place when fuel, most commonly a fossil fuel, reacts with the oxygen in air to produce heat.

- The heat created by the burning of a fossil fuel is used in the operation of equipment such as boilers, furnaces, kilns, and engines.

- Along with heat, CO_2 (carbon dioxide) and H_2O (water) are created as byproducts of the exothermic reaction.

$$CH_4 + 2O_2 \rightarrow CO_2 + 2H_2O + \text{Heat}$$
$$C + O_2 \rightarrow CO_2 + \text{Heat}$$
$$2H_2 + O_2 \rightarrow 2H_2O + \text{Heat}$$

- By monitoring and regulating some of the gases in the stack or exhaust, it is easy to improve combustion efficiency, which conserves fuel and lowers expenses.

- Combustion efficiency is the calculation of how effectively the combustion process runs. To achieve the highest levels of combustion efficiency, complete combustion should take place.

- Complete combustion occurs when all of the energy in the fuel being burned is extracted and none of the Carbon and Hydrogen compounds are left unburned.

- Complete combustion will occur when the proper amounts of fuel and air (fuel/air ratio) are mixed for the correct amount of time under the appropriate conditions of turbulence and temperature.

- Although theoretically stoichiometric combustion provides the perfect fuel to air ratio, which thus lowers losses and extracts all of the energy from the fuel; in reality, stoichiometric combustion is unattainable due to many varying factors.

- Heat losses are inevitable thus making 100% efficiency impossible. In practice, in order to achieve complete combustion, it is necessary to increase the amounts of air to the combustion process to ensure the burning of all of the fuel.

- The amount of air that must be added to make certain all energy retrieved is known as excess air.

- In most combustion processes, some additional chemicals are formed during the combustion reactions. Some of the products created such as CO (carbon monoxide), NO (nitric oxide), NO_2 (nitrogen dioxide), SO_2 (sulfur dioxide), soot, and ash should be minimized and accurately measured.

- The EPA has set specific standards and regulations for emissions of some of these products, as they are harmful to the environment. Combustion analysis is a vital step to properly operate and control any combustion process in order to obtain the highest combustion efficiency with the lowest emissions of pollutants.

Objectives of Combustion:

- The objective of combustion is to retrieve energy from the burning of fuels in the most efficient way possible.

- To maximize combustion efficiency, it is necessary to burn all fuel material with the least amount of losses.

- The more efficiently fuels are burned and energy is gathered, the cheaper the combustion process becomes.

Complete Combustion:

- Complete combustion occurs when 100% of the energy in the fuel is extracted. It is important to strive for complete combustion to preserve fuel and improve the cost efficiency of the combustion process.

- There must be enough air in the combustion chamber for complete combustion to occur.

- The addition of excess air greatly lowers the formation of CO (carbon monoxide) by allowing CO to react with O_2.

- The less CO remaining in the flue gas, the closer to complete combustion the reaction becomes.

- This is because the toxic gas carbon monoxide (CO) still contains a very significant amount of energy that should be completely burned.

Stoichiometric Combustion:

- Stoichiometric combustion is the theoretical point at which the fuel to air ratio is ideal so that there is complete combustion with perfect efficiency.

- Although stoichiometric combustion is not possible, it is striven for in all combustion processes to maximize profits.

Three T's of Combustion:

- Combustion efficiency can be further explained in terms of the three T's; Time, Temperature and Turbulence.

- Simply stated, thermal oxidation is the effective employment of a process which provides thorough mixing of an organic substance with sufficient oxygen at a high enough temperature for a sufficient time to cause the organics to oxidize to the desired degree of completion.

- To achieve successful thermal oxidation, the thermal oxidizer design must include what is known as "The Three T's of Combustion". These are;

    (a) Turbulence - Thorough mixing

    (b) Temperature - Oxidizing temperature (typically 1200°F – 1650°F)

    (c) Time - Combustion chamber residence time (typically 0.5 seconds - 2.0 seconds)

- The "Three T's of Combustion" along with sufficient oxygen are essential and interrelated in all thermal oxidizer designs. The level of turbulence (mixing), the necessary reaction temperature, and the amount of time (residence time) is primarily dependent on the fuel characteristics.

4.6 ENERGY EFFICIENT TECHNOLOGY

4.6.1 Maximum Demand Controller   (S-12)

What is Maximum Demand ?

- Maximum Demand is the power consumed over a predetermined period of time, which is usually between 8 – 30 minutes.

- The most common period of time, in the majority of countries, is 15 minutes.

- This power is calculated and billed by a kW demand meter, which records the highest kW value in one 15 minutes period, over a month's time.

- There are three terms that appear on the majority of electric company bills:
  - Active energy consumption (kWh)
  - Reactive energy consumption (kVArh)
  - Maximum Demand

- Traditionally, utility companies have concentrated their energy saving efforts on two items:
  - Reduction of Kilowatt Hour consumption
  - Improving the electrical system's Power Factor

- There is a third item to consider when reducing the amount of the electric company bill, proper kW Demand management which allows:
  - The reduction of the contracted power
  - Adjusting to the new kW limit
  - Avoiding kW Demand limit penalties

How to control maximum demand ?

- The purpose of controlling the demand is, not to exceed the contracted maximum demand limit.

- One way to do this is to shed non-critical loads. Possible loads to be disconnected are:
  - Lights
  - Compressors
  - Air conditioners
  - Pumps
  - Fans and extractors
  - Packaging machinery
  - Shredders
  - Others.

- Generally, all those machines which do not affect the main production process or which are not essential.

- In addition to controlling kW demand, the following equipment is suitable for processes which have large variations in kW demand and low loading factors, such as companies in the smelting, mining, automobile, textile, paper industries, etc.

- Maximum Demand Controller is a device designed to meet the need of industries conscious of the value of load management. Alarm is sounded when demand approaches a preset value.

- If corrective action is not taken, the controller switches off non-essential loads in a logical sequence. This sequence is predetermined by the user and is programmed jointly by the user and the supplier of the device.

- The plant equipments selected for the load management are stopped and restarted as per the desired load profile.

- Demand control scheme is implemented by using suitable control contactors. Audio and visual annunciations could also be used.

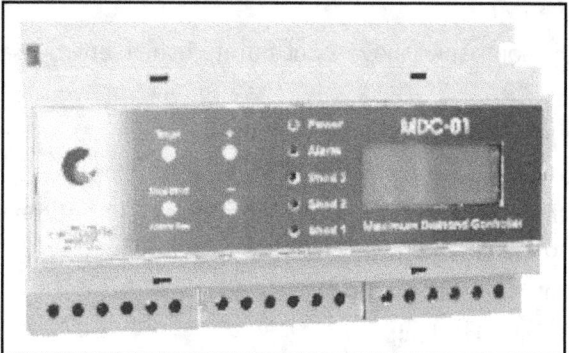

Fig. 4.10

Automatic Power Factor Controller:

- Power factor is the ratio between the useful (true) power (kW) to the total (apparent) power (kVA) consumed by an item of AC electrical equipment or a complete electrical installation.

- It is a measure of how efficiently electrical power is converted into useful work output.

- The ideal power factor is unity, or one. Anything less than one means that extra power is required to achieve the actual task at hand.

- All current flow causes losses both in the supply and distribution system. A load with a power factor of 1.0 results in the most efficient loading of the supply.

- A load with a power factor of, say, 0.8, results in much higher losses in the supply system and a higher bill for the consumer.

- A comparatively small improvement in power factor can bring about a significant reduction in losses since losses are proportional to the square of the current. Reactive power can also be interpreted as wattless, magnetising or wasted power and it represents an extra burden on the electricity supply system and on the consumer's bill.

- A poor power factor is usually the result of a significant phase difference between the voltage and current at the load terminals, or it can be due to a high harmonic content or a distorted current waveform.

- A poor power factor is generally the result of an inductive load such as an induction motor, a power transformer, a ballast in a luminaire, a welding set or an induction furnace.

- A distorted current waveform can be the result of a rectifier, an inverter, a variable speed drive, a switched mode power supply, discharge lighting or other electronic loads.

- A poor power factor due to inductive loads can be improved by the addition of power factor correction equipment, but a poor power factor due to a distorted current waveform requires a change in equipment design or the addition of harmonic filters.

- Power factor correction is the process of compensating for the lagging current by creating a leading current by connecting capacitors to the supply.

- A sufficient capacitance is connected so that the power factor is adjusted to be as close to unity as possible.

- Consider a single-phase induction motor. If the motor presented a purely resistive load to the supply, the current flowing would be in-phase with the voltage. This is not the case. The motor has a magnet and the magnetizing current is not in phase with the voltage.

- Consider a motor with a current draw of 10 A and a power factor of 0.75. The useful current is 7.5 A. The useful power from the motor is 230 × 7.5 = 1.725 kW but the total power that has to be supplied is 230 × 10 = 2.3 kVA.

- Without power factor correction, to achieve the required output of 1.725 kW (7.5 A) a power of 2.3 kVA (10 A) has to be supplied. A current of 10 A is flowing but only 7.5 A of that current is producing useful output.

Power factor correction:

- Power factor correction is the term given to a technology that has been used since the turn of the 20th century to restore the power factor to as close to unity as is economically viable.

- This is normally achieved by the addition of capacitors to the electrical network which compensate for the reactive power demand of the inductive load and thus reduce the burden on the supply.

- There should be no effect on the operation of the equipment.

- To reduce losses in the distribution system, and to reduce the electricity bill, power factor correction, usually in the form of capacitors, is added to neutralize as much of the magnetizing current as possible.

- Capacitors contained in most power factor correction equipment draw current that leads the voltage, thus producing a leading power factor.

- If capacitors are connected to a circuit that operates at a nominally lagging power factor, the extent that the circuit lags is reduced proportionately.

- Typically, the corrected power factor will be 0.92 to 0.95. Some power distributors offer incentives for operating with a power factor of better than 0.9, for example, and some penalize consumers with a poor power factor.
- There are many ways that this is metered but the net result is that in order to reduce wasted energy in the distribution system, the consumer is encouraged to apply power factor correction. Most Network Operating companies now penalize for power factors below 0.95 or 0.9.

Why improve power factor ?

- The benefits that can be achieved by applying the correct power factor correction are:
  - Environmental benefit. Reduction of power consumption due to improved energy efficiency. Reduced power consumption means less greenhouse gas emissions and fossil fuel depletion by power stations.
  - Reduction of electricity bills.
  - Extra kVA available from the existing supply.
  - Reduction of I2R losses in transformers and distribution equipment.
  - Reduction of voltage drop in long cables.
  - Extended equipment life – Reduced electrical burden on cables and electrical components.

How to improve power factor ?

- Power factor correction is achieved by the addition of capacitors in parallel with the connected motor or lighting circuits and can be applied at the equipment, distribution board or at the origin of the installation.
- Static power factor correction can be applied at each individual motor by connecting the correction capacitors to the motor starter.
- A disadvantage can occur when the load on the motor changes and can result in under or over correction. Static power factor correction must not be applied at the output of a variable speed drive, solid state soft starter or inverter as the capacitors can cause serious damage to the electronic components.
- Over-correction should not occur if the power factor correction is correctly sized. Typically, the power factor correction for an individual motor is based on the non-load (magnetizing) power since the reactive load of a motor is comparatively constant compared to actual kW load over compensation should be avoided.
- Care should be taken when applying power factor correction star/delta type control so that the capacitors are not subjected to rapid on-off-on conditions.
- Typically, the correction would be placed on either the Main or Delta contactor circuits. Power factor correction applied at the origin of the installation consists of a controller monitoring the VAr's and this controller switches capacitors in or out to maintain the power factor better than a preset limit (typically 0.95).

- Where 'bulk' power factor correction is installed, other loads can in theory be connected anywhere on the network.

Fig. 4.11

4.6.2 Energy Efficient Lighting and Control

Occupancy Sensors: (S-12; W-13)

- Occupancy linked control can be achieved using infra-red, acoustic, ultrasonic or microwave sensors, which detect either movement or noise in room spaces.
- These sensors switch lighting on when occupancy is detected, and off again after a set time period, when no occupancy movement detected.
- They are designed to override manual switches and to prevent a situation where lighting is left on in unoccupied spaces.
- With this type of system it is important to incorporate a built-in time delay, since occupants often remain still or quiet for short periods and do not appreciate being plunged into darkness if not constantly moving around.

Daylight Linked Control:

- Photoelectric cells can be used either simply to switch lighting on and off, or for dimming. They may be mounted either externally or internally. It is however important to incorporate time delays into the control system to avoid repeated rapid switching caused, for example, by fast moving clouds.
- By using an internally mounted photoelectric dimming control system, it is possible to ensure that the sum of daylight and electric lighting always reaches the design level by

sensing the total light in the controlled area and adjusting the output of the electric lighting accordingly.

- If daylight alone is able to meet the design requirements, then the electric lighting can be turned off. The energy saving potential of dimming control is greater than a simple photoelectric switching system. Dimming control is also more likely to be acceptable to room occupants.

Compact Fluorescent Lamp (CFL):

- Compact fluorescent lamps (CFLs) combine the energy efficiency of fluorescent lighting with the convenience and popularity of incandescent fixtures.
- CFLs work much like standard fluorescent lamps. They consist of two parts: a gas-filled tube, and a magnetic or electronic ballast.
- The gas in the tube glows with ultraviolet light when electricity from the ballast flows through it.
- This in turn excites a white phosphor coating on the inside of the tube, which emits visible light throughout the surface of the tube.
- Compact fluorescent lamps (CFLs) come in a variety of sizes and shapes including (a) twin-tube integral, (b and c) triple-tube integral, (d) integral model with casing that reduces glare, (e) modular circline and ballast, and (f) modular quad-tube and ballast.
- CFLs can be installed in regular incandescent fixtures, and they consume less than one-third as much electricity as incandescent lamps do.

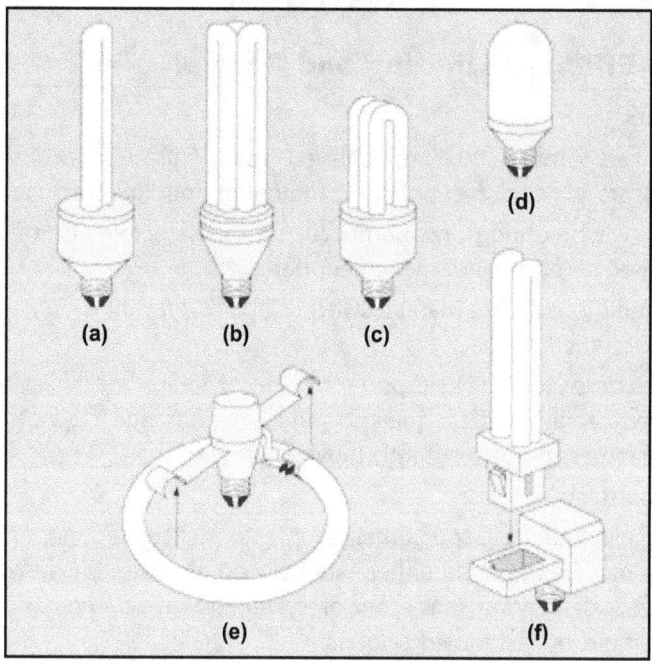

Fig. 4.12: Compact Fluorescent Lamps

Efficient: CFLs are four times more efficient and last upto 10 times longer than incandescents. A 22 watt CFL has about the same light output as a 100 watt incandescent. CFLs use 50 - 80% less energy than incandescents.

Less Expensive: Although initially more expensive, you save money in the long run because CFLs use 1/3 the electricity and last upto 10 times as long as incandescents. A single 18 watt CFL used in place of a 75 watt incandescent will save about 570 kWh over its lifetime. At 8 cents per kWh, that equates to a $45 savings.

Reduces Air and Water Pollution: Replacing a single incandescent bulb with a CFL will keep a half-ton of CO_2 out of the atmosphere over the life of the bulb. If everyone in the U.S. used energy-efficient lighting, we could retire 90 average size power plants. Saving electricity reduces CO_2 emissions, sulfur oxide and high-level nuclear waste.

High-Quality Light: Newer CFLs give a warm, inviting light instead of the "cool white" light of older fluorescents. They use rare earth phosphors for excellent colour and warmth. New electronically ballasted CFLs don't flicker or hum.

Versatile: CFLs can be applied nearly anywhere that incandescent lights are used. Energy-efficient CFLs can be used in recessed fixtures, table lamps, track lighting, ceiling fixtures and porchlights. 3-way CFLs are also now available for lamps with 3-way settings. Dimmable CFLs are also available for lights using a dimmer switch.

LED Lighting:

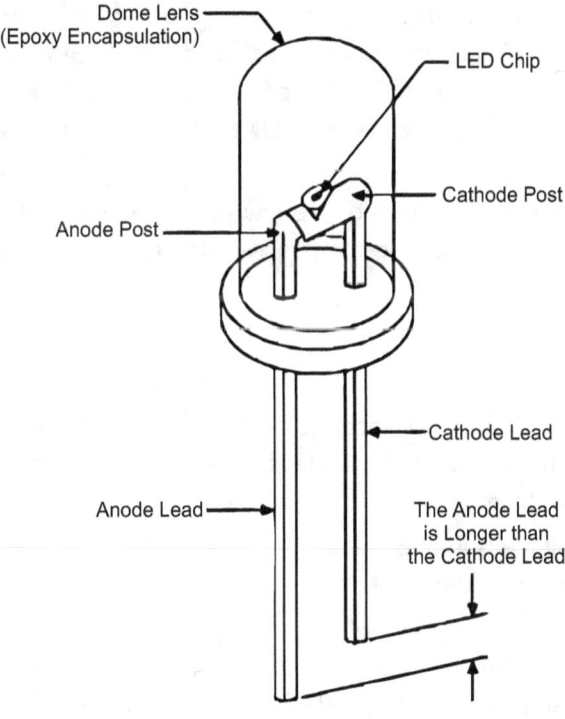

Fig. 4.13

- LEDs (Light Emitting Diodes) are small, solid light bulbs which are extremely energy-efficient. Until recently, LEDs were limited to single-bulb use in applications such as instrument panels, electronics, pen lights and, more recently, strings of indoor and outdoor lights.
- Recent improvements in manufacture have lowered the cost of LEDs, which has expanded their application.
- The bulbs are now available in clusters, from 2 to 36 bulbs, and are popular especially for battery powered items such as flashlights and headlamps.
- LEDs are also available in arrays which fit standard AC and DC receptacles, lamps, recessed and track lights.

LED:

Long-lasting: LED bulbs last 10 times as long as compact fluorescents, and 133 times longer than typical incandescents.

Durable: Since LEDs do not have a filament, they are not damaged under circumstances when a regular incandescent bulb would be broken. Because they are solid, LED bulbs hold up well to jarring and bumping.

Cool: These bulbs do not cause heat build-up; LEDs produce 3.4 btus/hour, compared to 85 for incandescent bulbs.

Energy-saving: LEDs use a fraction of the wattage of incandescent bulbs. Batteries will last 10 to 15 times longer than with incandescent bulbs. Also, because these bulbs last for years, energy is saved in maintenance and replacement costs. Many cities in the US are replacing their incandescent traffic lights with LED arrays because the electricity costs can be reduced by 80% or more.

Light for remote areas - because of the low power requirement for LEDs, using solar panels becomes more practical and less expensive than running an electric line or using a generator for lighting.

Electronic Ballast:

Role of Ballast:

- In an electric circuit the ballast acts as a stabilizer. Fluorescent lamp is an electric discharge lamp. The two electrodes are separated inside a tube with no apparent connection between them.
- When sufficient voltage is impressed on these electrodes, electrons are driven from one electrode and attracted to the other.
- The current flow takes place through an atmosphere of low pressure mercury vapour. Since the fluorescent lamps cannot produce light by direct connection to the power source, they need an ancillary circuit and device to get started and remain illuminated.
- The auxillary circuit housed in a casing is known as ballast.

Conventional versus Electronic Ballasts:

- The conventional ballasts make use of the kick caused by sudden physical disruption of current in an inductive circuit to produce the high voltage required for starting the lamp and then rely on reactive voltage drop in the ballast to reduce the voltage applied across the lamp.

- On account of the mechanical switch (starter) and low resistance of filament when cold the uncontrolled filament current, generally tend to go beyond the limits specified by Indian standard specifications.

- With high values of current and flux densities, the operational losses and temperature rise are on the higher side in conventional choke.

- The high frequency electronic ballast overcomes the above drawbacks.

- The basic functions of electronic ballast are:

  1.   To ignite the lamp.

  2.   To stabilize the gas discharge.

  3.   To supply the power to the lamp.

- The electronic ballasts (see Fig. 4.14) make use of modern power semi-conductor devices for their operation.

- The circuit components form a tuned circuit to deliver power to the lamp at a high resonant frequency (in the vicinity of 25 kHz) and voltage is regulated through an inbuilt feedback mechanism.

- It is now well established that the fluorescent lamp efficiency in the kHz range is higher than those attainable at low frequencies.

- At lower frequencies (50 or 60 Hz) the electron density in the lamp is proportional to the instantaneous value of the current because the ionisation state in the tube is able to follow the instantaneous variations in the current.

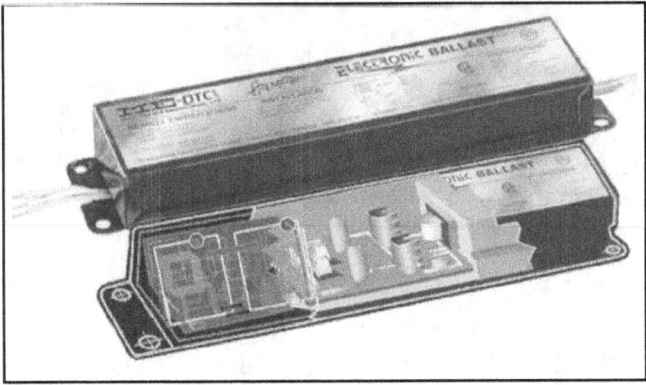

Fig. 4.14: Electronic Ballast

- At higher frequencies (kHz range), the ionisation state cannot follow the instantaneous variations of the current and hence the ionisation density is approximately a constant, proportional to the RMS (Root Mean Square) value of the current.

- Another significant benefit resulting from this phenomenon is the absence of stroboscopic effect, thereby significantly improving the quality of light output.

- One of largest advantages of an electronic ballast is the enormous energy savings it provides. This is achieved in two ways.

- The first is its amazingly low internal core loss, quite unlike old fashioned magnetic ballasts.

- And second is increased light output due to the excitation of the lamp phosphors with high frequency. If the period of frequency of excitation is smaller than the light retention time constant for the gas in the lamp, the gas will stay ionized and, therefore, produce light continuously.

- This phenomenon along with continued persistence of the phosphors at high frequency will improve light output from 8–12 per cent. This is possible only with high frequency electronic ballast.

Energy Efficient Motors: (W-13)

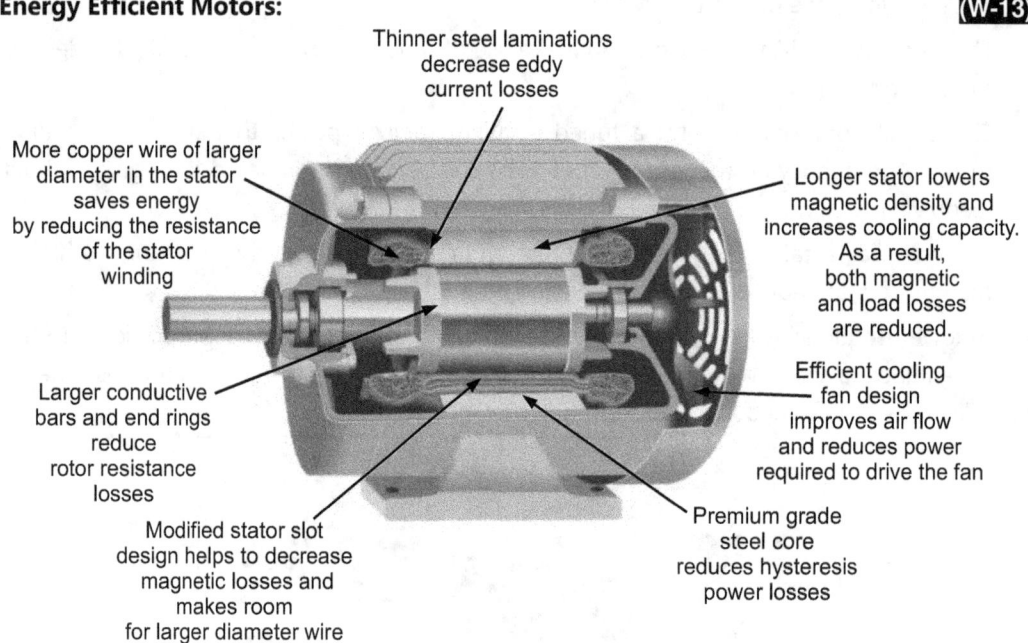

Fig. 4.15

- Electric motors are industry's basic need. Electric motors consume around 70% of the total electricity used in the industrial sector.

- As motors are the largest users of electrical energy, even small efficiency improvements can produce very large savings across the country.

- Energy conservation measure taken by individual consumers in this direction can improve the national economy and benefit the environment on global scale.
- An energy efficient motor produces the same shaft output power but draws less input power than a standard motor. Hence EE motor consumes less electricity than comparable standard motor.
- Energy efficient motors are manufactured using the same frame as a standard T-frame motor, but these have:
  - Low loss special grade of thinner laminations. This reduces the iron loss even at partial loads.
  - Thicker conductors and more copper contents reduce copper loss due to lower resistance.
  - Longer core length, reduced and uniform air gap between stator and rotor to reduce stray losses.
  - Special design of fan and fan cover to reduce windage losses.

Benefits:

- Improved efficiency is available from 60% to 100% load. The efficiency curve is almost flat resulting in higher energy savings as in most of the cases the motor is not always fully loaded.
- The special design features also result in lower operating temperatures, which enhance the life of motor and reduce the maintenance costs.
- These motors have inherently low noise and vibration and help in conservation of environment.
- These motors are with highest power factor in the industry due the special exclusive designs available.
- The higher power factor reduces the currents in the cables supplying power to motor and this reduces cable loss, improving the system efficiency sometimes by even 2%. Sometimes this allows even a lower cable size saving tremendously on capital costs. Reducing capacitors required improving power factor also makes saving.

Payback Time:

Following example shows simple payback period for Energy Efficient (EE) motor.

Efficiency of Standard motor	: 89.0%
Efficiency of EE motor	: 91.0%
Motor Power	: 11 kW
Number of hours of operation per year	: 5000
Energy saved per annum @ ₹ 4/kWh	: ₹ 5432.77
Additional cost of EE motor	: ₹ 2700.00
Payback period	: 6 months

Variable Speed Drives:

Speed Control of Induction Motors:

- Induction motor is the workhorse of the industry. It is cheap rugged and provides high power to weight ratio.

- On account of high cost-implications and limitations of D.C.

- System, induction motors are preferred for variable speed application, the speed of which can be varied by changing the supply frequency.

- The speed can also be varied through a number of other means, including, varying the input voltage, varying the resistance of the rotor circuit, using multi speed windings, using Scherbius or Kramer drives, using mechanical means such as gears and pulleys and eddy-current or fluid coupling, or by using rotary or static voltage and frequency converters.

Variable Frequency Drive:

- The VFD operates on a simple principle. The rotational speed of an AC induction motor depends on the number of poles in that stator and the frequency of the applied AC power.

- Although the number of poles in an induction motor cannot be altered easily, variable speed can be achieved through a variation in frequency. The VFD rectifies standard 50 cycle AC line power to DC, then synthesizes the DC to a variable frequency AC output.

- Motors connected to VFD provide variable speed mechanical output with high efficiency.

- These devices are capable of up to a 9: 1 speed reduction ratio (11 per cent of full speed), and a 3: 1 speed increase (300 per cent of full speed). In recent years, the technology of AC variable frequency drives (VFD) has evolved into highly sophisticated digital microprocessor control, along with high switching frequency IGBTs (Insulated Gate Bi Polar Transistors) power devices.

- This has led to significantly advanced capabilities from the ease of programmability to expanded diagnostics.

- The two most significant benefits from the evolution in technology have been that of cost and reliability, in addition to the significant reduction in physical size.

Variable Torque Versus Constant Torque:

- Variable speed drives, and the loads that are applied to, can generally be divided into two groups: constant torque and variable torque. The energy savings potential of variable torque applications is much greater than that of constant torque applications.

- Constant torque loads include vibrating conveyors, punch presses, rock crushers, machine tools, and other applications where the drive follows a constant V/Hz ratio.

- Variable torque loads include centrifugal pumps and fans, which make up the majority of HV AC applications.

Why Variable Torque Loads Offer Greatest Energy Savings:

- In variable torque applications, the torque required varies with the square of the speed, and the horsepower required varies with the cube of the speed, resulting in a large reduction of horsepower for even a small reduction in speed.

- The motor will consume only 25% as much energy at 50% speed than it will at 100% speed.

- This is referred to as the **Affinity Laws**, which define the relationships between speed, flow, torque, and horsepower. The following laws illustrate these relationships:
  - Flow is proportional to speed
  - Head is proportional to $(speed)^2$
  - Torque is proportional to $(speed)^2$
  - Power is proportional to $(speed)^3$

Extended Equipment Life and Reduced Maintenance:

- Single-speed starting methods start motors abruptly, subjecting the motor to a high starting torque and to current surges that are upto 10 times the full-load current.

- Variable speed drives, on the other hand, gradually ramp the motor upto operating speed to lessen mechanical and electrical stress, reducing maintenance and repair costs, and extending the life of the motor and the driven equipment.

4.6.3 Standards and Labeling

- Government of India established Bureau of Energy Efficiency (BEE) in 2002 under the energy conservation act 2001 for promoting efficient use of energy and its conservation. BEE stared labeling system that rates electrical appliances on the basis of energy efficiency.

- BEE label follows star rating system which goes from 1 star (least energy efficient system) to 5 star (most energy efficient system).

- Energy labeling program is being introduced for the first time in the Indian market.

- The program is being initially launched on voluntary basis for two appliances, namely, Frost Free Refrigerators and Tubular Fluorescent lamps. Subsequently, more appliances would be included in a phased manner and the scheme will be made mandatory.

- With the BEE labeled products coming in the market, consumers will have the choice of making informed purchases based on energy efficiency or energy consumption of the products.

- They will benefit through lower operating cost of the higher efficiency products.

- The star rating and labeling scheme will substantially expand the market for energy efficient appliances.

- Retailers will benefit from increased sales of energy efficient appliances.

- Energy Labeled products are expected to be available in market (starting with Frost Free Refrigerators and Fluorescent Tube Lamps) starting July 2006.

- BEE's Labeling program marks a significant step towards ensuring efficient use of scarce energy resources.
- It would result in substantial energy savings for the consumers and the nation. As more and more products come under the scope of the labeling program, the impact will be even greater.
- Direct cool refrigerators, General purpose Electric Motors, Air-conditioners and Ceiling fans will be included in the program by 2007.

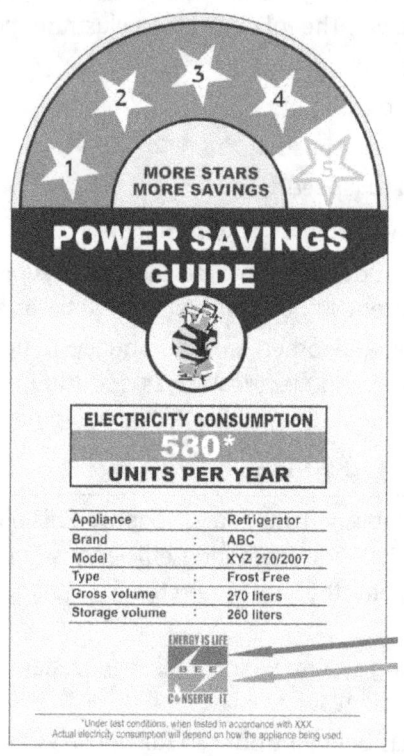

Fig. 4.16: Sample BEE label for refrigerator

Star rating for air conditioner:

Star Rating	EER (W/W)	
	Minimum	**Maximum**
1 Star *	2.70	2.89
2 Star **	2.90	3.09
3 Star ***	3.10	3.29
4 Star ****	3.30	3.49
5 Star *****	3.50	3.49

Star rating for transformer:

Rating	1 star		2 star		3 star		4 star		5 star	
kVA	Max Losses at 50% (watts)	Max Losses at 100% (watts)	Max Losses at 50% (watts)	Max Losses at 100% (watts)	Max Losses at 50% (watts)	Max Losses at 100% (watts)	Max Losses at 50% (watts)	Max Losses at 100% (watts)	Max Losses at 50% (watts)	Max Losses at 100% (watts)
16	200	555	165	520	150	480	135	440	120	400
25	290	785	235	740	210	695	190	635	175	595
63	490	1415	430	1335	380	1250	340	1140	300	1050
100	700	2020	610	1910	520	1800	475	1650	435	1500
160	1000	2800	880	2550	770	2200	670	1950	570	1700
200	1130	3300	1010	3000	890	2700	780	2300	670	2100

Star rating for Tubular fluorescent lamp:

Star Rating	*	**	***	****	*****
Lumens per watt at 0100 hrs of use	< 61	>= 61 & < 67	>= 67 & < 86	>= 86 & < 92	>= 92
Lumens per watt at 2000 hrs of use	< 52	>= 52 & < 57	>= 57 & < 77	>= 77 & < 83	>= 83
Lumens per watt at 3500 hrs of use	< 49	>= 49 & < 54	>= 54 & < 73	> 73 & < 78	>= 78

Practice Questions

1. What is NPSH of a pump and effect of inadequate NPSH ?
2. State the affinity laws as applicable to centrifugal pump.
3. Explain what do you understand by static head and friction head.
4. What are various methods of pump capacity control normally adopted ?
5. Explain with diagram the energy loss due to throttling in a centrifugal pump.
6. What are the effects of oversizing of pump ?
7. How does the pump performance vary with impeller diameter ?
8. List out energy conservation opportunities in pumping system.
9. What do you understand by the following terms with respect to cooling towers:
   (i) Approach
   (ii) Cooling duty
   (iii) Range
   (iv) Effectiveness.
10. Explain with diagram different types of cooling towers.
11. List the factors affecting cooling tower performance.
12. List out energy conservation opportunities in a cooling tower system.
13. Explain how maximum demand control works.
14. Explain the principle of automatic power factor controller.
15. What are the advantages of energy efficient motors ?
16. Explain working of a soft starter and its advantages over conventional starters.

MSBTE Questions and Answers (As Per 'E' Scheme)

Summer 2012

1. Differentiate between electronic ballast and magnetic ballast.

Ans. Please refer to Section 4.4.2.

2. Differentiate between conventional fuel and alternative fuel (four points).

Ans. Please refer to Section 4.3.

3. Explain construction and working of centrifugal pump.

Ans. Please refer to Section 4.1.3.

4. State the importance of any four properties of liquid petroleum fuel.

Ans. Please refer to Sections 4.3.1 and 4.3.2.

5. Write down names of four energy efficient technologies. Explain any one in detail.

Ans. Please refer to Section 4.4.1.

6. What are three T's of combustion? Explain their role.

Ans. Please refer to Section 4.3.5.

7. Define range and approach of cooling tower. Ideally how much cooling is possible in cooling tower?

Ans. Please refer to Sections 4.2 and 4.2.1.

8. What are the different types of fuels used in the industry? Classify them according to their physical state. What is the difference between GCV and NCV of fuel?

Ans. Please refer to Sections 4.3 and 4.3.1.

9. Define NPSH. Why it is important in pumping operation ?

Ans. Please refer to Sections 4.1.4 and 4.1.1.

10. Calculate stoichiometric (kg) amount of air required for complete combustion of 100 kg liquid fuel using the following data:

Constituents	% by weight
Carbon	85.9
Hydrogen	12.0
Oxygen	0.7
Nitrogen	0.5
Sulfur	0.5
Water	0.35
Ash	0.05

11. Calculate the power required for pump using the following data:

Flow rate = 12.5 lps

Head = 30 m

Motor efficiency = 90%

Pump efficiency = 60%

Density = 1000 kg/m^3

Winter 2013

1. Define pump. Draw characteristics curves of pump.

Ans. Please refer to Section 4.15.

2. Calculate the stiochiometric air/fuel ratio by mass and the percentage composition of the products of combustion per kg of alcohol. Chemical formula for alcohol is C_2H_6O.

3. How are cooling tower classified? Explain working of any one type.

Ans. Please refer to Section 4.2.

4. Explain the concept of energy efficiency in electrical utilities.

Ans. Please refer to Section 4.1.6.

5. What are the main features of energy efficient motor?

Ans. Please refer to Section 4.4.2.

6. Why excess air is required in combustion of fuel?

Ans. Please refer to Section 4.3.5.

7. How throttle valve pumping system can be replaced by any other four types of energy efficient pumping system?

Ans. Please refer to Section 4.1.6.

8. Compare centrifugal pump and reciprocating pump.

Ans. Please refer to Section 4.1.2 and 4.1.3.

9. What are the factors affecting the cooling of water in a cooling tower.

Ans. Please refer to Section 4.3.

Chapter 5

ENERGY PERFORMANCE ASSESSMENT

Objectives

Students will study and understand the following:

- State steps for performance assessment of heat exchanger, water pumps and boilers
- Working of boilers, heat exchangers, pumps and cooling towers
- Types of boilers, heat exchangers, pumps and cooling towers

5.1 WATER PUMP (W-13)

- The centrifugal pump pumps the difference between the suction and the discharge heads. There are three kinds of discharge head:
  - **Static head:** The height we are pumping to, or the height to the discharge piping outlet that is filling the tank from the top. Note that if you are filling the tank from the bottom, the static head will be constantly changing.
  - **Pressure head:** If we are pumping to a pressurized vessel (like a boiler), we must convert the pressure units (psi or kg) to head units (feet or metres).
  - **System or Dynamic head:** Caused by friction in the pipes, fittings, and system components. We get this number by making the calculations from published charts.
- Suction head is measured the same way.
  - If the liquid level is above the pump centre line, that level is a positive suction head. If the pump is lifting a liquid level from below its centre line, it is a negative suction head.
  - If the pump is pumping liquid from a pressurized vessel, you must convert this pressure to a positive suction head. A vacuum in the tank would be converted to a negative suction head.
  - Friction in the pipes, fittings, and associated hardware is a negative suction head.
  - Negative suction heads are added to the pump discharge head, positive suctions heads are subtracted from the pump discharge head.

5.1.1 Hydraulic Pump Power

- The ideal hydraulic power to drive a pump depends on the mass flow rate, the liquid density and the differential height - either it is the static lift from one height to an other, or the friction head loss component of the system - can be calculated as

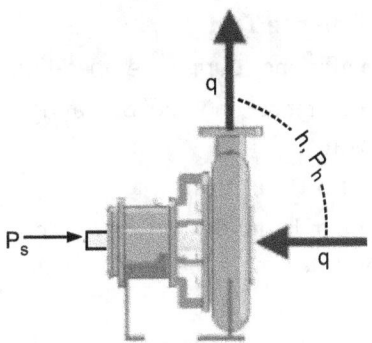

Fig. 5.1

$$P_h = \frac{q\rho g h}{3.6 \times 10^6}$$

where, P_h = Power (kW)

         q = Flow capacity (m³/h)

         ρ = Density of fluid (kg/m³)

         g = Gravity (9.81 m/s²)

         h = Differential head (m)

Shaft Pump Power

The shaft power: The power required is transferred from the motor to the shaft of the pump, depends on the efficiency of the pump and can be calculated as

$$P_s = \frac{P_h}{\eta}$$

where, P_s = Shaft power (kW)

         η = Pump efficiency

5.1.2 Assessment of Water Pumps

- Pumping is the process of addition of kinetic and potential energy to a liquid for the purpose of moving it from one point to another. This energy will cause the liquid to do work such as flow through a pipe or rise to a higher level.

- A centrifugal pump transforms mechanical energy from a rotating impeller into a kinetic and potential energy required by the system.

- The most critical aspect of energy efficiency in a pumping system is matching of pumps to loads. Hence even if an efficient pump is selected, but if it is a mismatch to the system then the pump will operate at very poor efficiencies.

- In addition, efficiency drop can also be expected over time due to deposits in the impellers.

- Performance assessment of pumps would reveal the existing operating efficiencies in order to take corrective action.

5.1.2.1 Purpose of the Performance Test

- Determination of the pump efficiency during the operating condition.
- Determination of system resistance and the operating duty point of the pump and compare the same with design.

5.1.2.2 Performance Terms and Definitions

Pump Capacity, Q = Volume of liquid delivered by pump per unit time, m^3/hr or m^3/sec. Q is proportional to N, where N- rotational speed of the pump.

Total developed head:

$$H = \text{The difference of discharge and suction pressure}$$

The pump head represents the net work done on unit weights of a liquid in passing from inlet of the pump to the discharge of the pump.

There are three heads in common use in pumps namely:

(i) Static head

(ii) Velocity head

(iii) Friction head.

The frictional head in a system of pipes, valves and fittings varies as a function (roughly as the square) of the capacity flow through the system.

System resistance: The sum of frictional head in resistance and total static head.

Pump Efficiency: Fluid power and useful work done by the pump divided by the power input in the pump shaft.

$$\text{Pump efficiency} = \frac{\text{Hydraulic power, } p_h}{\text{Power input to the pump shaft}} \times 100$$

where, Hydraulic power, p_h (kW) = $Q \times (h_d - h_s) \times \rho \times g / 100$

Q = Volume flow rate (m^3/s),

ρ = Density of the fluid (kg/m^3),

g = Acceleration due to gravity (m/s^2),

$(h_d - h_s)$ = Total head in m,

5.1.3 Field Testing for Determination of Pump Efficiency

- To determine the pump efficiency, three key parameters are required: Flow, Head and Power. Of these, flow measurement is the most crucial parameter as normally online flow meters are hardly available, in a majority of pumping system.
- The following methods outlined below can be adopted to measure the flow depending on the availability and site conditions.

1. **Flow Measurement, Q:**

   The following are the methods for flow measurements:
   - Tracer method BS5857

- Ultrasonic flow measurement
- Tank filling method
- Installation of an on-line flowmeter.

Tracer Method:

- The Tracer method is particularly suitable for cooling water flow measurement because of their sensitivity and accuracy.
- This method is based on injecting a tracer into the cooling water for a few minutes at an accurately measured constant rate.
- A series of samples is extracted from the system at a point where the tracer has become completely mixed with the cooling water. The mass flow rate is calculated from:

$$Q_{cw} = q_1 \times C_1/C_2$$

where,

q_{cw} = Cooling water mass flow rate, kg/s,

q_1 = Mass flow rate of injected tracer, kg/s,

C_1 = Concentration of injected tracer, kg/kg,

C_2 = Concentration of tracer at downstream position during the 'plateau' period of constant concentration, kg/kg.

- The tracer normally used is sodium chloride.

Ultrasonic Flow Meter:

- Operating under Doppler effect principle these meters are non-invasive, meaning measurements can be taken without disturbing the system.
- Scales and rust in the pipes are likely to impact the accuracy.
- Ensure measurements are taken in a sufficiently long length of pipe free from flow disturbance due to bends, tees and other fittings.
- The pipe section where measurement is to be taken should be hammered gently to enable scales and rusts to fall out.
- For better accuracy, a section of the pipe can be replaced with new pipe for flow measurements.

Tank Filing Method:

- In open flow systems such as water getting pumped to an overhead tank or a sump, the flow can be measured by noting the difference in tank levels for a specified period during which the outlet flow from the tank is stopped.
- The internal tank dimensions should be preferable taken from the design drawings, in the absence of which direct measurements may be resorted to.

Installation of an On-line Flow Meter:

If the application to be measured is going to be critical and periodic then the best option would be to install an on-line flowmeter which can get rid of the major problems encountered with other types.

2. Determination of Total Head, H:

Suction head (h_s):

This is taken from the pump inlet pressure gauge readings and the value to be converted in to metres (1 kg/cm^2 = 10 m). If not the level difference between sump water level to the centerline of the pump is to be measured. This gives the suction head in metres.

Discharge Head (h_d):

This is taken from the pump discharge side pressure gauge. Installation of the pressure gauge in the discharge side is a must, if not already available.

3. Determination of Hydraulic Power (Liquid horse power):

Hydraulic power, $\qquad$ P_h (kW) $= Q \times (h_d - H_s) \times \rho/1000$

Where, $\qquad\qquad\qquad$ Q = Volume flow rate (m^3/s),

$\qquad\qquad\qquad\qquad\quad \rho$ = Density of the fluid (kg/m^3),

$\qquad\qquad\qquad\qquad\quad g$ = Acceleration due to gravity (m/s^2),

$\qquad\qquad (h_d - h_s)$ = Total head in metres.

4. Measurement of Motor Input Power:

The motor input power P_m can be measured by using a portable power analyser.

5. Pump Shaft Power:

The pump shaft power P_s is calculated by multiplying the motor input power by motor efficiency at the existing loading.

$$P_s = P_m \times \eta_{Motor}$$

6. Pump Efficiency:

This is arrived at by dividing the hydraulic power by pump shaft power

$$\eta_{Pump} = \frac{P_h}{P_s}$$

Example of Pump Efficiency Calculation:

Illustration of calculation method outlined

A chemical plant operates a cooling water pump for process cooling and refrigeration applications. During the performance testing the following operating parameters were measured;

Measured Data:

Pump flow, Q	0.40 m^3/s
Power absorbed, P	325 kW
Suction head (Tower basin level), h_1	+ 1 m
Delivery head, h_2	55 m
Height of cooling tower	5 m
Motor efficiency	88%
Type of drive	Direct coupled
Density of water	996 kg/m^3

Pump efficiency:

Flow delivered by the pump	0.40 m³/s
Total head, $h_2 - (+ h_1)$	54 m
Hydraulic power	$0.40 \times 54 \times 996 \times 9.81/1000 = 211$ kW
Actual power consumption	325 kW
Overall system efficiency	$(211 \times 100)/325 = 65\%$
Pump efficiency	**65/0.88 = 74%**

5.1.4 Determining the System Resistance and Duty Point

- Determination of the system resistance curve and imposing the pump curve over it will give an idea of the operating efficiency of the pump and also the drop in efficiencies when the system curve changes from normal design.
- The example following from the earlier example outlines the method of constructing a system curve.

Example:

Location of equipments:

- The Refrigeration plant is located at +0.00 level and the process plant condensers are located at +15 m level. One cooler having a design pressure drop of 1.9 kg/cm² is located at the 0.00 level (ground level).
- Other relevant data can be inferred from the earlier section. See schematic in Fig. 5.2.

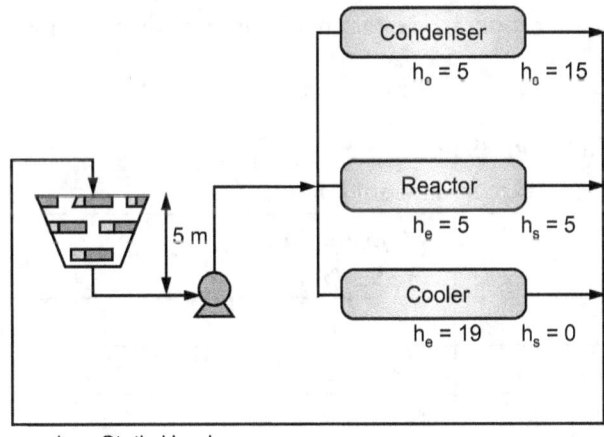

h_s = Static Head
h_e = Equipment Pressure Drop

Fig. 5.2: Schematic of the system

- The step-by-step approach for determining system resistance curve is given below.

Step 1: Divide system resistance into static and dynamic head.

Find static head,

Static head (Condenser floor height), 15 m

Find dynamic head,

$$\text{Dynamic head} = \text{Total head} - \text{Static head}$$

$$\text{Dynamic head} = (54 - 15) = 39 \text{ m}$$

Step 2: Check the maximum resistance circuit.

Resistance in the different circuits is as under:

Sr. No.	System	Condenser loop resistance, m	Reactor loop resistance, m	Cooler loop resistance, m
1.	Supply line from pump	15	10	15
2.	Static head	15	5	Nil (cooler at ground level)
3.	Equipment	5	5	19
4.	Return line from equipment to CT	15	10	15
5.	Tower head	–	–	5
6.	Total	50	30	54

It can be noted that at full load the condenser and cooler circuits offer the maximum resistance to flow.

Step 3: Draw system resistance curve.

Choose the condenser loop as it offers maximum resistance and is also having a static head component.

Static head: 15 m.

Dynamic head at full load: 39 m.

Compute system resistance at different flow rates.

Sr. No.	Flow (%)	Dynamic head = $39 \times (\% \text{ flow})^2$	Static head, m	Total head m
1.	100	39	15	54
2.	75	21.9	15	36.9
3.	50	9.75	15	24.75
4.	25	2.44	15	17.44

Step 4: Plot the system resistance against flow in the pump efficiency curves (see Fig. 5.3) provided by the vendor and compare actual operating duty point and see whether it operates at maximum efficiency. In the example provided it is found that the pump system efficiency is lower by 4% due to change in operating conditions.

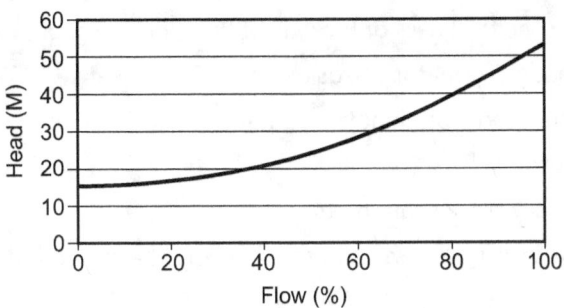

Fig. 5.3: System resistance curve

5.2 HEAT EXCHANGER

- A **heat exchanger** is a device built for efficient *heat transfer* from one medium to another, whether the media are separated by a solid wall so that they never mix, or the media are in direct contact.

- They are widely used in *space heating, refrigeration, air conditioning, power plants, chemical plants, petrochemical plants, petroleum refineries*, and *natural gas processing*.

- One common example of a heat exchanger is the *radiator* in a car, in which a hot engine-cooling fluid, like *antifreeze*, transfers heat to air flowing through the radiator.

5.2.1 Types of Heat Exchangers   (S-12; W-13)

Shell and Tube Heat Exchangers: (W-13)

- Shell and tube heat exchangers consist of a series of tubes. One set of these tubes contains the fluid that must be either heated or cooled. The second fluid runs over the tubes that are being heated or cooled so that it can either provide the heat or absorb the heat required.

- A set of tubes is called the tube bundle and can be made up of several types of tubes: plain, longitudinally finned etc. Shell and Tube heat exchangers are typically used for high pressure applications (with pressures greater than 30 bar and temperatures greater than 260°C).

- This is because the shell and tube heat exchangers are robust due to their shape.

- There are several thermal design features that are to be taken into account when designing the tubes in the shell and tube heat exchangers. These include:

  o **Tube diameter:** Using a small tube diameter makes the heat exchanger both economical and compact. However, it is more likely for the heat exchanger to foul up faster and the small size makes mechanical cleaning of the fouling difficult. To prevail over the fouling and cleaning problems, larger tube diameters can be used. Thus to determine the tube diameter, the available space, cost and the fouling nature of the fluids must be considered.

o Tube thickness: The thickness of the wall of the tubes is usually determined to ensure:

- There is enough room for corrosion.

- That flow-induced vibration has resistance.

- Axial strength.

- Ability to easily stock spare parts cost.

Sometimes the wall thickness is determined by the maximum pressure differential across the wall.

o **Tube length:** Heat exchangers are usually cheaper when they have a smaller shell diameter and a long tube length. Thus, typically there is an aim to make the heat exchanger as long as possible. However, there are many limitations for this, including the space available at the site where it is going to be used and the need to ensure that there are tubes available in lengths that are twice the required length (so that the tubes can be withdrawn and replaced). Also, it has to be remembered that long, thin tubes are difficult to take out and replace.

o **Tube pitch:** When designing the tubes, it is practical to ensure that the tube pitch (i.e. the centre-centre distance of adjoining tubes) is not less than 1.25 times the tubes outside diameter.

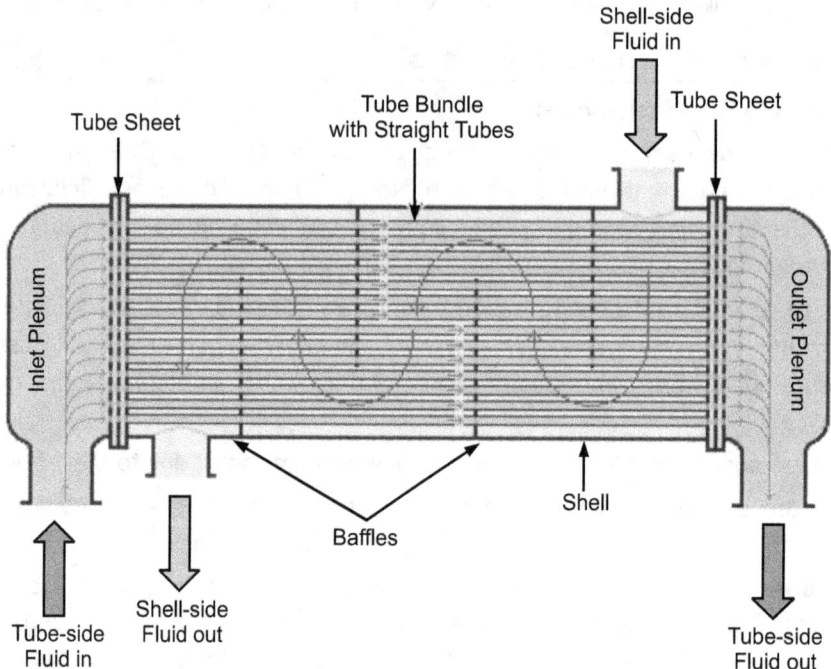

Fig. 5.4: Straight-tube heat exchanger (one pass tube-side)

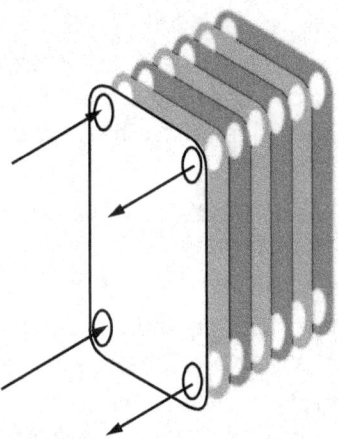

Fig. 5.5: Conceptual diagram of a plate and frame heat exchanger

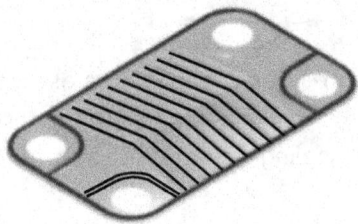

Fig. 5.6: A single-plate heat exchanger

Plate Heat Exchanger:

- Another type of heat exchanger is the *plate heat exchanger*. One is composed of multiple, thin, slightly-separated plates that have very large surface areas and fluid flow passages for heat transfer.

- This stacked-plate arrangement can be more effective, in a given space, than the shell and tube heat exchanger. Advances in *gasket* and *brazing* technology have made the plate-type heat exchanger increasingly practical.

- In HVAC applications, large heat exchangers of this type are called *plate-and-frame*; when used in open loops, these heat exchangers are normally of the gasketed type to allow periodic disassembly, cleaning, and inspection.

- There are many types of permanently-bonded plate heat exchangers, such as dip-brazed and vacuum-brazed plate varieties, and they are often specified for closed-loop applications such as *refrigeration*.

- Plate heat exchangers also differ in the types of plates that are used, and in the configurations of those plates.

- Some plates may be stamped with "chevron" or other patterns, where others may have machined fins and/or grooves.

Regenerative Heat Exchanger:

- A third type of heat exchanger is the *regenerative heat exchanger*. In this, the heat from a process is used to warm the fluids to be used in the process, and the same type of fluid is used either side of the heat exchanger (these heat exchangers can be either plate-and-frame or shell-and-tube construction).

- These exchangers are used only for gases and not for liquids. The major factor for this is the heat capacity of the heat transfer matrix.

Adiabatic Wheel Heat Exchanger:

- A fourth type of heat exchanger uses an intermediate fluid or solid store to hold heat, which is then moved to the other side of the heat exchanger to be released.

- Two examples of this are adiabatic *wheels*, which consist of a large wheel with fine threads rotating through the hot and cold fluids, and fluid heat exchangers.

- This type is used when it is acceptable for a small amount of mixing to occur between the two streams.

Fluid Heat Exchangers:

- This is a heat exchanger with a gas passing upwards through a shower of fluid (often water), and the fluid is then taken elsewhere before being cooled.

- This is commonly used for cooling gases whilst also removing certain impurities, thus solving two problems at once.

- It is widely used in espresso machines as an energy-saving method of cooling super-heated water to be used in the extraction of espresso.

Dynamic Scraped Surface Heat Exchanger:

- Another type of heat exchanger is called "dynamic heat exchanger" or "scraped-surface heat exchanger".

- This is mainly used for heating or cooling with high-*viscosity* products, *crystallization* processes, *evaporation* and high-*fouling* applications.

- Long running times are achieved due to the continuous scraping of the surface, thus avoiding *fouling* and achieving a sustainable heat transfer rate during the process.

Phase-change Heat Exchangers:

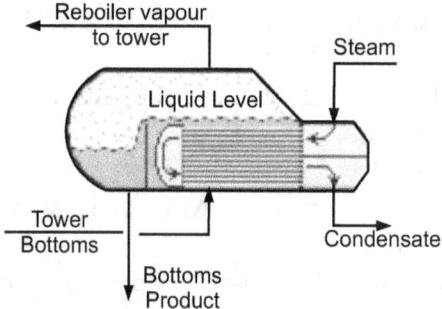

Fig. 5.7: Typical kettle reboiler used for industrial distillation towers

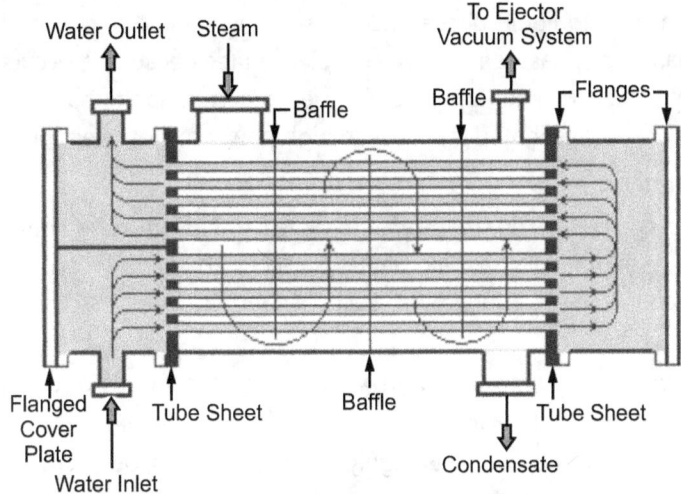

Fig. 5.8: Typical water-cooled surface condenser

- In addition to heating up or cooling down fluids in just a single phase, heat exchangers can be used either to heat a *liquid* to evaporate (or boil) it or used as *condensers* to cool a *vapour* and *condense* it to a liquid.

- In *chemical plants* and *refineries, reboilers* used to heat incoming feed for *distillation* towers are often heat exchangers.

- Distillation set-ups typically use condensers to condense distillate vapours back into liquid.

- *Power plants* which have *steam*-driven *turbines* commonly use heat exchangers to boil *water* into *steam*.

- Heat exchangers or similar units for producing steam from water are often called *boilers* or steam generators.

- In the nuclear power plants called *pressurized water reactors*, special large heat exchangers which pass heat from the primary (reactor plant) system to the secondary (steam plant) system, producing steam from water in the process, are called *steam generators*.

- All fossil-fueled and nuclear power plants using steam-driven turbines have *surface condensers* to convert the exhaust steam from the turbines into condensate (water) for re-use.

- In order to conserve energy and cooling capacity in chemical and other plants, regenerative heat exchangers can be used to transfer heat from one stream that needs to be cooled to another stream that needs to be heated, such as distillate cooling and reboiler feed pre-heating.

- This term can also refer to heat exchangers that contain a material within their structure that has a change of phase.

- This is usually a solid to liquid phase due to the small volume difference between these states. This change of phase effectively acts as a buffer because it occurs at a constant temperature but still allows for a heat exchanger to accept additional heat. One example where this has been investigated is for use in high power aircraft electronics.

Spiral Heat Exchangers:

- A *spiral* heat exchanger (SHE), may refer to a *helical* (coiled) tube configuration, more generally, the term refers to a pair of flat surfaces that are coiled to form the two channels in a counter-flow arragement. Each of the two channels has one long curved path.

- A pair of fluid ports are connected *tangentially* to the outer arms of the spiral, and axial ports are common, but optional.

- The main advantage of the SHE is its highly efficient use of space. This attribute is often leveraged and partially reallocated to gain other improvements in performance, according to well known tradeoffs in heat exchanger design. (A notable tradeoff is capital cost versus operating cost.)

- A compact SHE may be used to have a smaller footprint and thus lower all-around capital costs, or an over-sized SHE may be used to have less *pressure* drop, less pumping *energy*, higher thermal *efficiency*, and lower energy costs.

Self Cleaning:

- SHEs are often used in the heating of fluids which contain solids and thus have a tendency to *foul* the inside of the heat exchanger.

- The low pressure drop gives the SHE its ability to handle fouling more easily.

- The SHE uses a "self cleaning" mechanism, whereby fouled surfaces cause a localized increase in fluid velocity, thus increasing the *drag* (or fluid *friction*) on the fouled surface, thus helping to dislodge the blockage and keep the heat exchanger clean.

- "The internal walls that make up the heat transfer surface are often rather thick, which makes the SHE very robust, and able to last a long time in demanding environments."

- They are also easily cleaned, opening out like an *oven* where any build up of foulant can be removed by *pressure washing*.

Flow Arrangement:

- Heat exchangers may be classified according to their flow arrangement. In *parallel-flow* heat exchangers, the two fluids enter the exchanger at the same end, and travel in parallel to one another to the other side.

- In *counter-flow* heat exchangers the fluids enter the exchanger from opposite ends.

- The counter-current design is most efficient, in that it can transfer the most heat. See *counter-current exchange*.

- In a *cross-flow* heat exchanger, the fluids travel roughly perpendicular to one another through the exchanger.

- For efficiency, heat exchangers are designed to maximize the surface area of the wall between the two fluids, while minimizing resistance to fluid flow through the exchanger.
- The exchanger's performance can also be affected by the addition of fins or corrugations in one or both directions, which increase surface area and may channel fluid flow or induce turbulence.
- The driving temperature across the heat transfer surface varies with position, but an appropriate mean temperature can be defined.
- In most simple systems, this is the *log mean temperature difference* (LMTD).
- Sometimes direct knowledge of the LMTD is not available and the *NTU method* is used.

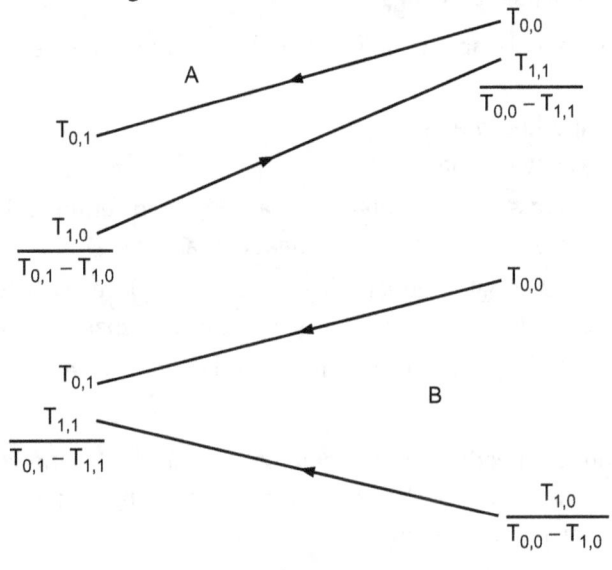

Fig. 5.9

Monitoring and Maintenance:

- Integrity inspection of plate and tubular heat exchanger can be tested in-situ by the conductivity or helium gas methods.
- These methods confirm the integrity of the plates or tubes to prevent any cross contamination and the condition of the gaskets.
- Condition monitoring of heat exchanger tubes may be conducted through non-destructive methods such as eddy current testing.
- The mechanics of water flow and deposits are often simulated by computational fluid dynamics or CFD.
- *Fouling* is a serious problem in some heat exchangers. River water is often used as cooling water, which results in biological debris entering the heat exchanger and building layers, decreasing the heat transfer coefficient.
- Another common problem is scale, which is made up of deposited layers of chemicals such as calcium carbonate or magnesium carbonate.

Fouling:

- Fouling occurs when a fluid goes through the heat exchanger, and the impurities in the fluid precipitate onto the surface of the tubes.

- Precipitation of these *impurities* can be caused by:

  o Frequent use of the Heat Exchanger.

  o Not cleaning the Heat Exchanger regularly.

  o Reducing the velocity of the fluids moving through the heat exchanger.

  o Over-sizing of the heat exchanger.

- Effects of fouling are more abundant in the cold tubes of the heat exchanger, than in the hot tubes.

- This is because impurities are less likely to be dissolved in a cold fluid. This is because solubility increases as temperature increases.

- Fouling reduces the cross-sectional area for heat to be transferred and causes an increase in the resistance to heat transfer across the heat exchanger.

- This is because the thermal conductivity of the fouling layer is low. This reduces the overall *heat transfer coefficient* and efficiency of the heat exchanger.

- This in turn, can lead to an increase in pumping and maintenance costs.

Maintenance:

- Plate heat exchangers need to be dissembled and cleaned periodically. Tubular heat exchangers can be cleaned by such methods as acid cleaning, *sandblasting, high-pressure water jet*, bullet cleaning, or drill rods.

- In large-scale cooling water systems for heat exchangers, water treatment such as purification, addition of chemicals, and testing, is used to minimize fouling of the heat exchange equipment.

- Other water treatment is also used in steam systems for power plants, etc. to minimize fouling and corrosion of the heat exchange and other equipment.

- A variety of companies have started using waterborne oscillations technology to prevent biofouling. Without the use of chemicals, this type of technology has helped in providing a low-pressure drop in heat exchangers.

Instruments for Monitoring:

- The test and evaluation of the performance of the heat exchanger equipment is carried out by measurement of operating parameters upstream and downstream of the exchanger.

- Due care needs to be taken to ensure the accuracy and correctness of the measured parameter. The instruments used for measurements require calibration and verification prior to measurement.

Table 5.1

Parameters	Units	Instruments used
Fluid flow	kg/h	Flow can be measured with instruments like Orifice flow meter, Vortex flow meter, Venturi meters, Coriollis flow meters, Magnetic flow meter as applicable to the fluid service and flow ranges.
Temperature	°C	Thermo gauge for low ranges, RTD, etc.
Pressure	Bar g	Liquid manometers, Draft gauge, Pressure gauges, Bourdon and diaphragm type, Absolute pressure transmitters, etc.
Density	kg/m^3	Measured in the laboratory as per ASTM standards, hydrometer, etc.
Viscosity	MPa.s	Measured in the laboratory as per ASTM standards, viscometer, etc.
Specific heat capacity	J/(kg.K)	Measured in the laboratory as per ASTM standards.
Thermal conductivity	W/(m.K)	Measured in the laboratory as per ASTM standards.
Composition	% wt (or) % vol	Measured in the laboratory as per ASTM standards using Chemical analysis, HPLC, GC, Spectrophotometer etc.

5.2.2 Methodology of Heat Exchanger Performance Assessment

(S-12)

Procedure for determination of overall heat transfer coefficient, U at field: This is a fairly rigorous method of monitoring the heat exchanger performance by calculating the overall heat transfer coefficient periodically. Technical records are to be maintained for all the exchangers, so that problems associated with reduced efficiency and heat transfer can be identified easily. The record should basically contain historical heat transfer coefficient data versus time/date of observation. A plot of heat transfer coefficient versus time permits rational planning of an exchanger-cleaning program.

The heat transfer coefficient is calculated by the equation

$$U = Q/(A \times LMTD)$$

where Q is the heat duty, A is the heat transfer area of the exchanger and LMTD is temperature driving force.

The step by step procedure for determining of overall heat transfer coefficient are described below.

Step A: Monitoring and reading of steady state parameters of the heat exchanger under evaluation are tabulated as below:

Parameters	Units	Inlet	Outlet
Hot fluid flow, W	kg/h		
Cold fluid flow, w	kg/h		
Hot fluid temperature, T	°C		
Cold fluid temperature, t	°C		
Hot fluid pressure, P	bar g		
Cold fluid pressure, p	bar g		

Step B: With the monitored test data, the physical properties of the stream can be tabulated as required for the evaluation of the thermal data.

Parameters	Units	Inlet	Outlet
Hot fluid density, ρ_h	kg/m^3		
Cold fluid density, ρ_c	kg/m^3		
Hot fluid viscosity, μ_h	MPas*		
Cold fluid viscosity, μ_c	MPas		
Hot fluid thermal conductivity, k_h	kW/(m.K)		
Cold fluid thermal conductivity, k_c	kW/(m.K)		
Hot fluid specific heat capacity, C_{ph}	kJ/(kg.K)		
Cold fluid specific heat capacity, C.$_{pc}$	kJ/(kg.K)		

* MPas – Mega Pascal Second.

Density and viscosity can be determined by analysis of the samples taken from the flow stream at the recorded temperature in the plant laboratory. Thermal conductivity and specific heat capacity if not determined from the samples can be collected from handbooks.

Step C : Calculate the thermal parameters of heat exchanger and compare with the design data.

Parameters	Units	Test Data	Design Data
Heat duty, Q	kW	*	
Hot fluid side pressure drop, ΔP_h	bar	*	
Cold fluid side pressure drop, ΔP_c	bar	*	
Temperature range hot fluid, ΔT	°C		
Temperature range cold fluid, Δt	°C		
Capacity ratio, R	–		
Effectiveness, S	–		
Corrected LMTD, MTD	°C		
Heat transfer coefficient, U	kW/(m².K)		

    *   The pressure drop for the design flow can be rated with the relation.

        Pressure drop is proportional to $(Flow)^{1.75}$

Step D: The following formulae are used for calculating the thermal parameters:

1.   Heat duty, $Q = q_s + q_l$

where, q_s is the sensible heat and q_l is the latent heat.

For Sensible heat

$$q_s = W \times C_{ph} \times (T_i - T_o)/1000/3600 \text{ in kW}$$

or $q_s = w \times C_{pc} \times (t_o - t_i)/1000/3600 \text{ in kW}$

For latent heat:

$$q_l = W \times \lambda_h$$

$$\lambda_h - \text{Latent hat of condensation of a hot condensing vapour}$$

or $q_l = w \times \lambda_c$, where λ_c – Latent heat of vaporization

2.   Hot fluid pressure drop, $\Delta P_h = P_i - P_o$

3.   Cold fluid pressure drop, $\Delta P_c = p_i - p_o$

4.   Temperature range hot fluid, $\Delta T = T_i - T_o$

5.   Temperature range cold fluid, $\Delta t = t_o - t_i$

6.   Capacity ratio, $R = W \times C_{ph}/w \times C_{pc}$ or $(T_i - T_o)/(t_o - t_i)$

7.   Effectiveness, $S = (t_o - t_i)/(T_i - t_i)$.

8.   LMTD.

(a)

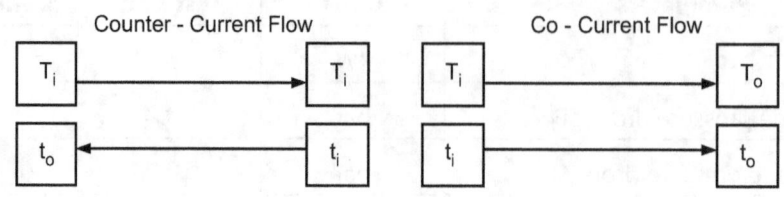

Fig. 5.10

LMTD counter-current flow = $[(T_i - t_o) - (T_o - t_i)]/\ln[(T_i - t_o)/(T_o - t_i)]$

LMTD co-current flow = $[(T_i - t_i) - (T_o - t_o)]/\ln[(T_i - t_i)/(T_o - t_o)]$

(b) Correction factor for LMTD to account for cross flow.

$$F = \frac{(R + 1)^{1/2} \times \ln[(1 - SR)/(1 - S)]}{(1 - R) \times \ln\left\{\dfrac{2 - S[R + 1 - (R + 1)^{1/2}]}{2 - S[R + 1 + (R + 1)^{1/2}]}\right\}}$$

9. Corrected LMTD $= F \times$ LMTD.

10. Overall heat transfer co-efficient

$$U = Q/(A \times \text{Corrected LMTD})$$

Examples:

(a) Liquid – liquid exchanger:

A shell and tube exchanger of following configuration is considered being used for oil cooler with oil at the shell side and cooling water at the tube side.

Tube side:

* 460 Nos. × 25.4 mm OD × 2.11 mm thick × 7211 mm long.

* Pitch – 31.75 mm 30° triangular.

* 2 pass.

Shell side:

* 787 mm ID

* Baffle space – 787 mm

* 1 pass.

The monitored parameters are as below:

Parameters	Units	Inlet	Outlet
Hot fluid flow, W	kg/h	719800	719800
Cold fluid flow, w	kg/h	881150	881150
Hot fluid temperature, T	°C	145	102
Cold fluid temperature, t	°C	25.5	49
Hot fluid pressure, P	bar g	4.1	2.8
Cold fluid pressure, p	bar g	6.2	5.1

Calculation of Thermal data:

Heat transfer area $= 264.55 \text{ m}^2$

1. Heat duty:

$$Q = q_s + q_l$$

Hot fluid, $Q = 719800 \times 2.847 \times (145 - 102)/3600 = 24477.4 \text{ kW}$

Cold fluid, $Q = \dfrac{881150 \times 4.187 \times (49 - 25.5)}{3600} = 24083.4 \text{ kW}$

2. Hot fluid pressure drop,

Pressure drop $= P_i - P_o = 4.1 - 2.8 = 1.3 \text{ bar g}$

3. Cold fluid pressure drop

Pressure drop $= p_i - p_o = 6.2 - 5.1 = 1.1 \text{ bar g.}$

4. Temperature range of hot fluid

Temperature range $\Delta T = T_i - T_o = 145 - 102 = 43°C$

5. Temperature range cold fluid

Temperature range $\Delta t = t_o - t_i = 48 - 25.5 = 23.5°C$

6. Capacity ratio

Capacity ratio, $R = \dfrac{T_i - T_o}{t_o - t_i} = \dfrac{43}{23.5} = 1.83$

7. Effectiveness

Effectiveness, $S = \dfrac{t_o - t_i}{T_o - T_i} = \dfrac{49 - 25.5}{145 - 25.5} = 23.5/119.5 = 0.20$

8. LMTD

   (a) LMTD, counter flow $= (96 - 76.5)/\ln (96/76.5) = 85.9°C$

   (b) Correction factor to account for cross flow.

$$F = \dfrac{(R + 1)^{1/2} \times \ln (1 - SR)/(1 - S)}{(1 - R) \times \ln \left\{ \dfrac{2 - S (R + 1 - (R + 1)^{1/2})}{2 - S (R + 1 + (R + 1)^{1/2})} \right\}}$$

   $F = 0.977$

9. Corrected LMTD

$$= F \times LMTD = 0.977 \times 85.9 = 83.9°C$$

10. Overall heat transfer co-efficient

$$U = Q/A\Delta T = \dfrac{2447.4}{(264.55 \times 83.9)} = 1.104 \text{ kW/m}^2.\text{K}$$

Comparison of calculated data with design data:

Parameters	Units	Test Data	Design Data
Duty, Q	kW	24477.4	25623
Hot fluid side pressure drop, ΔP_h	Bar	1.3	1.34
Cold fluid side pressure drop, ΔP_c	Bar	1.1	0.95
Temperature range hot fluid, ΔT	°C	43	45
Temperature range cold fluid, Δt	°C	23.5	25
Capacity ratio, R	–	1.83	0.556
Effectiveness, S	–	0.20	0.375
Corrected LMTD, MTD	°C	83.8	82.2
Heat transfer coefficient, U	kW/(m^2.K)	1.104	1.178

Inference:

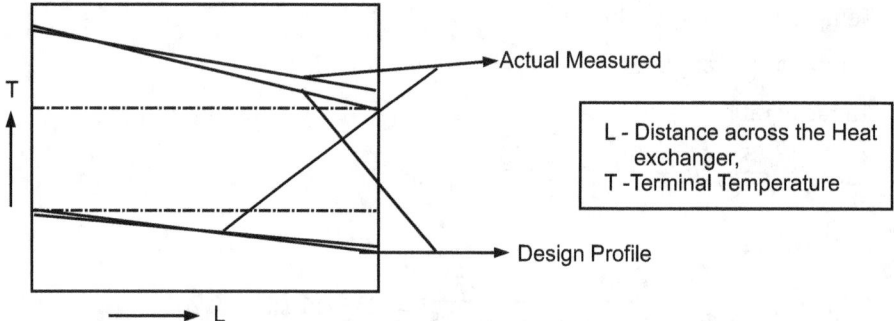

Fig. 5.11

Observation after monitoring performance of heat exchanger:

Heat duty: Actual duty differences will be practically negligible as there duty differences could be because of the specific heat capacity deviation with the temperature. Also, there could be some heat loss due to radiation from the hot shell side.

Pressure drop: Also, the pressure drop in the shell side of the hot fluid is reported normal (only slightly less than the design figure). This is attributed with the increased average bulk temperature of the hot side due to decreased performance of the exchanger.

Temperature range: As seen from the data the deviation in the temperature ranges could be due to the increased fouling in the tubes (cold stream), since a higher pressure drop is noticed.

Heat transfer coefficient: The estimated value has decreased due to increased fouling that has resulted in minimized active area of heat transfer.

Physical properties: If available from the data or lab analysis can be used for verification with the design data sheet as a cross check towards design considerations.

Trouble shooting: Fouled exchanger needs cleaning.

SOLVED PROBLEMS

Problem 5.1:

A textile processing industry is operating a 10 TPH, furnace oil fired boiler at 7 kg/cm^2 (g) pressure. Energy manager of the plant has conducted a quick test to determine boiler efficiency by direct method. The following are the measured and collected data during the test. Find out the efficiency and evaporation ratio of the boiler.

Duration of testing	=	2 hrs
Furnace oil tank size	=	1 m × 2 m × 2 m
Furnace oil level reduction during the 2 hours test	=	500 mm
Boiler feed water tank size	=	3 m × 5 m × 4 m
Feed water level reduction during the test period	=	850 mm
Specific gravity of furnace oil	=	0.92
GCV of furnace oil	=	10400 kcal/kg
Boiler inlet feed water temperature	=	60°C
Enthalpy of saturated steam at 7 kg/cm^2 (g)	=	660 kcal/kg

Solution:

1. Duration of test = 2 hours

2. **Determine fuel consumption per hour:**

Furnace oil tank size	=	1 m × 2 m × 2 m
Furnace oil level reduction during the 2 hours test period	=	500 mm
Furnace oil consumption for 2 hrs	=	1 × 2 × 0.5 = 1 m^3
Furnace oil consumption/hour	=	0.5 m^3/hr
Specific gravity of furnace oil	=	0.92
Furnace oil consumption	=	0.5 × 0.92
	=	0.46 TPH = 460 kg/hr

3. **Determine water consumption per hour:**

Feed water tank size	=	3 m × 5 m × 4 m
Feed water level reduction	=	850 mm
Water consumption during test period (2 hrs)	=	3 × 5 × 0.85
	=	12.75 m^3
Water consumption/hour	=	12.75/2
	=	6.37 m^3/hr
	=	6.37 TPH = 6370 kg/hr

Boiler efficiency by direct method:

4. **Boiler efficiency:**

$$= \frac{\text{Output heat}}{\text{Input heat}} \times 100$$

$$= \frac{6370 \times (660 - 60)}{460 \times 10400} \times 100$$

$$= \textbf{79.89\%}$$

5. **Evaporation ratio:**

$$= \frac{\text{Quantity of steam generated}}{\text{Quantity of fuel consumed}}$$

$$= \frac{6370}{460}$$

$$= \textbf{13.8}$$

Problem 5.2:

A chemical plant is generating saturated at 10 kg/cm^2 (g) pressure at the rate of 9 TPH for meeting the process requirement. To estimate the dry flue gas loss, flue gas analysis was carried out. The following measurements were done during boiler efficiency trial.

Oxygen in flue gas	= 4.2 %
Exhaust flue gas temperature	= 220°C
Theoretical air requirement	= 14 kg of air/kg of oil
Ambient temperature	= 30°C
GCV of fuel oil	= 10500 kcal/kg
Specific heat of flue gas	= 0.23 kcal/kg°C

After adjusting air inlet damper, the oxygen in flue gas is reduced to 2.5%. However the flue gas temperature remains same at 220°C.

Determine the % reduction in dry flue gas loss by this excess air control.

Solution:

Before damper adjustment:

1. O_2 % in flue gas = 4.2%

2. Excess air level

$$= \left(\frac{O_2}{21 - O_2}\right) \times 100$$

$$= \frac{4.2}{21 - 4.2} \times 100$$

$$= 25\%$$

3. Actual air supplied

$$= \left\{1 + \frac{\text{Excess air}}{100}\right\} \times \text{Theoretical air}$$

$$= \left(1 + \frac{25}{100}\right) \times 14$$

$$= 17.5 \text{ kg of air/kg of oil}$$

4.　Dry flue gas loss
$$= \frac{m \times C_p \times \Delta T}{GCV} \times 100$$

m = Weight of flue gas

= Actual mass of air supplied/kg of fuel + Mass of fuel (1 kg)

m = 17.5 + 1 = 18.5 kg/kg of oil

Dry flue gas loss
$$= \frac{18.5 \times 0.23 \times (220.30)}{10500} \times 100$$

= 7.69%

After damper adjustment

The oxygen level in flue gas was reduced to 2.5% by closing the air inlet damper.

O_2 % in flue gas　　　　= 2.5%

Excess air level
$$= \frac{O_2}{21 - O_2} \times 100$$

$$= \frac{2.5}{21 - 2.5} \times 100$$

= 13.5%

Actual air supplied
$$= \left\{ 1 + \frac{\text{Excess air}}{100} \right\} \times \text{Theoretical air}$$

= 1.135 × 14

= 15.89 kg of air/kg of oil

Dry flue gas loss
$$= \frac{m \times C_p \times \Delta T}{GCV} \times 100$$

m = 15.89 + 1 – 16.89 kg/kg of oil

Dry flue gas loss
$$= \frac{16.89 \times 0.23 \times (222 - 30)}{10500} \times 100$$

– **7.1%**

% Reduction in dry flue gas loss　= 7.69 – 7.1

= **0.59%**

Problem 5.3:

A heat treatment furnace was retrofitted with waste heat recovery after estimating the flue gas loss. The performance data before and after retrofitting are given below. Estimate the % reduction in flue gas loss after retrofitting with waste heat recovery. Theoretical air required/kg of oil can be assumed as 14 kg.

Before installation of waste heat recovery:

- Flue gas temperature　　　　= 825°C
- Ambient temperature　　　　= 35°C

After installation of waste heat recovery:

- Flue gas temperature   = 485°C
- O_2 % in flue gas   = 4%

Solution:

Dry flue gas loss before waste heat recovery:

Excess air level
$$= \frac{O_2 \times 100}{21 - O_2}$$

$$= \frac{5.5 \times 100}{21 - 5.5}$$

$$= 35\%$$

Actual air supplied
$$= \left\{ 1 + \frac{\text{Excess air}}{100} \right\} \times \text{Theoretical air}$$

$$= 1.35 \times 14$$

$$= 18.9 \text{ kg of air/kg of oil}$$

Dry flue gas loss
$$= \frac{m \times C_p \times \Delta T}{GCV} \times 100$$

m = Weight of flue gas

  = Actual mass of air supplied/kg of fuel + mass of fuel (1 kg)

m = 18.9 + 1 – 19.9 kg/kg of oil

Dry flue gas loss
$$= \frac{19.9 \times 0.24 \times (825 - 35)}{10500} \times 100$$

$$= 35.93\%$$

Dry flue gas loss after waste heat recovery O_2 % = 4%

Excess air level
$$= \frac{O_2 \times 100}{21 - O_2}$$

$$= \frac{4 \times 100}{21 - 4}$$

$$= 23.5\%$$

Actual air supplied
$$= \left\{ 1 + \frac{\text{Excess air}}{100} \right\} \times \text{Theoretical air}$$

$$= 1.235 \times 14$$

$$= 17.29 \text{ kg of air/kg of oil}$$

Dry flue gas loss
$$= \frac{m \times C_p \times \Delta T}{GCV} \times 100$$

$$= \frac{(17.29 + 1) \times 0.24 \times (485 - 35)}{10500} \times 100$$

$$= 18.81\%$$

$$= 35.93 - 18.81$$

% Reduction in flue gas loss   **= 17.12%**

Problem 5.4:

A heat treatment furnace is used to heat the billet for extrusion in an engineering industry. Billet is charged through a door, which is opened always. The door opening hole size is 800 mm × 800 mm square hole. Furnace wall thickness is 400 mm. The furnace operating temperature is 1250°C. Take emissivity as 0.8.

Calculate the direct radiation heat loss through openings using graph and convert the heat loss in terms of oil equivalent loss if GCV of oil is 10200 kcal/kg.

Solution:

The shape of the opening is square and D/X	= 0.8/0.4 = 2
The factor of radiation	= 0.7
Black body radiation corresponding to 1250°C	= 30.00 kcal/cm²/hr
Area of opening	= 80 cm × 80 cm
	= 6400 cm²
Emissivity	= 0.8

Total heat loss through opening:

= Black body radiation × Area of opening × Factor of radiation × Emissivity

= 30 × 6400 × 0.7 × 0.8

= 1,07,520 kcal/hr

Equivalent oil loss = 1075200/10,200

= 10.54 kg/hr

Problem 5.5:

A chemical industry needs saturated steam at 5 kg/cm² (g) and 10 kg/cm² (g) pressure level for process heating. A fluidized bed boiler generates steam at 22 kg/cm² (g) pressure at the rate of 22 TPH. About 4 TPH of steam is reduced through PRDS for meeting the 10 kg/cm² (g) pressure steam requirement. The balance steam is passed through a back pressure stream turbine. The turbine back pressure steam at 5 kg/cm² (g) is sent to process in the plant.

Total steam flow rate	= 18,000 kg/hr
Efficiency of steam turbine	= 40%
Efficiency of alternator	= 93%
Losses in gear transmission	= 3%

Find out the power output of the alternator in kW.

Solution:

Step 1:

Total heat of steam at turbine inlet conditions at 22 kg/cm^2 and 280°C, h_1 = 708 kcal/kg.

Step 2:

Total heat of steam at turbine outlet conditions at 5 kg/cm^2 and 159°C, h_2 = 658 kcal/kg.

Step 3:

Enthalpy drop across the turbine per kg of inlet steam $(h_1 - h_2)$ = (708 − 658) = 50 kcal/kg.

Step 4:

Total steam flow rate through turbine	= 18000 kg/hr
Total enthalpy drop across the turbine	= 18000 × 50
	= 900,000 kcal/hr

Step 5:

Efficiency of steam turbine	= 40%
Efficiency of alternator	= 93%
% losses in gear transmission	= 3% (i.e. efficiency = 97%)
Overall efficiency of the turbo alternator	= 0.40 × 0.93 × 0.97
	= 0.36 = 36%

Overall efficiency of the turbo alternator $= \dfrac{\text{Energy output}}{\text{Energy input}} \times 100$

Energy output of turbine $= \dfrac{36 \times 900000}{100}$

= 324000 kcal/hr

Power output of the alternator in kW $= \dfrac{324000}{860}$ = **376.7 kW**

Problem 5.6:

A gas turbine was running with naphtha as a fuel. The following are the data collected during the gas turbine operation:

Fuel (Naphtha) consumption	= 180 kg/hr
GCV of naphtha fuel	= 11500 kcal/kg
Overall efficiency of gas turbine which includes air compressor and alternator	= 30%
Cost of naphtha fuel	= ₹ 15000/Ton

Find out the cost of generating one unit of electricity.

Solution:

Heat input to turbine	= 11500 × 180
	= 2070000 kcal/hr

Efficiency of gas turbine	=	30%
Gas turbine output	=	$\dfrac{2070000 \times 0.3}{860}$
	=	722 kWh
Cost of generating 722 units of electricity	=	180 kg × ₹ 15
	=	₹ 2700
Cost of one unit of electricity generation	=	2700/722
	=	**₹ 3.74**

Problem 5.7:

A counter flow liquid-to-liquid, shell and tube heat exchanger is provided for diesel generating set system. Lubricating oil of the DG set is cooled by cooling water from cooling tower operation. Determine the heat exchanger performance such as capacity ratio, effectiveness and overall heat transfer co-efficient with the following data:

Inlet lubricating oil flow rate	=	4000 kg/hr
Inlet lubricating oil temperature	=	90°C
Outlet lubricating oil temperature	=	80°C
Cooling water inlet flow rate	=	7600 kg/hr
Cooling water inlet temperature	=	30°C
Cooling water outlet temperature	=	35°C
Heat transfer area	=	250 m^2

Solution:

1. Heat duty

$$\text{Heat duty in hot fluid} = M \times C_{ph} \times \Delta T = 4000 \times 4.187 \times (90 - 80)$$

$$= 167480 \text{ kJ/hr} = \frac{167480}{860 \times 4.187} = 46.51 \text{ kW}$$

$$\text{Heat duty in cold fluid} = m \times C_{pc} \times \Delta T = 7600 \times 4.187 \times (35 - 30)$$

$$= 159106 \text{ kJ/hr} = \frac{159106}{860 \times 4.187} = 44.19 \text{ kW}$$

2. Temperature range hot fluid

$$\text{Temperature range} = \Delta T = T_i - T_o = 90 - 80 = 10°C$$

3. Temperature range cold fluid

$$\text{Temperature range} = \Delta t = t_o - t_i = 35 - 30 = 5°C$$

4. Capacity ratio, R

$$\text{Capacity ratio, R} = \frac{T_i - T_o}{t_o - t_i} = \frac{90 - 80}{35 - 30} = 2$$

5. Effectiveness, S

$$\text{Effectiveness, S} = \frac{t_o - t_i}{T_i - t_i} = \frac{35 - 30}{90 - 30} = 0.08$$

6. LMTD

(a)   LMTD, Counter flow $= \dfrac{(T_i - t_o)\,(T_o - t_i)}{\ln\left(\dfrac{T_i - t_o}{T_o - t_i}\right)} = \dfrac{(90 - 35) - (80 - 30)}{\ln\left(\dfrac{90 - 35}{80 - 30}\right)} = 53$

7. Overall heat transfer co-efficient

$$U = \frac{Q}{A \times LMTD} = \frac{46.51}{250 \times 53} = 0.035 \ kW/m^2 k$$

Problem 5.8:

Hot effluent having a flow rate of 1450 kg/hr at 80°C from the process is sent to a counter flow heat exchanger for recovery of heat through hot water generation. The outlet temperature of effluent in the heat exchanger is 38°C. The cold water having a flow rate of 2970 kg/hr enters the heat exchanger at 30°C and leaves at 50°C. Find out the capacity ratio, effectiveness and overall heat transfer coefficient.

Solution:

1. Heat duty:

$$\text{Heat duty in hot fluid} = M \times C_{ph} \times \Delta T = 1450 \times 4.187 \times (80 - 38)$$

$$= 254988.3 \ kJ/hr = \frac{254988.3}{860 \times 4.187} = 70.81 \ kW$$

$$\text{Heat duty in cold fluid} = m \times C_{pe} \times \Delta t = 2970 \times 4.187 \times (50 - 30)$$

$$= 248707.8 \ kJ/hr = \frac{248707.8}{860 \times 4.187} = 69.07 \ kW$$

2. Temperature range hot fluid:

$$\text{Temperature range, } \Delta T = T_i - T_o = 80 - 38 = 42°C$$

3. Temperature range cold fluid:

$$\text{Temperature range, } \Delta t = t_o - t_i = 50 - 30 = 20°C$$

4. Capacity ratio:

$$\text{Capacity ratio, } R = \frac{T_i - T_o}{t_o - t_i} = \frac{80 - 38}{50 - 30} = 2.1$$

5. Effectiveness:

$$S = \frac{t_o - t_i}{T_i - ti} = \frac{50 - 30}{80 - 30} = 0.4$$

6. LMTD:

$$\text{LMTD, counter flow} = \frac{(T_i - t_o) - (T_o - t_1)}{\ln\left(\dfrac{T_i - t_o}{T_o - t_i}\right)} = \frac{(80 - 50) - (38 - 30)}{\ln\left(\dfrac{80 - 50}{38 - 30}\right)} = 16.64$$

7. Overall heat transfer co-efficient:

$$U = \frac{Q}{A \times LMTD} = \frac{70.81}{250 \times 16.64} = 0.02 \ kW/m^2 k$$

Problem 5.9:

A motor loading survey was carried out in pumping system. The name plate details of the motor are collected as shown below:

$$\text{Rated power} = 10 \text{ kW}$$
$$\text{Voltage} = 415 \text{ V}$$
$$\text{Current} = 15 \text{ A}$$
$$\text{Speed} = 1440 \text{ rpm}$$
$$\text{Efficiency} = 90\%$$

The operating parameters such as voltage, current and power factor were measured with meter as given below:

$$\text{Operating voltage} = 415 \text{ V}$$
$$\text{Operating current} = 10 \text{ A}$$
$$\text{Operating power factor} = 0.75$$

Find out the motor operating load.

Solution: Step I: Find out the rated input power of the motor.

$$\text{Rated power output} = 10 \text{ kW}$$
$$\text{Rated efficiency of the motor} = 90\%$$
$$\text{Rated power input} = \frac{10}{0.9} = 11.11 \text{ kW}$$

Step II: Find out the actual input power during operation.

$$\text{Actual power drawn} = \sqrt{3} \times V \times I \times \cos \phi$$
$$= 1.732 \times 0.415 \times 10 \times 0.7$$
$$= 5.39 \text{ kW}$$

Step III: Calculate % motor loading

$$\% \text{ motor loading} = \frac{\text{Actual load}}{\text{Rated load}} \times 100$$
$$= \frac{5.39 \times 100}{11.11}$$

$$\text{Motor loading} = \textbf{48.5\%}$$

Problem 5.10:

An industrial fan is directly coupled with an induction motor of rated capacity 30 kW and full load rated speed of 1440 rpm. The fan is running 3 shift (8 hrs/shift) per day continuously. The % flow during three shifts and power drawn are given below. The damper is manually operated to achieve the part load operation.

	% Flow	Power Consumed
I. Shift	100%	32 kW
II. Shift	50%	26 kW
III. Shift	50%	26 kW

Estimate the electrical energy saving potential per day if the fan is controlled with variable speed driven (VSD) instead of throttling the damper.

Solution:

Step I: Power consumption with damper control.

	Operating hours	Power consumed	Power × Operating hours	Energy consumed
I. Shift	8 hrs	32 kW	32 × 8	256
II. Shift	8 hrs	26 kW	26 × 8	208
III. Shift	8 hrs	26 kW	26 × 8	208
Total energy consumption per day				**672**

Step II: If flow is reduced to 50%, the speed has to be reduced to 50% i.e. 1440 rpm will have to run at 720 rpm. The new power at 720 rpm will be full flow power $\times \left(\dfrac{1440}{720}\right)^3$

$= \dfrac{32}{8} = 4$ kW.

Step III: Power consumption with VSD control.

	Operating hours	Power consumed	Power × Operating hours	Energy consumed
I. Shift	8 hrs	32 kW	32 × 8	256
II. Shift	8 hrs	4 kW	4 × 8	32
III. Shift	8 hrs	4 kW	4 × 8	32
Total energy consumption per day				**320**

Energy saving potential per day = 672 – 320 = 352 kWh/day.

Problem 5.11:

The following are the details of fume extraction fan. A test was conducted to determine the fan static efficiency.

Name plate rating:

$$\text{Flow} = 5,00,000 \ \text{m}^3/\text{hr}$$

$$\text{Static pressure} = 53 \ \text{mm WC}$$

The test results of the fan are given below:

$$\text{Damper opening} = 80\%$$
$$\text{Ambient temperature} = 40°C$$
$$\text{Density of air at } 0°C = 1.293 \text{ kg/m}^3$$
$$\text{Velocity pressure} = 15 \text{ mm WC}$$
$$\text{Pilot tube constant} = 0.85$$
$$\text{Static pressure at inlet} = 10 \text{ mm WC}$$
$$\text{Static pressure at outlet} = 30 \text{ mm WC}$$
$$\text{Diameter of duct} = 3.5 \text{ m}$$
$$\text{Motor power drawn} = 106 \text{ kW}$$
$$\text{Motor efficiency} = 90\%$$

Find out the fan static efficiency.

Solution:

(a) $\dfrac{\text{Gas density}}{\text{(Corrected to NTP)}} = \dfrac{273 \times 1.293}{273 + T°C}$ (at site condition)

$$= \dfrac{273 \times 1.293}{273 + 40°C} \text{ (at site condition)}$$

$$= 1.13 \text{ kg/m}^3$$

(b) $\text{Volume} = \dfrac{C_p \times A \times \sqrt{2 \times 9.81 \times \Delta P \times \gamma}}{1.15}$

where, $C_p = $ Pitot tube constant $= 0.85$

$$A = \text{Area of duct in m}^2 = \dfrac{\pi \times (3.5)^2}{4} = 9.62 \text{ m}^2$$

$$\Delta P = \text{Average velocity pressure} = 15 \text{ mm WC}$$

$$\gamma = \text{Density at test condition, } 1.13 \text{ kg/m}^3$$

$$\text{Volume} = \dfrac{0.85 \times 9.62 \times \sqrt{2 \times 9.81 \times 1.5 \times 1.13}}{1.15} = 130 \text{ m}^3/\text{sec}$$

(d) $P = $ Power input to the fan shaft

     $= $ Power input to the motor (kW) $\times$ Efficiency of motor (%) at the operating load $\times$ Transmission efficiency

$$= 106 \times 0.9 \times 1$$

$$= 95.4 \text{ kW}$$

(e) $\text{Static fan efficiency \%} = \dfrac{\text{Volume in m}^3/\text{sec} \times \text{Total static pressure in mmWC}}{102 \times \text{Power input to the shaft in (kW)}}$

where, 102 is a conversion constant.

$$\text{Total static pressure, mmWC} \atop (\Delta P_{Static}, \text{ across the fan})} = 30 - (-10) = 40\text{mmWC}$$

$$\text{Static fan efficiency} = \frac{130 \times 40}{102 \times 95.4} \times 100 = 53\%$$

Problem 5.12:

In an air conditioning duct 0.5 m × 0.5 m, the average velocity of air measured by vane anemometer is 28 m/s. The static pressure at inlet of the fan is 20 mm WC and at the outlet is 30 mmWC. The motor draws 10.8 A at 415 V and power factor of 0.9. Find out the efficiency of the fan if motor efficiency = 90% (Neglect density correction).

Solution:

Volume flow rate of the fan, Q = Velocity × Area

$$= 28 \times (0.5 \times 0.5)$$

$$= 7 \text{ m}^3/\text{s}$$

Power input to the fan shaft = Motor input power × Motor efficiency

$$= \left(\sqrt{3} \times 0.415 \times 10.8 \times 0.9\right) \times 0.9$$

$$= \textbf{6.3 kW}$$

$$\text{Fan efficiency} = \frac{\text{Volume in m}^3/\text{sec} \times \text{Total pressure in mmWC}}{102 \times \text{Power input to the shaft in (kW)}}$$

$$= \frac{7 \times (30 - (-20))}{102 \times 6.3} \times 100$$

Fan efficiency = 54.5%

Problem 5.13:

Water is pumped to an overhead tank in an industry for general and drinking purpose daily. The following are the details of the pumping system. Find out the operating efficiency of the pump.

Suction head	= 2 m below the pump level
Height of the overhead tank from pump center line	= 40 m
Overhead tank dimensions	= 5 m × 4 m
Tank level difference during test period	= 2 m
Time taken for filling up to 2 m level in the tank	= 30 minutes
Density of water	= 1000 kg/m^3
Motor efficiency	= 90%
Power drawn by the motor	= 14.3 kW

Find out the efficiency of the pump.

Solution:

Pump efficiency	$= \dfrac{\text{Hydraulic power, } P_h \times 100}{\text{Pump shaft power}}$
Hydraulic power, P_h(kW)	$= Q(\text{m}^3/\text{s}) \times$ Total head, $(h_d - h_s)$ (m) $\times \rho(\text{kg/m}^3) \times g(\text{m/s}^2)/1000$

where,

Q = Volume flow rate, ρ = Density of the fluid,

g = Acceleration due to gravity

Time taken to fill 40 m^3 (5 m $\times$ 4 m $\times$ 2 m)	= 30 minutes
Volume flow rate, Q	= 40/30 m^3/min
	= 0.022 m^3/sec
Total head, $(h_d - h_s)$	= 40 $-$ ($-$ 2) = 42 m
Hydraulic power	$= \dfrac{0.022 \times 42 \times 1000 \times 9.81}{1000}$
	= 9.06 kW
Pump shaft power	= Motor input power $\times$ Motor efficiency
	= 14.3 $\times$ 0.9
Pump shaft power	= 12.87 kW
Pump efficiency	$= \dfrac{\text{Hydraulic power}}{\text{Pump shaft power}} \times 100$
	$= \dfrac{9.06 \times 10}{12.87}$
Pump efficiency	**= 70.4%**

Problem 5.14:

A process in a plant needs a water flow of 180 m^3/hr for cooling. The pump supplier has two pumps (Pumps A and B) that can be supplied to the user. The details of the pump are given below:

Pump A:

Flow rate = 300 m^3/hr

Heat required in the system with throttling = 30 m

Efficiency of the pump under throttling condition = 60%

Pump B:

Flow rate = 180 m^3/hr

System head for 180 m^3/hr flow without throttling = 20 m

Efficiency of the pump at this operating point = 70%.

1. Assuming motor efficiency to be 90%, density of water as 1000 kg/m^3 in both the cases, find out the difference in power consumption between pump A and pump B.

2. What are the two parameters which are responsible for difference in power consumption between two pumps.

Solution:

Hydraulic power, P_h(kW) $= Q(m^3/s) \times$ Total head, $(h_d - h_s)$ (m) $\times \rho(kg/m^3) \times g(m/s^2)/1000$

where,

Q = Volume flow rate, ρ = Density of the fluid,

g = Acceleration due to gravity

Pump A:

Hydraulic power $= \dfrac{0.05 \times 30 \times 1000 \times 9.81}{1000}$

$= 14.7$ kW

Pump shaft power $= \dfrac{\text{Hydraulic power}}{\text{Pump efficiency}}$

$= 14.7/0.6$

$= 24.5$ kW

Motor input power $= \dfrac{\text{Pump shaft power}}{\text{Motor efficiency}}$

$= \dfrac{24.5}{0.9}$

Motor input power for pump A $= $ **27.2 kW**

Pump B:

Hydraulic power $= \dfrac{0.05 \times 20 \times 1000 \times 9.81}{1000}$

$= 9.81$ kW

Pump shaft power $= \dfrac{\text{Hydraulic power}}{\text{Pump efficiency}}$

$= \dfrac{9.81}{0.7}$

$= 14$ kW

Motor input power $= \dfrac{\text{Power shaft power}}{\text{Motor efficiency}} = \dfrac{14}{0.9}$

Motor input power for pump B $= $ **15.6 kW**

Difference in power consumption $= 27.2 - 15.6$

1. Difference in power consumption $= $ **11.6 kW**

2. The two parameters which are responsible for increased power consumption in pump A than pump B are throttling done in pump A and the other is the efficiency of the pump which is higher for pump B then pump A.

Problem 5.15:

A reciprocating compressor of 600 cfm (1014 m³/hr) capacity was tested with nozzle method to find out the FAD. The details of the test are given below:

$$\text{Receiver pressure, } P_2 = 6 \text{ kg/cm}^2 \text{ (g)}$$
$$\text{Inlet air pressure, } P_1 = 1.04 \text{ kg/cm}^2 \text{ (a)}$$
$$\text{Inlet air temperature, } T_1 = 33°C$$
$$\text{Pressure before nozzle, } P_3 = 1 \text{ kg/cm}^2 \text{ (g)}$$
$$\text{Temperature before the nozzle, } T_3 = 44°C$$

Pressure drop across the nozzle,

$$(P_3 - P_4) = 0.009 \text{ kg/cm}^2$$
$$\text{Gas constant, } R_a = 287 \text{ Joules/kg K}$$

(a) Calculate the free air delivered.

(b) Calculate the isothermal power requirement.

Solution:

$$\text{Free air delivered, } Q_f = k \times \frac{\pi}{4} \times d^2 \times \frac{T_1}{P_1} \times \left(\frac{2(P_3 - P_4)\ (P_3 \times P_a)}{T_3} \right)^{1/2}$$

$$= 1 \times \frac{\pi}{4} \times (0.08)^2 \times \frac{306}{1.04} \times \left(\frac{2(0.009)\ (2 \times 287)}{317} \right)^{1/2}$$

$$= 0.267 \text{ m}^3/\text{sec}$$

(a)   **Free air delivered, Q_f = 961 m³/hr**

$$\text{Isothermal power (kW)} = \frac{P_1 \times O_f \times \log_e r}{36.7}$$

$$\text{Compression ratio, } r = \frac{P_2}{P_1}$$

$$= \frac{7}{1.04}$$

$$= 6.73$$

$$\text{Isothermal power} = \frac{1.04 \times 961 \times \log_e 6.73}{36.7}$$

(b)   **Isothermal power = 52 kW**

Problem 5.16:

A pump up test was conducted in a screw compressor of 850 m³/hr capacity to access the actual free air delivered. The following are the test results.

Atmospheric pressure, P_0	= 1.04 kg/cm² (a)
Atmospheric temperature	= 35°C
Receiver volume	= 9 m³

Volume of connecting pipe from compressor to receiver　　　$= 0.84 \text{ m}^3$

Initial receiver pressure, P_1　　　$= 1 \text{ kg/cm}^2 \text{ (g)}$

Final receiver pressure after pumping test, P_2　　　$= 7 \text{ kg/cm}^2 \text{ (g)}$

Time taken to fill the receiver from 1 kg/cm^2 (g) to 7 kg/cm^2 (g) = 4 minutes

Receiver air temperature after pumping test　　　$= 50\ °C$

Calculate the free air delivered (FAD).

Solution:

$$\text{Free air delivered} = \frac{P_2 - P_1}{P_0} \times \frac{V}{T} \text{ m}^3/\text{min}$$

$$\text{Total volume, } V = 9 + 0.84$$

$$= 9.84 \text{ m}^3$$

$$\text{FAD} = \frac{6}{1.04} \times \frac{9.84}{4}$$

$$= 14.19 \text{ m}^3/\text{min}$$

$$= 851 \text{ m}^3/\text{hr}$$

$$\text{Corrected FAD} = 851 \times \left(\frac{273 + 35}{273 + 50}\right)$$

Corrected FAD $= 811 \text{ m}^3/\text{hr}$

Problem 5.17:

The following is the schematic diagram of the HVAC system.

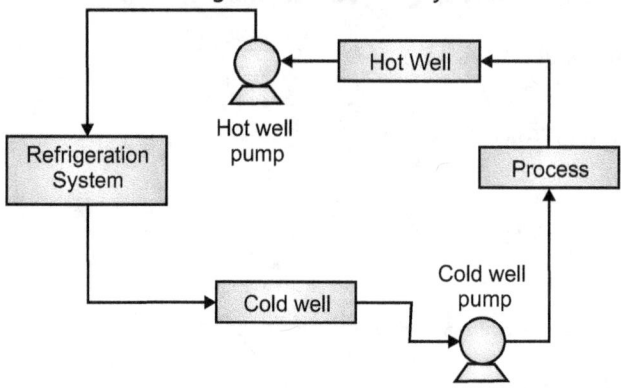

Fig. 5.12

Test data:

$$\text{Hot well temperature} = 11°C$$

$$\text{Cold well temperature} = 5°C$$

$$\text{Cold well tank dimensions} = 3 \text{ m} \times 2 \text{ m}$$

Flow rate was measured by switching off the cold well pump, running the hot well pump and by measurement of tank level difference in the cold well. Time taken for level rise of 1 m in cold well = 10 minutes. Current drawn by the motor is measured as 131 A, at a voltage of 0.415 kV and power factor of 0.9. Find out the kW/TR, COP and EER.

Solution:

$$\text{Flow delivered by the pump in 10 minutes} = 3 \times 2 \times 1$$

$$= 6 \text{ m}^3$$

$$\text{Flow rate, m} = \frac{6}{10} \text{ m}^3/\text{min}$$

$$= 36 \text{ m}^3/\text{hr}$$

$$\text{m} = 36000 \text{ kg/hr}$$

$$\text{Net refrigeration capacity (TR)} = \frac{\text{m} \times C_p \times (t_{in} - t_{out})}{3024}$$

$$= \frac{36000 \times 1 \times (11 - 5)}{3024}$$

$$\text{Net refrigeration capacity kW/ton rating} = 71.4 \text{ TR}$$

$$= \frac{\text{Measured compressor power, kW}}{\text{Net refrigeration capacity (TR)}}$$

$$\text{Compressor power} = \sqrt{3} \times 0.415 \times 131 \times 0.9$$

$$= 84.7 \text{ kW}$$

$$\text{kW/ton rating} = \frac{84.7}{71.4}$$

$$\textbf{kW/ton rating} = \textbf{1.2 kW/TR}$$

$$\text{COP} = \frac{3.516}{\text{kW/TR}}$$

$$= \frac{3.516}{1.2}$$

$$\textbf{COP} = \textbf{3}$$

$$\text{EER} = \frac{12}{\text{kW/TR}} = \frac{12}{1.2}$$

$$\textbf{EER} = \textbf{10.1}$$

Problem 5.18: The following are the heat loads in the process.

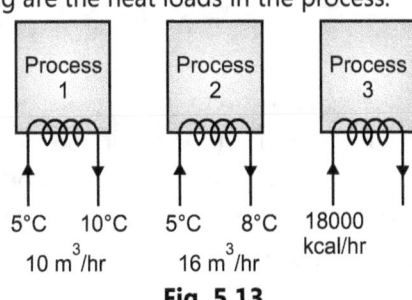

Fig. 5.13

Chilled water is used to remove these heat loads through a common refrigeration plant. The motor draws a current of 61.5 A at 440 V and 0.9 PF. Find out the kW/TR, COP and EER of the common refrigeration plant.

Solution:

$$\text{Heat load} = m \times C_p \times \text{Temperature difference}$$

$$= \{10000 \times 1 \times (10 - 5) + (16000 \times 1 \times (8 - 5)\}$$

$$+ \ 18000$$

$$\text{Total heat load} = 116000 \text{ kcal/hr}$$

$$\text{Net refrigeration capacity (TR)} = \frac{\text{Total heat load}}{3024}$$

$$= \frac{116000}{3024}$$

$$\begin{array}{l}\text{Net refrigeration capacity} \\ \text{kW/ton rating}\end{array} = 38.36 \text{ TR}$$

$$= \frac{\text{Measured compressor power, kW}}{\text{Net refrigeration capacity (TR)}}$$

$$\text{Compressor power consumption} = \sqrt{3} \times 0.415 \times 61.5 \times 0.9$$

$$= 39.7 \text{ kW}$$

$$\text{kW/ton rating} = \frac{39.7}{38.36}$$

$$\text{kW/ton rating} = 1.03 \text{ kW/TR}$$

$$\text{COP} = \frac{3.516}{\text{kW/TR}} = \frac{3.516}{1.03}$$

$$\textbf{COP = 3.4}$$

$$\text{EER} = \frac{12}{\text{kW/TR}} = \frac{12}{1.03}$$

$$\textbf{EER = 11.6}$$

Problem 5.19:

The dimension of an office hall is 12 m × 7 m. The lamp is located at a height of 3 metres from ground level. The total electrical circuit watt for the office hall is 1600 watts. The average lux level measured in the room is 650 lux. The office works for 8 hours a day for 300 days a year. Calculate the energy saving potential per annum. Other relevant data required for calculation can be taken from the book.

Solution:

Step 1:

Floor area of the interior: $\qquad = 12 \times 7 = 84 \text{ m}^2$

Step 2:

Room Index (RI) $\qquad = \dfrac{L \times W}{H_m \, (L + W)}$

H_m (the mounting height, which is the height of the $\quad = \quad 3 - 0.75$

lighting fittings above the horizontal working plane.

The working plane is assumed as 0.75 m above the

floor in offices)

$$RI = 2.25 \text{ m}$$

$$= \dfrac{12 \times 7}{2.25 \, (12 + 7)}$$

Room Index (RI) $\qquad = 1.96$

Step 3:

Total circuit watts of the installation $\qquad = 1600 \text{ W}$

Step 4:

Watts per m^3 $\qquad = \dfrac{1600}{84}$

Watts per m^2 $\qquad = 19.04 \text{ W/m}^2$

Step 5:

Average lux level measured $\qquad = 650 \text{ lux}$

Step 6:

Actual lux per watt/m^2 $\qquad = \dfrac{650}{19.04}$

$$= 34.13 \text{ lux/W/m}^2$$

Step 7:

Target lux/W/m^2 lux for type of the office
application and RI of 1.96 $\qquad = 46 \text{ lux/W/m}^2$

Step 8: Installed Load Efficiency Ratio (ILER) $= \dfrac{34.13}{46}$

　　ILER　　　　　　　　　　　　　= **0.74**

　　Annual energy wastage　　　　= 0.74

　　　　　　　　　　　　　　　　= (1 – ILER) × watts × No. of operating hours

　　　　　　　　　　　　　　　　= (1 – 0.74) × 1600 × 8 hrs/day × 300 days

　　　　　　　　　　　　　　　　= 998400 watts

　　　　　　　　　　　　　　　　= 998400/1000 kWh/year

　　Energy saving potential　　　= **998 kWh/year**

Practice Questions

1. What are the different kinds of discharge head ?
2. Explain the following terms:
   (i) Hydraulic pump power.
   (ii) Shaft pump power.
3. How will you determine the pump efficiency?
4. What are the different types of heat exchangers?
5. Explain monitoring and maintenance of plate and tabular heat exchanger.
6. What do you mean by fouling?
7. Explain methodology of heat exchanger performance assessment.

MSBTE Questions and Answers (As Per 'E' Scheme)

Summer 2012

1. What are the different modes of heart transfer? Explain which mode of heat transfer is used to generate steam in boiler.

Ans. Please refer to Section 5.2.1.

2. Give equations to calculate LMTD in heat exchanger for parallel and counter flow.

Ans. Please refer to Section 5.2.2.

Winter 2013

1. Explain with neat sketch constructional features of water pump.

Ans. Please refer to Section 5.1.

2. The flow rates of hot and cold water streams running through a parallel-flow heat exchanger are 0.2 kg/s and 0.5 kg/s respectively. The inlet temperature on the hot and cold sides are 75ºC and 20ºC respectively. The exit temperature of hot water is 45ºC. If the individual heart transfer coefficents on both sides are 65- W/m^2 ºC. Calculate the area of the heat exchanger.

3. Explain shell and tube type heat exchangers in brief.

Ans. Please refer to Section 5.2.1.

4. How are heat exchanger classified? give one example of each.

Ans. Please refer to Section 5.2.1.

Chapter 6

NON-CONVENTIONAL ENERGY SOURCES

Objectives

Students will study and understand the following:

- Describe method of generating electricity by solar thermal energy
- Calculate power available in wind
- Compare conventional and non-conventional energy on given point

6.1 INTRODUCTION (S-12)

- **Renewable energy** is energy generated from natural resources - such as sunlight, wind, rain, tides and geothermal heat - which are renewable (naturally replenished).

- Renewable energy technologies range from solar power, wind power, hydroelectricity/micro hydro, biomass and biofuels for transportation.

- In 2006, about 18% of global final energy consumption came from renewables, with 13% coming from traditional biomass, such as wood-burning. Hydropower was the next largest renewable source, providing 3%, followed by hot water/heating, which contributed 1.3%.

- Modern technologies, such as geothermal, wind, solar, and ocean energy together provided some 0.8% of final energy consumption.

- The technical potential for their use is very large, exceeding all other readily available sources.

- India is blessed with a variety of renewable energy sources, the main ones being biomass, biogas, the sun, wind, and small hydro power. (Large hydro power is also renewable in nature, but has been utilized all over the world for many decades, and is generally not included in the term 'new and renewable sources of energy'.)

- Municipal and industrial wastes can also be useful sources of energy, but are basically different forms of biomass.

- Advantages of renewable energy are that it is
  - o perennial,
  - o available locally and does not need elaborate arrangements for transport,

- o usually modular in nature, i.e. small-scale units and systems can be almost as economical as large-scale ones,
- o environment-friendly,
- o well suited for decentralized applications and use in remote areas.
- The Ministry of Non-Conventional Energy Sources has been implementing comprehensive programmes for the development and utilization of various renewable energy sources in the country.
- As a result of efforts made during the past quarter century, a number of technologies and devices have been developed and have become commercially available.
- These include biogas plants, improved wood stoves, solar water heaters, solar cookers, solar lanterns, street lights, pumps, wind electric generators, water-pumping wind mills, biomass gasifiers, and small hydro-electric generators.
- Energy technologies for the future such as hydrogen, fuel cells, and bio-fuels are being actively developed. India is implementing one of the world's largest programmes in renewable energy.
- The country ranks second in the world in biogas utilization and fifth in wind power and photovoltaic production.
- Renewable sources already contribute to about 5% of the total power generating capacity in the country.
- The major renewable energy sources and devices in use in India are listed in Table 6.1 along with their potential and present status in terms of the number of installations or total capacity.

Table 6.1: Renewable Energy in India at a Glance

Source/System	Estimated potential	Cumulative installed capacity/number*
Wind power	45,000 MW	3595 MW
Biomass power	16000 MW	302.53 MW
Bagasse cogeneration	3500 MW	447.00 MW
Small hydro (upto 25 MW)	15000 MW	1705.63 MW
Waste to energy		
• Municipal solid waste	1700 MW	17 MW
• Industrial waste	1000 MW	29.50 MW
Family-size biogas plants	12 million	3.71 million
Improved chulhas	120 million	35.20 million
Solar street lighting systems	–	54795

Contd...

Home lighting systems	–	342607
Solar lanterns	–	560295
Solar photovoltaic power plants	–	1566 kWp
Solar water heating systems	140 million m^2 of collector area	1 million m^2 of collector area
Box-type solar cookers	–	575000
Solar photovoltaic pumps	–	6818
Wind pumps	–	1087
Biomass gasifiers	–	66.35 MW
* as on 31st March 2005.		

6.2 SOLAR ENERGY   (W-13)

Solar Power:

- Even though most of the energy of the earth would not be present without the sun, only a few forms of power are considered to be solar power.

- In the context of renewable energy, solar power is associated with the harnessing of the sun's present emissions of heat or light.

- Solar power, besides providing heat and light, also causes the wind that we feel here on Earth.

- Winds are created when various layers of the atmosphere absorb different amounts of heat and therefore expand differently.

- This creates regions of lower and higher pressure, resulting in masses of air that circulate both at ground level and at higher altitudes.

- Solar power is also responsible for fossil fuels such as petroleum and coal. These substances are the result of large masses of decayed plant matter, which during their lifetime, absorbed solar energy.

- Fossil fuels are merely concentrated stores of the solar energy that these plants had while alive.

- Power from the sun comes to the Earth as heat and light. This heat and light are the effect of the Sun's constant nuclear fusion of hydrogen nuclei.

- The process of fusion produces helium nuclei along with large amounts of energy.

- This energy is expressed as electromagnetic radiation (light is a specific frequency range of this radiation) as well as radiated temperatures of more than 6,100 °C.

- This is actually fairly cool compared with the corona and core of the sun that burn at several million °C.

- A small fraction of these extreme levels of energy that are released by the Sun come into contact with the Earth. The average amount of energy that contacts the Earth's surface in a day is 200 W/m^2. This means that the average home has more than enough roof space to produce enough electricity to supply all of its power needs.

- In fact, each day, more energy reaches the Earth from the sun than would be consumed by the global population in 27 years.

Why is solar power renewable?

- Solar power is renewable as long as the sun keeps burning the massive amount of hydrogen it has in its core.

- Even with the sun expending 700 billion tons of hydrogen every second, it is expected to keep burning for another 4.5 billion years. Therefore, technically, solar power is not a completely renewable power source because it will be depleted in 4.5 billion years.

Are there different types of technologies associated with solar power?

- There are a variety of types of technologies associated with solar power. These technologies can be divided into two groups.

- The first groups are those that use the sun to generate heat, called solar thermal technologies.

- Solar thermal technologies include solar concentrator power systems, flat plate solar collectors, and passive solar heating.

- The other group of solar power technologies directly convert solar radiation into electricity through the photoelectric effect by using photovoltaics (also known as PV).

Solar thermal technologies:

- Concentrating solar power systems generate electricity with heat. Concentrating solar collectors use mirrors and lenses to concentrate and focus sunlight onto a receiver mounted at the system's focal point.

- The receiver absorbs and converts the sunlight into heat. This heat is then transported by means of a heated fluid (either water or molten salt) through pipes to a steam generator or engine where it is converted into electricity. Flat plate solar collectors are usually large flat boxes with one or more glass covers.

- Inside the boxes are dark coloured metal plates that absorb heat. Air or liquid, such as water, flows through the tubes and is warmed by heat stored in the plates. These systems are particularly useful for providing hot water to households and 83% of households in Israel were using solar collectors by 1994.

- As of 1992, over 4.5 million buildings in Japan were using solar hot water systems.

- Passive solar heating design methods use features such as large south-facing windows and building materials that absorb the sun's thermal energy.

- Passive solar methods can be used to greatly lower heating bills and can even be used to cool a building using natural ventilation.

- The simplest and perhaps most common of the passive solar technologies is referred to as direct solar gain.

- A direct gain system includes south-facing windows and a large mass, usually of composed of stone, brick, or concrete, placed within the space to receive the most direct sunlight in cold weather and the least direct sunlight in hot weather.

- The result is that in cold weather the large thermal mass in the room absorbs solar energy and radiates heat throughout the room.

- During warmer times, due to its strategic placement away from the windows most concentrated light, the thermal mass absorbs only the warm air already in the room. This leaves the air cooled in warmer seasons and heated in cooler seasons.

- Solar thermal technologies come in various sizes. There are small portable solar cookers that utilize a parabolic concentrating disk to cook food and boil water. There are also large centralized solar power plants, known as "power towers", that use many acres of mirrors to collect and focus the sun's power.

- This focused heat turns water into steam that is used to power a generator.

- The "Solar One" and "Solar Two" power plants, both with 10 MW capacities, are examples of these large scale solar thermal power plants.

- The "Solar Two" produces enough power for 10,000 households. Engineers hope to build larger versions in the future with capacities of 30-200 MW.

- One beneficial and not immediately apparent application of solar thermal technology is the use of sunlight to cool buildings.

- Solar thermal energy is used to cool buildings in two ways. The first is by using absorption cooling devices that run on a normal refrigerator cycle by condensing and evaporating a refrigerant fluid.

- The second method uses desiccants cooling systems, which use a drying agent to absorb water vapor, reduce humidity, and cool the air through evaporation.

How much does solar power cost?

- Currently, solar power is more expensive than other methods of producing electricity. However, utilities using fossil fuels and nuclear are able to provide a lower price, in part, because of government subsidies and incentives as well as the avoided cost of pollution control, and NO_x credits in some places.

- It is also important to remember that as supplies of fossil fuels continue to be depleted their price will increase.

- Solar technologies on the other hand will become less expensive as they evolve into more efficient forms. With solar power, alongwith some batteries for backup, one is also paying for the extra reliability with their increased resistance to the simple line failures of standard utility electricity.

- There are different parts of the whole system to consider when looking at price. There is the price per watt of the solar cell, price per watt of the module (whole panel), and the price per watt of the entire system.

- It is important to remember that all systems are unique in their quality and size, making it difficult to make broad generalizations about price. The average PV cell price was $2.01 per peak watt in 1999 and the average per peak watt cost of a module was $3.62 in the same year.

- The module price however does not include the design costs, land, support structure, batteries, an inverter, wiring, and lights/appliances. With all of these included, to buy a full system it can cost anywhere from $7 per watt to $20 per watt. So, for example, if you wanted to put in a 10 kilowatt-hour per day system in an area with on average 5 hours of sun a day, you will need a 2 kilowatt system.

- At $7 a watt it would cost about $14,000. With most average homes drawing from 1 kilowatt to 2 kilowatts, a system of this size would offset a significant portion of load during hours of maximum sunlight, maintenance free for 15-20 years.

- **Solar energy** is the heat and light radiated from the Sun that powers Earth's climate and supports life.

- Solar technologies allow controlled use of this energy resource.

- **Solar power** is a synonym of solar energy or refers specifically to the conversion of sunlight into electricity by photovoltaics, concentrating solar thermal devices and various experimental technologies.

- The controlled use of solar energy is an important consideration in building design. Thermal mass is used to conserve the heat that sunshine delivers to all buildings.

- Daylighting techniques optimize the use of light in buildings. Solar water heaters heat swimming pools and provide domestic hot water. In agriculture, greenhouses grow specialty crops and photovoltaic-powered pumps provide water for grazing animals.

- Evaporation ponds find applications in the commercial and industrial sectors where they are used to harvest salt and clean waste streams of contaminants.

- Solar distillation and disinfection techniques produce potable water for millions of people worldwide.

- Family-scale solar cookers and larger solar kitchens concentrate sunlight for cooking, drying and pasteurization. More sophisticated concentrating technologies magnify the rays of the Sun for high-temperature material testing, metal smelting and industrial chemical production.

- A range of prototype solar vehicles provide ground, air and sea transportation.

- Earth continuously receives 174 PW of incoming solar radiation (insolation) at the upper atmosphere. Approximately 30% is reflected back to space while the rest is absorbed by the atmosphere, oceans and land masses.

- After passing through the atmosphere, the insolation spectrum is mostly split between the visible and infrared ranges with a small part in the ultraviolet.

- The absorption of solar energy by atmospheric convection (sensible heat transport) and evaporation and condensation of water vapor (latent heat transport) powers the water cycle and drives the winds.

- Sunlight absorbed by the oceans and land masses keeps the surface at an average temperature of 14 °C. The conversion of solar energy into chemical energy via photosynthesis produces food, wood and the biomass from which fossil fuels are derived.

- Solar radiation along with secondary solar resources such as wind and wave power, hydroelectricity and biomass account for over 99.9% of the available flow of renewable energy on Earth.

- The flows and stores of solar energy in the environment are vast in comparison to current human energy needs.

  o The total solar energy absorbed by Earth's atmosphere, oceans and land masses is approximately 3,850 zettajoules (ZJ) per year.

  o Global wind energy at 80 m is estimated at 2.25 ZJ per year.

  o Photosynthesis captures approximately 3 ZJ per year in biomass.

  o Worldwide electricity consumption was approximately 0.0567 ZJ in 2005.

  o Worldwide primary energy consumption was 0.487 ZJ in 2005.

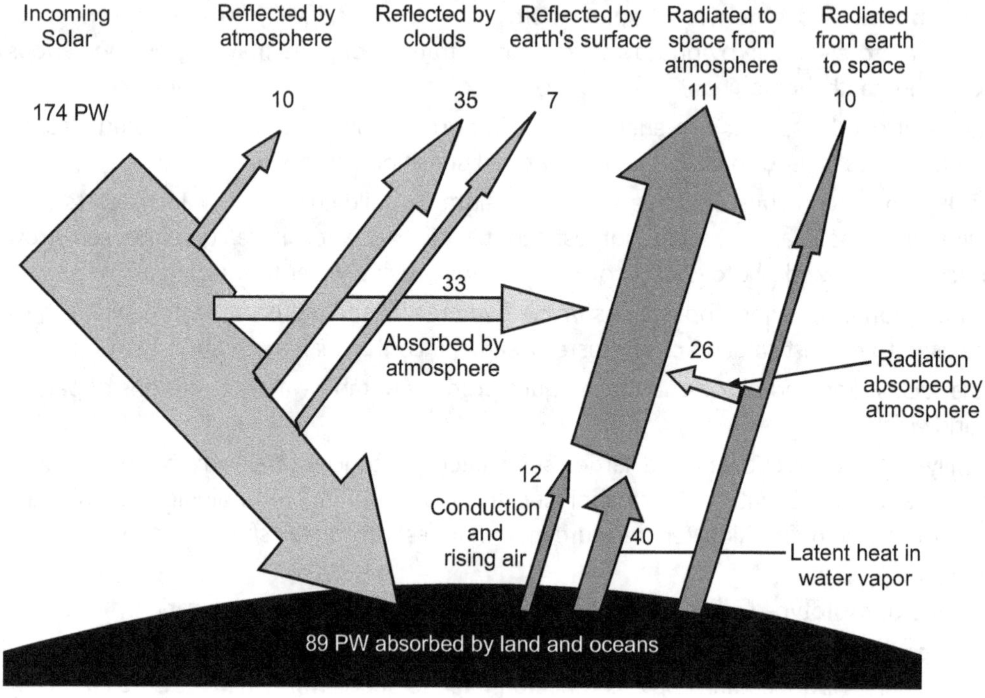

Fig. 6.1

- Solar energy technologies use solar radiation for practical ends. Technologies that use secondary solar resources such as biomass, wind, waves and ocean thermal gradients can be included in a broader description of solar energy but only primary resource applications are discussed here.

- Because the performance of solar technologies varies widely between regions, solar technologies should be deployed in a way that carefully considers these variations.
- Solar technologies such as photovoltaics and water heaters increase the supply of energy and may be characterized as supply side technologies. Technologies such as passive design and shading devices reduce the need for alternate resources and may be characterized as demand side.
- Optimizing the performance of solar technologies is often a matter of controlling the resource rather than simply maximizing its collection.

6.2.1 Architecture and Urban Planning

Fig. 6.2

- Darmstadt University of Technology won the 2007 Solar Decathlon with this passive house designed specifically for the humid and hot subtropical climate in Washington, D.C.
- Sunlight has influenced building design since the beginning of architectural history. Fully developed solar architecture and urban planning methods were first employed by the Greeks and Chinese who oriented their buildings toward the south to provide light and warmth.
- The elemental features of passive solar architecture are Sun orientation, compact proportion (a low surface area to volume ratio), selective shading (overhangs) and thermal mass.
- When these features are tailored to the local climate and environment they can produce well-lit spaces that stay in a comfortable temperature range.
- Socrates' Megaron House is a classic example of passive solar design.
- The most recent approaches to solar design use computer modeling to tie together solar lighting, heating and ventilation systems in an integrated solar design package.
- Active solar equipment such as pumps, fans and switchable windows can also complement passive design and improve system performance.
- Urban heat islands (UHI) are metropolitan areas with higher temperatures than the surrounding environment.
- These higher temperatures are the result of urban materials such as asphalt and concrete that have lower albedos and higher heat capacities than the natural environment.

- A straightforward method of counteracting the UHI effect is to paint buildings and roads white and plant trees.
- Using these methods, a hypothetical "cool communities" program in Los Angeles has projected that urban temperatures could be reduced by approximately 3°C at an estimated cost of US$1 billion, giving estimated total annual benefits of US$530 million from reduced air-conditioning costs and health care savings.

6.2.2　Agriculture and Horticulture

Fig. 6.3

- Greenhouses like these in the Netherland's Westland municipality grow a wide variety of vegetables, fruits and flowers.
- Agriculture inherently seeks to optimize the capture of solar energy, and thereby plant productivity.
- Techniques such as timed planting cycles, tailored row orientation, staggered heights between rows and the mixing of plant varieties can improve crop yields. While sunlight is generally considered a plentiful resource, there are exceptions which highlight the importance of solar energy to agriculture.
- During the short growing seasons of the Little Ice Age, French and English farmers employed fruit walls to maximize the collection of solar energy.
- These walls acted as thermal masses and accelerated ripening by keeping plants warm.
- Early fruit walls were built perpendicular to the ground with a south facing orientation but over time sloping walls were developed to make better use of sunlight.
- In 1699, Nicolas Fatio de Duillier even suggested using a tracking mechanism which could pivot to follow the Sun.
- Solar energy is also used in many areas of agriculture aside from growing crops.
- Applications include pumping water, drying crops, brooding chicks and drying chicken manure.
- Greenhouses control the use of solar heat and light to grow plants in enclosed environments, enabling year-round production and the growth of specialty crops and other plants not naturally suited to the local climate.
- Primitive greenhouses were first used during Roman times to grow cucumbers year-round for the Roman emperor Tiberius.

- The first modern greenhouses were built in Europe in the 16th century to conserve exotic plants brought back from explorations abroad.

- Greenhouses remain an important part of horticulture today, while plastic transparent materials have also been used to similar effect in polytunnels and row covers.

6.2.3 Solar Lighting

Fig. 6.4

- Daylighting features such as this oculus at the top of the Pantheon in Rome have been in use since antiquity.

- The history of lighting is dominated by the use of natural light. The Romans recognized the Right to Light as early as the 6th century and English law echoed these judgements with the Prescription Act of 1832. In the 20th century, artificial lighting became the main source of interior illumination.

- Daylighting systems collect and distribute sunlight to provide interior illumination. These systems directly offset energy use by replacing artificial lighting, and indirectly offset non-solar energy use by reducing the need for air-conditioning.

- Although difficult to quantify, the use of natural lighting also offers physiological and psychological benefits compared to artificial lighting. Daylighting design carefully selects window type, size and orientation and may also consider exterior shading devices.

- Individual features include sawtooth roofs, clerestory windows, light shelves, skylights and light tubes.

- These features may be incorporated into existing structures but are most effective when integrated in a solar design package that accounts for factors such as glare, heat flux and time-of-use.

- When daylighting features are properly implemented they can reduce commercial lighting-related energy requirements by 25%.

- Hybrid solar lighting (HSL) is an active solar method of using sunlight to provide illumination. HSL systems collect sunlight using focusing mirrors that track the Sun and use optical fibers to transmit the light into a building's interior to supplement conventional lighting.

- In single-story applications, these systems are able to transmit 50% of the direct sunlight received.

- Although daylight saving time is promoted as a way to use sunlight to save energy, recent research is limited and reports contradictory results: several studies report savings, but just as many suggest no effect or even a net loss, particularly when gasoline consumption is taken into account.
- Electricity use is greatly affected by geography, climate and economics, making it hard to generalize from single studies.

6.2.4 Solar Thermal

- Solar thermal technologies can be used for water heating, space heating, space cooling and process heat generation.

6.2.5 Water Heating

Fig. 6.5

- Solar water heaters face the equator and are angled according to latitude to maximize solar gain.
- Solar hot water systems use sunlight to heat water. When sited in low latitudes (below 40 degrees), solar heating system can provide around 60 to 70% of domestic hot water use with temperatures upto 60 °C.
- The most common types of solar water heaters are evacuated tube collectors (44%) and glazed flat plate collectors (34%) generally used for domestic hot water; and unglazed plastic collectors (21%) used mainly to heat swimming pools.
- As of 2007, the total installed capacity of solar hot water systems is approximately 154 GW. China is the world leader in the deployment of solar hot water with 70 GW installed as of 2006 and a long term goal of 210 GW by 2020.
- Israel is the per capita leader in the use of solar hot water with 90% of homes using this technology. In the United States, Canada and Australia, heating swimming pools is the dominant application of solar hot water, with an installed capacity of 18 GW as of 2005.

6.2.6 Heating, Cooling and Ventilation

Fig. 6.6

- MIT's Solar House #1, built in 1939, used seasonal thermal storage for year-round heating.

- In the United States, heating, ventilation and air conditioning (HVAC) systems account for 30% (4.65 EJ) of the energy used in commercial buildings and nearly 50% (10.1 EJ) of the energy used in residential buildings.

- Solar heating, cooling and ventilation technologies can be used to offset a portion of this energy.

- Thermal mass, in the most general sense, is any material that has the capacity to store heat. In the context of solar energy, thermal mass materials are used to store heat from the Sun.

- Common thermal mass materials include stone, cement and water. These materials have historically been used in arid climates or warm temperate regions to keep buildings cool by absorbing solar energy during the day and radiating stored heat to the cooler atmosphere at night, but they can also be used in cold temperate areas to maintain warmth.

- The size and placement of thermal mass should consider several factors such as climate, daylighting and shading conditions.

- When properly incorporated, thermal mass maintains space temperatures in a comfortable range and reduces the need for auxiliary heating and cooling equipment.

- A solar chimney (or thermal chimney) is a passive solar ventilation system composed of a vertical shaft connecting the interior and exterior of a building.

- As the chimney warms, the air inside is heated causing an updraft that pulls air through the building. Performance can be improved by using glazing and thermal mass materials in a way that mimics greenhouses.

- These systems have been in use since Roman times and remain common in the Middle East.

- Deciduous trees and plants can be used to provide heating and cooling. When planted on the southern elevation of the building, the leaves can provide shade during the summer while the bare limbs allow light and warmth to pass during the winter.

6.2.7 Desalination and Disinfection

Fig. 6.7

- A SODIS application in Indonesia demonstrates the simplicity of this approach to water disinfection.

- Solar distillation is the production of potable water from saline or brackish water using solar energy.

- The first recorded use was by 16th century Arab alchemists. The first large-scale solar distillation project was constructed in 1872 in the Chilean mining town of Las Salinas.

- This 4,700 m^2 still could produce upto 22,700 L per day and operated for 40 years. Individual still designs include single-slope, double-slope (or greenhouse type), vertical, conical, inverted absorber, multi-wick and multiple effect.

- These stills can operate in passive, active or hybrid modes. Double slope stills are the most economical for decentralized domestic purposes while active multiple effect units are more suitable to large-scale applications.

- Solar water disinfection (SODIS) is a method of disinfecting water by exposing water-filled plastic PET bottles to several hours of sunlight.

- Exposure times vary according to weather and climate from a minimum of six hours to two days during fully overcast conditions. SODIS is recommended by the World Health Organization as a viable method for household water treatment and safe storage.

- Over two million people in developing countries use SODIS for their daily drinking water needs.

6.2.8 Cooking

Fig. 6.8

- The Solar Bowl in Auroville, India, concentrates sunlight on a movable receiver to produce steam for cooking.
- Solar cookers use sunlight for cooking, drying and pasteurization. These devices can be grouped into three broad categories: box cookers, panel cookers and reflector cookers.
- The simplest type of solar cooker is the box cooker first built by Horace de Saussure in 1767. A basic box cooker consists of an insulated container with a transparent lid.
- These cookers can be used effectively with partially overcast skies and will typically reach temperatures of 90-150°C.
- Panel cookers use a reflective panel to direct sunlight onto an insulated container and reach temperatures comparable to box cookers. Reflector cookers use various concentrating geometries (dish, trough, Fresnel mirrors) to focus light on a cooking container.
- These cookers reach temperatures of 315°C and above but require direct light to function properly and must be repositioned to track the Sun.
- The solar bowl is a unique concentrating technology employed by the Solar Kitchen in Auroville, India.
- The solar bowl is a stationary spherical reflector that focuses light along a line perpendicular to the sphere's interior surface and a computer control system moves the receiver to intersect this line.
- Steam is produced in the receiver at temperatures reaching 150°C and then used for process heat in the kitchen.
- A reflector developed by Wolfgang Scheffler in 1986 is used in many solar kitchens. Scheffler reflectors are flexible parabolic dishes that combine aspects of trough and power tower concentrators.
- Polar tracking is used to follow the Sun's daily course and the curvature of the reflector is adjusted for seasonal variations in the incident angle of sunlight.
- These reflectors can reach temperatures of 450-650 °C and have a fixed focal point which improves the ease of cooking. The world's largest Scheffler reflector system in Abu Road, Rajasthan, India is capable of cooking upto 35,000 meals a day.
- As of 2008, over 2,000 large Scheffler cookers had been built worldwide.

6.2.9 Process Heat

Fig. 6.9

- STEP parabolic dishes used for steam production and electrical generation.

- Concentrating solar technologies such as parabolic dish, trough and Scheffler reflectors can provide process heat for commercial and industrial applications.

- The first commercial system was the Solar Total Energy Project (STEP) in Shenandoah, Georgia where a field of 114 parabolic dishes provided 50% of the process heating, air conditioning and electrical requirements for a clothing factory.

- This cogeneration system generated 400 kW of electricity and 3 MW of thermal energy in the form of steam, and had a thermal storage system that allowed for peak-load shaving.

- Evaporation ponds are shallow pools that concentrate dissolved solids through evaporation. The use of evaporation ponds to obtain salt from sea water is one of the oldest applications of solar energy.

- Modern uses include concentrating brine solutions used in leach mining and removing dissolved solids from waste streams.

- Clothes lines, clothes horses, and clothes' racks, dry clothes through evaporation.

- These devices use wind and sunlight instead of electricity or natural gas.

- Florida legislation specifically protects the 'right to dry' and similar solar rights legislation has been passed in Utah and Hawaii.

- Unglazed transpired collectors (UTC) are perforated sun-facing walls used for preheating ventilation air.

- UTCs can raise the incoming air temperature up to 22°C and deliver outlet temperatures of 45-60°C. The short payback period of transpired collectors (3 to 12 years) makes them a more cost-effective alternative than glazed collection systems.

- As of 2003, over 80 systems with a combined collector area of 35,000 m² had been installed worldwide, including an 860 m² collector in Costa Rica used for drying coffee beans and a 1,300 m² collector in Coimbatore, India used for drying marigolds.

6.2.10 Solar Electricity

- Sunlight can be converted into electricity using photovoltaics (PV), concentrating solar power (CSP), and various experimental technologies. PV has mainly been used to power small and medium-sized applications, from the calculator powered by a single solar cell to off-grid homes powered by a photovoltaic array.

- For large-scale generation, CSP plants like SEGS have been the norm but recently multi-megawatt PV plants are becoming common.

- Completed in 2007, the 14 MW power station in Clark County, Nevada and the 20 MW site in Beneixama, Spain are characteristic of the trend toward larger photovoltaic power stations in the US and Europe.

6.2.11 Photovoltaics

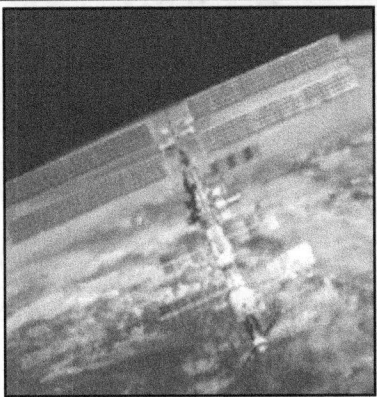

Fig. 6.10

- Solar cells power the International Space Station.

- A solar cell (or photovoltaic cell) is a device that converts light into direct current using the photoelectric effect. The first solar cell was constructed by Charles Fritts in the 1880s.

- Although the prototype selenium cells converted less than 1% of incident light into electricity, both Ernst Werner von Siemens and James Clerk Maxwell recognized the importance of this discovery.

- Following the fundamental work of Russell Ohl in the 1940s, researchers Gerald Pearson, Calvin Fuller and Daryl Chapin created the silicon solar cell in 1954. These early solar cells cost 286 USD/watt and reached efficiencies of 4.5-6%.

- The earliest significant application of solar cells was as a back-up power source to the Vanguard I satellite, which allowed the satellite to continue transmitting for over a year after its chemical battery was exhausted.

- The successful operation of solar cells on this mission was duplicated in many other Soviet and American satellites, and by the late 1960s PV had become the established source of power for satellites.

- Photovoltaics went on to play an essential part in the success of early commercial satellites such as Telstar and continue to remain vital to the telecommunications infrastructure today.

- The high cost of solar cells limited terrestrial uses throughout the 1960s. This changed in the early 1970s when prices reached levels that made PV generation competitive in remote areas without grid access.

- Early terrestrial uses included powering telecommunication stations, off-shore oil rigs, navigational buoys and railroad crossings.

- These and other off-grid applications have proven very successful and accounted for over half of worldwide installed capacity until 2004.

- Building-integrated photovoltaics cover the roofs of an increasing number of homes.

Fig. 6.11

- The 1973 oil crisis stimulated a rapid rise in the production of PV during the 1970s and early 1980s. Economies of scale which resulted from increasing production along with improvements in system performance brought the price of PV down from 100 USD/watt in 1971 to 7 USD/watt in 1985.

- Steadily falling oil prices during the early 1980s led to a reduction in funding for photovoltaic R&D and a discontinuation of the tax credits associated with the Energy Tax Act of 1978. These factors moderated growth to approximately 15% per year from 1984 through 1996.

- Since the mid-1990s, leadership in the PV sector has shifted from the US to Japan and Germany.

- Between 1992 and 1994 Japan increased R&D funding, established net metering guidelines, and introduced a subsidy program to encourage the installation of residential PV systems. As a result, PV installations in the country climbed from 31.2 MW in 1994 to 318 MW in 1999, and worldwide production growth increased to 30% in the late 1990s.

- Germany has become the leading PV market worldwide since revising its Feed-in tariff system as part of the Renewable Energy Sources Act. Installed PV capacity has risen from 100 MW in 2000 to approximately 4,150 MW at the end of 2007.

- Spain has become the third largest PV market after adopting a similar feed-in tariff structure in 2004, while France, Italy, South Korea and the US have also seen rapid growth recently due to various incentive programs and local market conditions.

6.2.12 Concentrating Solar Power

Fig. 6.12

- Dish engine systems eliminate the need to transfer heat to a boiler by placing a Stirling engine at the focal point.
- Concentrated sunlight has been used to perform useful tasks since the time of ancient China. A legend claims Archimedes used polished shields to concentrate sunlight on the invading Roman fleet and repel them from Syracuse.
- In 1866, Auguste Mouchout used a parabolic trough to produce steam for the first solar steam engine, and subsequent developments led to the use of concentrating solar-powered devices for irrigation, refrigeration and locomotion.
- Concentrating Solar Power (CSP) systems use lenses or mirrors and tracking systems to focus a large area of sunlight into a small beam.
- The concentrated light is then used as a heat source for a conventional power plant. A wide range of concentrating technologies exist; the most developed are the solar trough, parabolic dish and solar power tower.
- These methods vary in the way they track the Sun and focus light.
- In all these systems, a working fluid is heated by the concentrated sunlight, and is then used for power generation or energy storage.

Fig. 6.13

- The PS10 concentrates sunlight from a field of heliostats on a central tower.

Fig. 6.14

- A solar trough consists of a linear parabolic reflector that concentrates light onto a receiver positioned along the reflector's focal line.
- The reflector is made to follow the Sun during the daylight hours by tracking along a single axis.
- Trough systems are the most mature CSP technology. The SEGS plants in California and Acciona's Nevada Solar One near Boulder City, Nevada are representatives of this technology.

- A parabolic dish system consists of a stand-alone parabolic reflector that concentrates light onto a receiver positioned at the reflector's focal point. The reflector tracks the Sun along two axes.

- Parabolic dish systems give the highest efficiency among CSP technologies. The 50 kW Big Dish in Canberra, Australia is an example of this technology.

- A solar power tower uses an array of tracking reflectors (heliostats) to concentrate light on a central receiver atop a tower.

- Power towers are less advanced than trough systems but offer higher efficiency and better energy storage capability.

- The Solar Two in Barstow, California and the Planta Solar 10 in Sanlucar la Mayor, Spain are representatives of this technology.

6.3 WIND ENERGY (W-13)

Wind Power:

Wind power has many benefits that make it an attractive source of power for both utility-scale and small, distributed power generation applications. The beneficial characteristics of wind power include:

- **Clean and inexhaustible fuel:** Wind power produces no emissions and is not depleted over time. A single one megawatt (1 MW) wind turbine running for one year can displace over 1,500 tons of carbon dioxide, 6.5 tons of sulfur dioxide, 3.2 tons of nitrogen oxides and 60 pounds of mercury (based on the U.S. average utility generation fuel mix).

- **Local economic development:** Wind plants can provide a steady flow of income to landowners who lease their land for wind development, while increasing property tax revenues for local communities.

- **Modular and scalable technology:** Wind applications can take many forms, including large wind farms, distributed generation, and single end-use systems. Utilities can use wind resources strategically to help reduce load forecasting risks and stranded costs.

- **Energy price stability:** By further diversifying the energy mix, wind energy reduces dependence on conventional fuels that are subject to price and supply volatility.

- **Reduced reliance on imported fuels:** Wind energy expenditures are not used to obtain fuels from abroad, keeping funds closer to home, and lessening dependence on foreign governments that supply these fuels.

Resources and Technology:

- This section explains where wind comes from and how it is harnessed to produce electricity. Because wind power technology has been treated extensively elsewhere, this paper does not go into great technical detail.

- For detailed technical information see, for example, the web sites of the Danish Wind Industry Association (www.windpower.org) and the U.S.
- Department of Energy's National Wind Technology Center (www.nrel.gov/wind), as well as the Wind Energy Technical Information page of the American Wind Energy Association's web site (www.awea.org/faq).

Source of Wind Energy:

- Wind energy, like most terrestrial energy sources, comes from solar energy. Solar radiation emitted by the sun travels through space and strikes the Earth, causing regions of unequal heating over land masses and oceans.
- This unequal heating produces regions of high and low pressure, creating pressure gradients between these regions. The second law of thermodynamics requires that these gradients be minimized, nature seeks the lowest energy state in order to maximize entropy.
- This is accomplished by the movement of air from regions of high pressure to regions of low pressure, what we know as wind.
- Large scale winds are caused by the fact that the earth's surface is heated to a greater degree at the equator than at the poles.
- Prevailing winds combine with local factors, such as the presence of hills, mountains, trees, buildings and bodies of water, to determine the particular characteristics of the wind in a specific location. Because air has mass, moving air in the form of wind carries with it kinetic energy.
- A wind turbine converts this kinetic energy into electricity. The energy content of a particular volume of wind is proportional to the square of its velocity.
- Thus, a doubling of the speed with which this volume of air passes through a wind turbine will result in roughly a fourfold increase in power that can be extracted from this air.
- In addition, this doubling of wind speed will allow twice the volume of air to pass through the turbine in a given amount of time, resulting in an eightfold increase in power generated.
- This means that only a slight increase in wind velocity can yield significant gains in power production.

$E_k = \dfrac{1}{2} \cdot m \cdot v^2$	$P \sim v^3$
The amount of kinetic energy in an air mass (E_k) is equal to half the product of its mass (m) and the square of its velocity (v).	The amount of power (P) exerted by the wind is proportional to the cube of its velocity (v).

and 100 meters (131 and 328 feet) tall. A utility-scale wind installation, called a wind farm or wind park, consists of a collection of these turbines.

Environmental Benefits:

- The environmental benefits of wind power are felt locally, regionally and globally. Wind power can displace power from fossil fuel-powered plants, and thereby help to improve local air quality, mitigate regional effects such as acid rain, and reduce greenhouse gas emissions.

- On average, each MWh of electricity generated in the U.S. results in the emission of 1,341 pounds of carbon dioxide (CO_2), 7.5 pounds of sulphur dioxide (SO_2) and 3.55 pounds of nitrogen oxides (NO_x).

- Thus, the 10 million MWh of electricity generated annually by U.S. wind farms represents about 6.7 million tons in avoided CO_2 emissions, 37,500 tons of SO_2 and 17,750 tons of NO_x.

- This avoided CO_2 equals over 1.8 million tons of carbon, enough to fill 180 trains, each 100 cars long, with each car holding 100 tons of carbon every year.

- Note that these figures are national averages and do not account for regional differences in fuel mix.

- Wind has the potential to displace relatively more emissions in areas where more heavily polluting fuels predominate.

- Among the different renewable energy sources, wind energy is currently making a significant contribution to the installed capacity of power generation, and is emerging as a competitive option.

- The programme covers research and development, survey and assessment of wind resources, implementation of demonstration and private sector projects and promotional policies.

- As a result, India, with an installed capacity of about 3000 MW, ranks fifth in the world after Germany, USA, Spain and Denmark in wind power generation.

Table 6.2: Wind Power Potential

State	Gross Potential (MW) (a)	Technical Potential (MW) (b)
Andhra Pradesh	8275	1750
Gujarat	9675	1780
Karnataka	6620	1120
Kerala	875	605
Madhya Pradesh	5500	825
Maharashtra	3650	3020
Orissa	1700	680
Rajasthan	5400	895
Tamil Nadu	3050	1750
West Bengal	450	450
Total	**45195**	**12875**

- Wind is simple air in motion. It is caused by the uneven heating of the earth's surface by the sun.
- Since the earth's surface is made of very different types of land and water, it absorbs the sun's heat at different rates.
- During the day, the air above the land heats up more quickly than the air over water.
- The warm air over the land expands and rises, and the heavier, cooler air rushes in to take its place, creating winds. At night, the winds are reversed because the air cools more rapidly over land than over water.
- In the same way, the large atmospheric winds that circle the earth are created because the land near the earth's equator is heated more by the sun than the land near the North and South Poles.
- Today, wind energy is mainly used to generate electricity. Wind is called a renewable energy source because the wind will blow as long as the sun shines.

6.3.1 Wind Power

- **Wind power** is the conversion of wind energy into a useful form, such as electricity, using wind turbines.
- At the end of 2007, worldwide capacity of wind-powered generators was 94.1 gigawatts. Although wind currently produces about 1% of world-wide electricity use, it accounts for approximately 19% of electricity production in Denmark, 9% in Spain and Portugal, and 6% in Germany and the Republic of Ireland (2007 data).
- Globally, wind power generation increased more than fivefold between 2000 and 2007.

Fig. 6.15

6.3.2 Capacity Factor

- Since wind speed is not constant, a wind farm's annual energy production is never as much as the sum of the generator nameplate ratings multiplied by the total hours in a year.
- The ratio of actual productivity in a year to this theoretical maximum is called the capacity factor.

- Typical capacity factors are 20-40%, with values at the upper end of the range in particularly favourable sites. For example, a 1 megawatt turbine with a capacity factor of 35% will not produce 8,760 megawatt-hours in a year, but only $0.35 \times 24 \times 365 = 3,066$ MWh, averaging to 0.35 MW.

- Online data is available for some locations and the capacity factor can be calculated from the yearly output. Unlike fueled generating plants, the capacity factor is limited by the inherent properties of wind.

- Capacity factors of other types of power plant are based mostly on fuel cost, with a small amount of downtime for maintenance.

- Nuclear plants have low incremental fuel cost, and so are run at full output and achieve a 90% capacity factor.

- Plants with higher fuel cost are throttled back to follow load. Gas turbine plants using natural gas as fuel may be very expensive to operate and may be run only to meet peak power demand.

- A gas turbine plant may have an annual capacity factor of 5-25% due to relatively high energy production cost.

- According to a 2007 Stanford University study published in the Journal of Applied Meteorology and Climatology, interconnecting ten or more wind farms allows 33 to 47% of the total energy produced to be used as reliable, baseload electric power, as long as minimum criteria are met for wind speed and turbine height.

6.3.3 Wind Turbines

- Wind turbines, like aircraft propeller blades, turn in the moving air and power an **electric generator** that supplies an electric current.

- Simply stated, a wind turbine is the opposite of a fan.

- Instead of using electricity to make wind, like a fan, wind turbines use wind to make electricity.

- The wind turns the blades, which spin a shaft, which connects to a generator and makes electricity.

6.3.4 Wind Turbine Types

- Modern wind turbines fall into two basic groups; the **horizontal-axis** variety, like the traditional farm windmills used for pumping water, and the **vertical-axis** design, like the eggbeater-style Darrieus model, named after its French inventor.

- Most large modern wind turbines are horizontal-axis turbines.

Turbine Components:

- Horizontal turbine components include:
  - **blade** or **rotor**, which converts the energy in the wind to rotational shaft energy;
  - a **drive train**, usually including a gearbox and a generator;
  - a **tower** that supports the rotor and drive train; and

    o　other equipment, including controls, electrical cables, ground support equipment, and interconnection equipment.

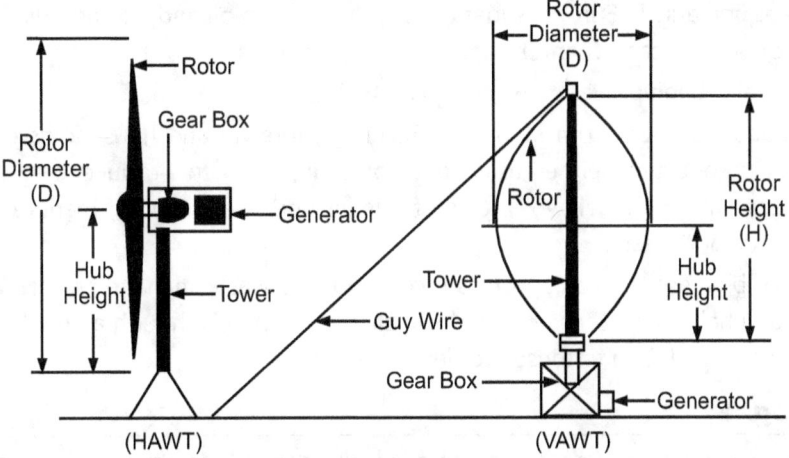

Fig. 6.16

6.4 BIOENERGY　　　(W-13)

- **Bioenergy** is renewable energy made available from materials derived from biological sources. In its most narrow sense, it is a synonym to biofuel, which is fuel derived from biological sources.
- In its broader sense, it does not include biomass, the biological material used as a biofuel, as well as the social, economic, scientific and technical fields associated with using biological sources for energy.
- This is a common misconception, as bioenergy is the energy extracted from the biomass, as the biomass is the fuel and the bioenergy is the energy contained in the fuel.
- Biomass is any organic material which has stored sunlight in the form of chemical energy. As a fuel it may include wood, wood waste, straw, manure, sugar cane, and many other byproducts from a variety of agricultural processes.
- Biomass is material derived from recently living organisms, which includes plants, animals and their byproducts. Manure, garden waste and crop residues are all sources of biomass.
- It is a renewable energy source based on the carbon cycle, unlike other natural resources such as petroleum, coal, and nuclear fuels.
- Animal waste is a persistent and unavoidable pollutant produced primarily by the animals housed in industrial-sized farms. Researchers from Washington University have figured out a way to turn manure into biomass.
- In April 2008, with the help of imaging technology, they noticed that vigorous mixing helps microorganisms turn farm waste into alternative energy.
- This is providing farmers with a simple way to treat their waste and convert it into energy.

- There are also agricultural products being grown for biofuel production. These include corn, switchgrass, and soybeans, primarily in the United States; rapeseed, wheat and sugar beet primarily in Europe; sugar cane in Brazil; palm oil and miscanthus in Southeast Asia; sorghum and cassava in China; and jatropha in India.

- Hemp has also been proven to work as a biofuel.

- Biodegradable outputs from industry, agriculture, forestry and households can be used for biofuel production, either using anaerobic digestion to produce biogas, or using second generation biofuels; examples of this include straw, timber, manure, rice husks, sewage, and food waste.

- The use of biomass fuels can therefore contribute to waste management as well as fuel security and help to prevent or slow down climate change, although alone they are not a comprehensive solution to these problems.

6.4.1 Biogas

- Biogas represents an alternative source of energy, derived mainly from organic wastes. In India, the use of biogas derived from animal waste, primarily cow dung, has been promoted for over three decades now.

- According to the 1997 Livestock Census, the cattle population in the country is about 290 million. The estimated potential of household biogas plants based on animal waste in India is 12 million.

- Till December 2004, under the National Biogas Programme, over 3.7 million biogas plants in the capacity of 1–6 m^3 had been installed.

- Larger units have also been set up in many villages, farms, and cattle houses. The estimated biogas production from these plants is over 3.5 million m^3 per day, which is equivalent to a daily supply of about 2.2 million m^3 of natural gas.

- These plants usually provide gas for cooking and lighting, the latter through specially designed mantles. By replacing up to 75% of the diesel in dual-fuel engines with biogas, mechanical and electrical power is also generated.

- Efforts are now under way to introduce small capacity engines to efficiently generate electricity from biogas in a decentralized mode. Standardized models of biogas plants – suitable for individual households and institutions/communities – are thus available.

- Along with development of plants and related infrastructure, a large pool of skilled manpower has been trained and deployed for plant construction and maintenance.

- The technology involved – anaerobic digestion – has been successfully extended to treat industrial and urban wastes on a large scale.

- This holds potential as a solution to numerous environmental problems, including waste and manure handling, water pollution, and carbon dioxide emission.

- Biogas is a clean fuel produced through anaerobic digestion of a variety of organic wastes: animal, agricultural, domestic, and industrial.

Anaerobic digestion comprises three steps.

- o Decomposition (hydrolysis) of plant or animal matter to break down complex organic materials into simple organic substances.
- o Conversion of decomposed matter into organic acids.
- o Conversion of acids into methane gas.

- As the process temperature affects the rate of digestion, it should be maintained in the mesophilic range (30°C–40°C) with an optimum of 35°C. It is also possible to operate plants in the thermophilic range (55°C–65°C) under controlled conditions.

- Apart from temperature, the rate of biogas production also depends on factors such as the carbon: nitrogen ratio, hydraulic retention time, solid concentration, and types of feedstock. Biogas consists of methane, carbon dioxide, and traces of other gases such as hydrogen, carbon monoxide, nitrogen, oxygen, and hydrogen sulphide.

- The gas mixture is saturated with water vapour and may contain dust particles. The relative percentages of these gases depend on the quality of feed material and the process conditions.

- The percentage of methane in the gas determines its calorific value as the other constituents do not contribute to the energy content.

- The methane content of biogas is appreciably high, at 60%. This provides a calorific value high enough to find use in many energy applications, including power generation. Table 6.3 provides a comparison of the calorific values of various fuels.

Table 6.3: Comparison of the calorific values of various fuels

Fuel	Calorific value (approximate)
Natural gas	8600 kcal per m^3
Liquefied petroleum gas	10,800 kcal per kg
Kerosene	10,300 kcal per kg
Diesel	10,700 kcal per kg
Biogas	5000 kcal per m^3

Components of Biogas Plants:

Mixing tank: The feed material (dung) is collected in the mixing tank. Sufficient water is added and the material is thoroughly mixed till a homogeneous slurry is formed.

- **Inlet pipe:** The substrate is discharged into the digester through the inlet pipe/tank.

- **Digester:** The slurry is fermented inside the digester and biogas is produced through bacterial action.

- **Gas holder or gas storage dome:** The biogas gets collected in the gas holder, which holds the gas until the time of consumption.

- **Outlet pipe:** The digested slurry is discharged into the outlet tank either through the outlet pipe or the opening provided in the digester.

- **Gas pipeline:** The gas pipeline carries the gas to the point of utilization, such as a stove or lamp.

6.4.2 Types of Biogas Plants

(i) Fixed-dome type:

The fixed-dome biogas plant consists of one lower segment (for the digester) and a hemisphere over it (for both digester and gas holder). The mixing tank is connected to the digester by a 15 cm asbestos cement pipe. Through the outlet hole provided in the digester, the slurry is pushed into the outlet tank and overflows through another hole provided in the outlet tank.

(ii) Floating-drum type:

The floating-drum biogas plant consists of a deep well-shaped underground digester connected by inlet and outlet pipes. A mild-steel gas storage drum, inverted over the slurry, rises and falls around a guide pipe corresponding to the accumulation and withdrawal of gas.

(iii) Bag type:

Made of rubberized nylon fabric, the bag-type biogas plant is a portable unit, which can conveniently be placed at any location. The appropriate model is selected on the basis of technical requirements such as location, distance between kitchen and cattle shed, availability of dung and water, preferences of the beneficiaries, and so on.

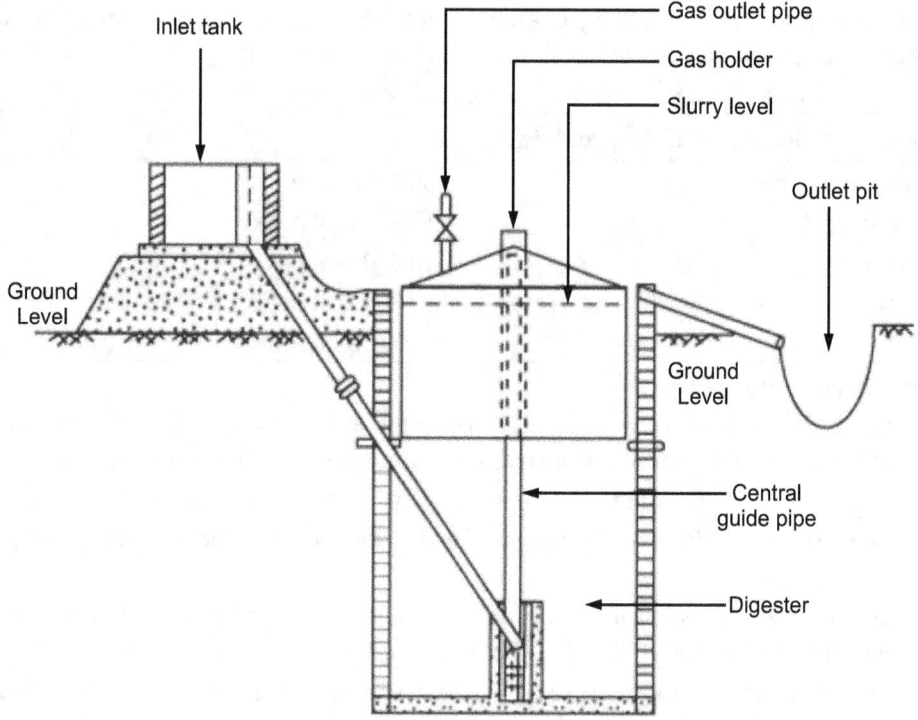

Fig. 6.17: Floating-dome type biogas digester

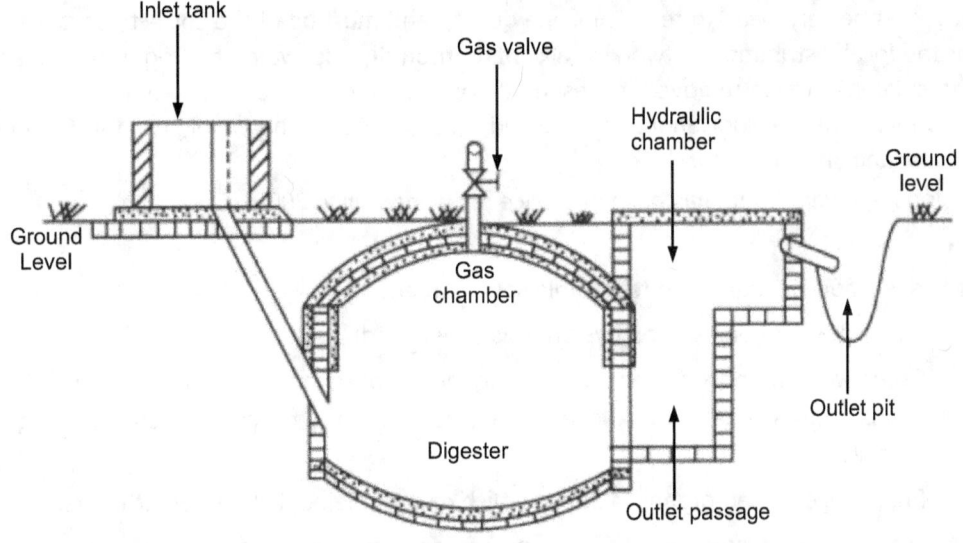

Fig. 6.18

Applications:

- Biogas can be utilized for electricity production, cooking, space heating, water heating and process heating.

- If compressed, it can replace compressed natural gas for use in vehicles, where it can fuel an internal combustion engine or fuel cells.

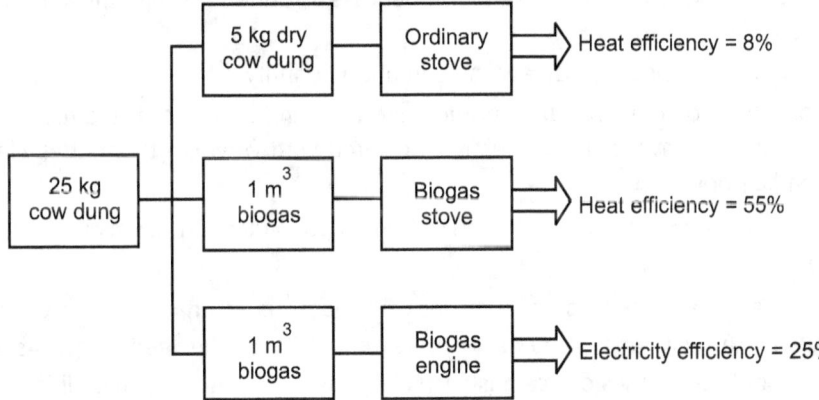

Fig. 6.19: Efficiency of energy conversion from cattle dung

- Methane within biogas can be concentrated to the same standards as natural gas than, it is called biomethane.

- If the local gas network permits it, the producer of the biogas may be able to utilize the local gas distribution networks.

- Gas must be very clean to reach pipeline quality, and must be of the correct composition for the local distribution network to accept. Carbon dioxide, water, hydrogen sulfide and particulates must be removed if present. If concentrated and compressed it can also be used in vehicle transportation. Compressed biogas is becoming widely used in Sweden, Switzerland and Germany.

- A biogas-powered train has been in service in Sweden since 2005.

Benefits:

Provides a non-polluting and renewable source of energy

- Efficient way of energy conversion (saves fuelwood).

- Saves women and children from drudgery of collection and carrying of firewood, exposure to smoke in the kitchen, and time consumed for cooking and cleaning of utensils.

- Produces enriched organic manure, which can supplement chemical fertilizers.

- Leads to improvement in the environment, and sanitation and hygiene.

- Provides a source for decentralized power generation.

- Leads to employment generation in the rural areas.

6.4.3 Biomass Briquetting

- Many of the developing countries produce huge quantities of agro residues but they are used inefficiently causing extensive pollution to the environment. The major residues are rice husk, coffee husk, coir pith, jute sticks, bagasse, groundnut shells, mustard stalks and cotton stalks.

- Sawdust, a milling residue is also available in huge quantity.

- Apart from the problems of transportation, storage, and handling, the direct burning of loose biomass in conventional grates is associated with very low thermal efficiency and widespread air pollution.

- The conversion efficiencies are as low as 40% with particulate emissions in the flue gases in excess of 3000 mg/Nm^3.

- In addition, a large percentage of unburnt carbonaceous ash has to be disposed off. In the case of rice husk, this amounts to more than 40% of the feed burnt. As a typical example, about 800 tonnes of rice husk ash are generated every day in Ludhiana (Punjab) as a result of burning 2000 tonnes of husk.

- Briquetting of the husk could mitigate these pollution problems while at the same time making use of this important industrial/domestic energy resource.

- Historically, biomass briquetting technology has been developed in two distinct directions. Europe and the United States has pursued and perfected the reciprocating ram/piston press while Japan has independently invented and developed the screw press technology.

- Although both technologies have their merits and demerits, it is universally accepted that the screw pressed briquettes are far superior to the ram pressed solid briquettes in terms of their storability and combustibility.

- Japanese machines are now being manufactured in Europe under licensing agreement but no information has been reported about the manufacturing of European machines in Japan.

- Worldwide, both technologies are being used for briquetting of sawdust and locally available agro-residues.

- Although the importance of biomass briquettes as substitute fuel for wood, coal and lignite is well recognized, the numerous failures of briquetting machines in almost all developing countries have inhibited their extensive exploitation.

- Briquetting technology is yet to get a strong foothold in many developing countries because of the technical constraints involved and the lack of knowledge to adapt the technology to suit local conditions.

- Overcoming the many operational problems associated with this technology and ensuring the quality of the raw material used are crucial factors in determining its commercial success.

- In addition to this commercial aspect, the importance of this technology lies in conserving wood, a commodity extensively used in developing countries and leading to the widespread destruction of forests.

- Biomass densification, which is also known as briquetting of sawdust and other agro residues, has been practiced for many years in several countries. Screw extrusion briquetting technology was invented and developed in Japan in 1945.

- As of April 1969, there were 638 plants in Japan engaged in manufacturing sawdust briquettes, known as 'Ogalite', amounting to a production of 0.81 MTY.

- The fact that the production of briquettes quadrupled from 1964 to 1969 in Japan speaks for the success of this technology. This technology should be differentialed from such processes as the 'Prest-o-log' technology of the United States, the 'Glomera' method in Switzerland and the 'Compress' method in West Germany.

- At present two main high pressure technologies: ram or piston press and screw extrusion machines, are used for briquetting.

- While the briquettes produced by a piston press are completely solid, screw press briquettes on the other hand have a concentric hole which gives better combustion characteristics due to a larger specific area.

- The screw press briquettes are also homogeneous and do not disintegrate easily. Having a high combustion rate, these can substitute for coal in most applications and in boilers.

- Briquettes can be produced with a density of 1.2 g/cm^3 from loose biomass of bulk density 0.1 to 0.2 g/cm^3.

- These can be burnt clean and therefore are eco-friendly arid also those advantages that are associated with the use of biomass are present in the briquettes.

- With a view to improving the briquetting scene in India, the Indian Renewable Energy Development Agency (IREDA) - a finance granting agency - has financed many briquetting projects, all of which are using piston presses for briquetting purposes.
- But the fact remains that these are not being used efficiently because of their technical flaws and also due to a lack of understanding of biomass characteristics.
- Holding meetings with entrepreneurs at different levels, providing technical back-up shells and educating entrepreneurs have to some extent helped some plants to achieve profitability and holds out hope of reviving the briquetting sector.

Fig. 6.20

6.4.4 Biomass Gasifier

- Biomass has been a major energy source, prior to the discovery of fossil fuels like coal and petroleum.
- Even though its role is presently diminished in developed countries, it is still widely used in rural communities of the developing countries for their energy needs in terms of cooking and limited industrial use.
- Biomass, besides using in solid form, can be converted into gaseous form through gasification route.

1. Concept and Principle:

- Gasification is the process of converting solid fuels to gaseous fuel. It is not simply pyrolysis; pyrolysis is only one of the steps in the conversion process.
- The other steps are combustion with air and reduction of the product of combustion, (water vapour and carbon dioxide) into combustible gases, (carbon monoxide, hydrogen, methane, some higher hydrocarbons) and inerts, (carbon dioxide and nitrogen).
- The process leads to a gas with some fine dust and condensable compounds termed tar, both of which must be restricted to less than about 100 ppm each if the gas is to be used in internal combustion engines.

2. Uses of Producer Gas:

- The producer gas obtained by the process of gasification can have end use for thermal application or for mechanical/electrical power generation.
- Like any other gaseous fuel, producer gas has the control for power when compared to that of solid fuel, in this solid biomass.
- This also paves way for more efficient and cleaner operation.
- The producer gas can be conveniently used in number of applications as mentioned below.

(i) Thermal:

- Thermal energy of the order of 5 MJ is released, by flaring 1 m^3 of producer gas in the burner. Flame temperatures as high as 1550 K can be obtained by optimal pre-mixing of air with gas. For applications which require thermal energy, gasifiers can be a good option as a gas generator, and retrofitted with existing devices. Few of the devices to which gasifier could be retrofitted are

  (a) Dryers: Drying is the most essential process in beverage and spices industry like tea and cardamom. This calls for hot gases in the temperature range of 120 - 130°C, in the existing designs. Typically the heat energy required is equivalent to 1 kg of wood for 1 kg made tea. Gasifier is an ideal solution for the above situation, where hot gas after combustion can be mixed with the right quantity of secondary air, so as to lower its temperature to the desired level for use in the existing dryers.

  (b) Kilns: Baking of tiles, potteries require hot environment in the temperature range of 800 - 950°C. This is presently being done by combusting large quantities of wood in an inefficient manner. Gasifiers could be suitable for such applications, which provide a better option of regulating the thermal environment. There will also be an added advantage of smokeless and sootless operation, whereby enhancing the product value.

  (c) Furnaces: In non-ferrous metallurgical and foundry industries, high temperatures (~650 - 1000°C) are required for melting metals and alloys. This is commonly done by using expensive fuel oils or electrical heaters. Gasifiers are well suited for such applications.

  (d) Boilers: Process industries which require steam or hot water, use either biomass or coal as fuel in the boilers. Biomass is used inefficiently with higher pollutants like NO_x and with little control with respect to power regulation. Therefore these devices are appropriate to be retrofitted with gasifiers for efficient energy usage.

  Apart from these, energy requirements in poultry farms, cold storage devices (vapour compression refrigerator), rubber industry and so on could be met using wood gasifiers.

(ii) Power Generation:

- Using wood gas, it is possible to operate a diesel engine on dual fuel mode. Diesel substitution of the order of 80 to 85% can be obtained at nominal loads. The mechanical energy thus derived can be used either for energising a water pump set for irrigational purpose or for coupling with an alternator for electrical power generation, either for local consumption or for grid synchronisation.

- An appropriate site to realise the above application is an unelectrified village or hamlet. The benefits derived from this could be many, right from irrigation of fields to the supply of drinking water, and illuminating the village to supporting village industries. The other suitable sites could be saw mills and coffee plantations, where waste wood (ofcourse of specified size) could be used as a feed stock in gasifiers.

3. Wood Gasifier:

- This system is meant for biomass having density in excess of 250 kg/m^3. Theoretically, the ratio of air-to-fuel required for the complete combustion of the wood, defined as stoichiometric combustion is 6: 1 to 6.5: 1, with the end products being CO_2 and H_2O.

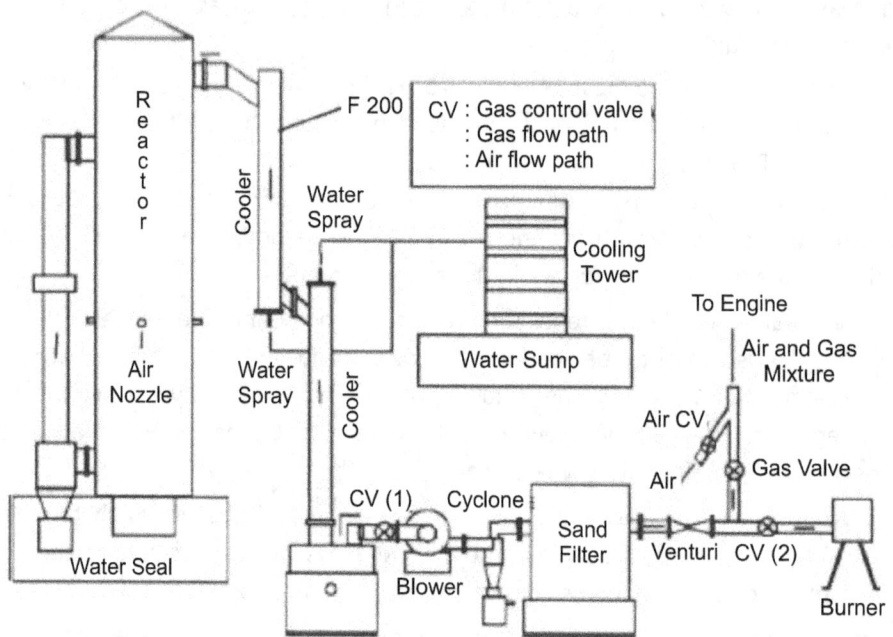

Fig. 6.21: Schematic of Wood Gasifier for Power Generation Application

- Whereas, in gasification, the combustion is carried at sub-stoichiometric conditions with air-to-fuel ratio being 1.5: 1 to 1.8: 1.

- The product gas thus generated during the gasification process is combustible. This process is made possible in a device called gasifier, in a limited supply of air.

- A gasifier system (Fig. 6.21) basically comprises of a reactor where the gas is generated, and is followed by a cooling and cleaning train which cools and cleans the gas.

- The clean combustible gas is available for power generation in diesel-gen-set. Whereas, for thermal use the gas from the reactor can be directly fed to the combustor using an ejector.

6.5 HYDRO ENERGY   (W-13)

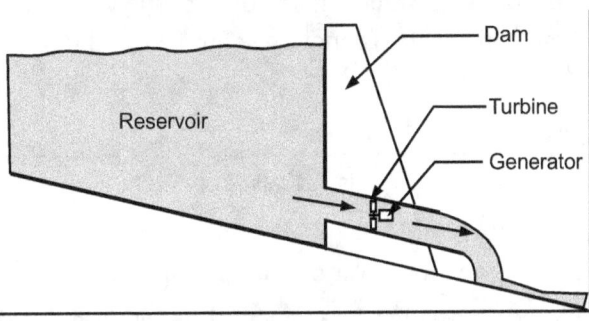

Fig. 6.22

- We have used running water as an energy source for thousands of years, mainly to grind corn.
- The first house in the world to be lit by hydroelectricity was Cragside House, in Northumberland, England, in 1878.
- In 1882 on the Fox river, in the USA, hydroelectricity produced enough power to light two paper mills and a house.
- Nowadays, there are many hydro-electric power stations, providing around 20% of the world's electricity. The name comes from "hydro", the Greek word for water.
- A dam is built to trap water, usually in a valley where there is an existing lake.
- Water is allowed to flow through tunnels in the dam, to turn turbines and thus drive generators.
- Notice that the dam is much thicker at the bottom than at the top, because the pressure of the water increases with depth.
- Hydro-electric power stations can produce a great deal of power very cheaply.
- When it was first built, the huge "Hoover Dam", on the Colorado river, supplied much of the electricity for the city of Las Vegas; however now Las Vegas has grown so much, the city gets most of its energy from other sources.
- Although there are many suitable sites around the world, hydro-electric dams are very expensive to build.
- However, once the station is built, the water comes free of charge, and there is no waste or pollution.
- Gravitational potential energy is stored in the water above the dam. Because of the great height of the water, it will arrive at the turbines at high pressure, which means that we

can extract a great deal of energy from it. The water then flows away downriver as normal.

- In mountainous countries such as Switzerland and New Zealand, hydro-electric power provides more than half of the country's energy needs.

- An alternative is to build the station next to a fast-flowing river. However with this arrangement the flow of the water cannot be controlled, and water cannot be stored for later use.

6.5.1 Advantages

- Once the dam is built, the energy is virtually free.
- No waste or pollution produced.
- Much more reliable than wind, solar or wave power.
- Water can be stored above the dam ready to cope with peaks in demand.
- Hydro-electric power stations can increase to full power very quickly, unlike other power stations.
- Electricity can be generated constantly.

6.5.2 Disadvantages

- The dams are very expensive to build. However, many dams are also used for flood control or irrigation, so building costs can be shared.
- Building a large dam will flood a very large area upstream, causing problems for animals that used to live there.
- Finding a suitable site can be difficult - the impact on residents and the environment may be unacceptable.
- Water quality and quantity downstream can be affected, which can have an impact on plant life.

6.5.3 Micro Hydro

- **Micro Hydro** is a term used for hydroelectric power installations that typically produce upto 100 kW of power.
- They are often used in water rich areas as a Remote Area Power Supply (RAPS).
- There are many of these installations around the world, including several delivering around 50 kW in the Solomon Islands, supplying energy for small communities.
- Micro hydro is frequently accomplished with a pelton wheel for high head, low flow water supply.
- The installation is often just a small dammed pool, at the top of a waterfall, with several hundred feet of pipe leading to a small generator housing.

- In low-head installations, maintenance and mechanism costs often become important. A low-head system moves larger amount of water, and is more likely to encounter surface debris.

- For this reason a Banki turbine, a pressurized self-cleaning crossflow waterwheel, is often preferred for low-head microhydropower systems.

- Though less efficient, its simpler structure is less expensive than other low-head turbines of the same capacity.

- Since the water flows in, then out of it, it cleans itself and is less prone to jam with debris.

- Micro hydro systems complement photovoltaic solar energy systems because in many areas, water flow, and thus available hydro power, is highest in the winter when solar energy is at a minimum.

6.5.4 Small Hydro

- **Small Hydro** is the development of hydroelectric power on a scale serving a small community or industrial plant.

- The definition of a small hydro project varies but a generating capacity of upto 10 megawatts (MW) is generally accepted as the upper limit of what can be termed as small hydro.

- This may be stretched to 25 MW and 30 MW in Canada and the USA. In contrast many hydroelectric projects are of enormous size, such as the generating plant at the Hoover Dam (2,074 megawatts) or the vast multiple projects of the Tennessee Valley Authority.

- Small hydro can be further subdivided into mini hydro, usually defined as less than 1,000 kW, and micro hydro which is less than 100 kW. Micro hydro is usually the application of hydroelectric power sized for small communities, single families or small enterprise.

- Small hydro plants may be connected to conventional electrical distribution networks as a source of low-cost renewable energy.

- Alternatively, small hydro projects may be built in isolated areas that would be uneconomic to serve from a network, or in areas where there is no national electrical distribution network.

- Since small hydro projects usually have minimal reservoirs and civil construction work, they are seen as having a relatively low environmental impact compared to large hydro.

6.6 TIDAL AND OCEAN ENERGY   (S-12; W-13)

- Tidal Energy, Coastal areas with huge and flowing tidal waters carry vast potential energy.
- 11th Century England was the first to harness this energy, using water wheels to produce mechanical power.
- Now a days the rise and fall of tides have become the basis to produce electrical power similar to the principles of hydroelectric power generation.

Origin:

- The daily rise and fall in the level of ocean water relative to the coastline is referred to as tide. Tides originate from the motions of the earth, moon and sun. The gravitational pull of the Moon and Sun along with the revolution of the Earth result in tides. (The magnitude of the gravitational attraction of an object is dependant upon the mass of an object and its distance.)

- The moon exerts a larger gravitational force on the earth, though it is much smaller in mass, because it is a lot closer than the sun. This force of attraction causes the oceans, which make up 71 percent of the earth's surface, to bulge along an axis pointing towards the moon.

- Tides are produced by the rotation of the earth beneath this bulge in its watery coating, resulting in the rhythmic rise and fall of coastal ocean levels.

- The gravitational attraction of the sun also affects the tides similarly, but to a lesser degree. As well as bulging towards the moon, the oceans also bulge slightly towards the sun.

- When the earth, moon and sun are positioned in a straight line i.e on the occasion of a full or new moon, the gravitational attractions are combined, resulting in very large spring tides.

- At half moon, the sun and moon are positioned at right angles, resulting in lower neap tides. Coastal areas experience two high and two low tides over a period of 24 hours and slightly above.

- The presence of geographical features such as bays and inlets result in higher tides. To produce enough amounts of power (electricity) that can be put to practical use, a difference of at least five meters between high and low tides is a must.

- There are about 40 suitable sites around the world with this kind of tidal range.

- The higher the tides the greater is the amount of electricity that can be generated from a given site. It is inversely proportional to the cost of electricity produced, making such sites also more economical.

- Approximately 3000 GW (1 Giga Watt = 1 GW = 1 billion watts) of energy are available from the tides, worldwide. However considering the limitations as mentioned above, only about 2% (= 60 GW) can potentially be exploited for electricity generation.

Generating tidal energy:

- The technology required to convert tidal energy into electricity is comparable to technology used in traditional hydroelectric power plants. The first requirement is a dam across a tidal bay or estuary.

- However building a dam is expensive and the best sites are those where a bay has a narrow opening, thus reducing the length of dam required.

- Gates and turbines are installed. When there is adequate difference in the levels of the water on the different sides of the dam, the gates are opened.

- This causes water to flow through the turbines, turning the generator to produce electricity.

- Electricity is generated by water flowing both inwards and out of a bay. There are periods of maximum generation every twelve hours, with no electricity generation at the six-hour mark in between. The turbines may also be used as pumps to pump extra water into the basin behind the dam at times when the demand on electricity is low.

- This water can later be released when the demand on the system is very high, thus allowing the tidal plant to function like a "pumped storage" hydroelectric facility.

Fig. 6.23

6.6.1 Advantages of Tidal Energy

- The most important advantage of tidal energy is its economical benefits, as tidal energy does not require any fuel. Tides rise and fall every day in a very consistent pattern. The economic life of a tidal plant is very high. A plant is expected to be in production for 75 to 100 years, in comparison with the 35 years of a conventional fossil fuel plant.

- Besides the economical factors, tidal energy is clean and renewable, unlike fossil fuels.

- Tidal energy offers a lot of potential to be a substitute for hydrocarbon and fossil fuels. A very important feature of tidal energy is that it is non-polluting.

- A tidal barrage can prevent approximately one million tons of CO_2 per TWH generated. A barrage can also safeguard coastlines from storms.

6.6.2 Disadvantages of Tidal Energy

- The altering of the ecosystem at the bay is the biggest drawback of tidal power. Damages like reduced flushing, winter icing and erosion can change the vegetation of the area and disrupt the balance.

- The alteration of tidal currents affects the habitat of the seabirds and the fish. Similar to other ocean energies, tidal energy has several prerequisites that make it only available in a small number of regions.

- For a tidal power plant to produce electricity effectively (about 85% efficiency), it requires a basin or a gulf that has a mean tidal amplitude (the differences between spring and neap tide) of 7 metres or above. It is also desirable to have semi-diurnal tides where there are two high and low tides everyday.

- Tides out in the ocean have maximum amplitude of about one meter.

- As you move closer to shore, this can increase to as high as 12 or more. This can depend on local features such as shelving or funneling meaning the tidal range can vary considerably along any given coastline.

- This can mean that a lot of places just aren't suitable.

- When planning the location major consideration has to be given to see whether the tides are high enough and if there is a suitable place for building the site.

6.6.3 Ocean Thermal Energy Conversion (OTEC)

- **Ocean thermal energy conversion (OTEC)** is a method for generating electricity which uses the temperature difference that exists between deep and shallow waters to run a heat engine.

- As with any heat engine, the greatest efficiency and power is produced with the largest temperature difference. This temperature difference generally increases with decreasing latitude, i.e. near the equator, in the tropics.

- However, evaporation prevents the surface temperature from exceeding 27°C (80°F). Also the subsurface water rarely falls below 5°C.

- Historically, the main technical challenge of OTEC was to generate significant amounts of power, efficiently, from this very small temperature ratio. Changes in efficiency of heat exchange in modern designs allow performance approaching the theoretical maximum efficiency.

- The Earth's oceans are continually heated by the sun and cover nearly 70% of the Earth's surface; this temperature difference contains a vast amount of solar energy which can potentially be harnessed for human use.

- If this extraction could be made cost effective on a large scale, it could provide a source of renewable energy needed to deal with energy shortages, and other energy problems.

- The total energy available is one or two orders of magnitude higher than other ocean energy options such as wave power, but the small magnitude of the temperature difference makes energy extraction comparatively difficult and expensive, due to low thermal efficiency. Earlier OTEC systems had an overall efficiency of only 1 to 3% (the theoretical maximum efficiency lies between 6 and 7%.

- Current designs under review will operate closer to the theoretical maximum efficiency.

- The energy carrier, seawater, is free, although it has an access cost associated with the pumping materials and pump energy costs.

- Although an OTEC plant operates at a low overall efficiency, it can be configured to operate continuously as a Base load power generation system.

- Any thorough Cost-benefit analysis should include these factors to provide an accurate assessment of performance, efficiency, operational and construction costs and returns on investment.

Fig. 6.24

- View of a land based OTEC facility at Keahole Point on the Kona coast of Hawaii (United States Department of Energy).

- The concept of a heat engine is very common in thermodynamics engineering, and much of the energy used by humans passes through a heat engine.

- A heat engine is a thermodynamic device placed between a high temperature reservoir and a low temperature reservoir.

- As heat flows from one to the other, the engine converts some of the heat energy to work energy.

- This principle is used in steam turbines and internal combustion engines, while refrigerators reverse the direction of flow of both the heat and work energy.

- Rather than using heat energy from the burning of fuel, OTEC power draws on temperature differences caused by the sun's warming of the ocean surface.

- The only heat cycle suitable for OTEC, is the Rankine cycle, using a low-pressure turbine. Systems may be either closed-cycle or open-cycle.

- Closed-cycle engines use working fluids that are typically thought of as refrigerants such as ammonia or R-134a.

- Open-cycle engines use the water heat source as the working fluid.

Practice Questions

1.　What are the advantages of renewable energy ?
2.　Explain wind energy by considering factors like wind power, wind turbines.
3.　Explain solar energy with respect to
　　(a)　Architecture and urban planning
　　(b)　Agriculture and horticulture
　　(c)　Solar lighting
　　(d)　Water heating
　　(e)　Cooking
　　(f)　Process heat
　　(g)　Photovoltaics.
4.　Give advantages and disadvantages of Tidal Energy.
5.　Explain ocean thermal energy conversion.
6.　Explain hydro energy and its advantages and disadvantages.
7.　Describe bio-energy as renewable energy source.
8.　What are the components of biogas plant ?
9.　What are the types of biogas plants and their benefits ?
10.　Explain with diagram wood gasifier for power generation.

MSBTE Questions and Answers (As Per 'E' Scheme)

Summer 2012

1.　Explain solar drying. State any two applications of it.

Ans.　Please refer to Section 6.2.3.

2.　State any four advantages and disadvantages of renewable energy.

Ans.　Please refer to Section 6.1.

3.　How energy is generated from tide and ocean?

Ans.　Please refer to Section 6.6.

4. What is hydroenergy? How it can be used.

Ans. Please refer to Section 6.5.

Winter 2013

1. Compare renewable energy sources and non-renewable energy sources.

Ans. Please refer to Section 6.1.

2. Write the advantages and disadvantages of tidal energy.

Ans. Please refer to Section 6.4.

3. Draw a neat sketch to generate bio energy and labelled it.

Ans. Please refer to Section 6.4.

4. Explain wind energy with one example illustrating to save energy.

Ans. Please refer to Section 6.3.

5. Write the advantages and disadvantages of solar energy.

Ans. Please refer to Section 6.2.

6. What are the different elements of hydroelectric power plant ? State the function of it.

Ans. Please refer to Section 6.5.

❑❑❑

www.ingramcontent.com/pod-product-compliance
Lightning Source LLC
Chambersburg PA
CBHW080904020726
47502CB00008B/2344